Dean scanned the area. "Where's Krysty?"

Startled, Ryan jerked his head around. One glance told him she wasn't in the tank with them. Rushing to a blasterport, the one-eyed man blew away the outside greenery with a single discharge and looked frantically at the alleyway. Ivy was everywhere, thickening by the second.

"Second floor!" Doc cried, standing at the rooftop periscope.

Ryan turned and found her, dangling from the grip of the mutie plant twenty feet in the air. Her .38 discharged once, pointing at nothing in particular. Then she was hauled over the rooftop and gone.

"Combat positions," Ryan ordered, striding past his friends and sliding into the driver's seat. "We're going after her."

JAMES AXLER

DEATH LANDS®

Pandora's Redoubt

A GOLD EAGLE BOOK FROM

WORLDWIDE®

TORONTO • NEW YORK • LONDON
AMSTERDAM • PARIS • SYDNEY • HAMBURG
STOCKHOLM • ATHENS • TOKYO • MILAN
MADRID • WARSAW • BUDAPEST • AUCKLAND

To Melissa and Lisa, for doing such a bang-up job.
Thanks, amigas.

First edition June 2000

ISBN 0-373-62560-X

PANDORA'S REDOUBT

Copyright © 2000 by Worldwide Library.

Printed in U.S.A.

It is the nature of a thing to be true to its essence: fire can only burn, a rock is unyielding, water flows. Men alone are both animal and intellect, and thus must choose if they shall stand erect and embrace the stars, or sprawl in the dirt and feast on blood like a lowly beast....

—*The Meditations of*
Marcus Aurelius, 167 A.D.

THE DEATHLANDS SAGA

This world is their legacy, a world born in the violent nuclear spasm of 2001 that was the bitter outcome of a struggle for global dominance.

There is no real escape from this shockscape where life always hangs in the balance, vulnerable to newly demonic nature, barbarism, lawlessness.

But they are the warrior survivalists, and they endure—in the way of the lion, the hawk and the tiger, true to nature's heart despite its ruination.

Ryan Cawdor: The privileged son of an East Coast baron. Acquainted with betrayal from a tender age, he is a master of the hard realities.

Krysty Wroth: Harmony ville's own Titian-haired beauty, a woman with the strength of tempered steel. Her premonitions and Gaia powers have been fostered by her Mother Sonja.

J. B. Dix, the Armorer: Weapons master and Ryan's close ally, he, too, honed his skills traversing the Deathlands with the legendary Trader.

Doctor Theophilus Tanner: Torn from his family and a gentler life in 1896, Doc has been thrown into a future he couldn't have imagined.

Dr. Mildred Wyeth: Her father was killed by the Ku Klux Klan, but her fate is not much lighter. Restored from predark cryogenic suspension, she brings twentieth-century healing skills to a nightmare.

Jak Lauren: A true child of the wastelands, reared on adversity, loss and danger, the albino teenager is a fierce fighter and loyal friend.

Dean Cawdor: Ryan's young son by Sharona accepts the only world he knows, and yet he is the seedling bearing the promise of tomorrow.

In a world where all was lost, they are humanity's last hope....

Chapter One

The handle of the door to the mat-trans chamber moved a fraction of an inch, the hinges screeching in protest at the intrusion. Muffled curses came from the other side as the stubborn handle grudgingly moved, and promptly jammed again. More curses. Then the locking mechanism disengaged with a echoing clank of heavy steel on steel. The door was muscled open, and seven armed people charged into the hexagonal chamber beyond. A badly scarred man with a patch covering one eye was the last inside, and he stood ready to close the door behind them to trigger a jump.

"Dark night, we made it," J. B. Dix gasped. The short wiry man removed his well-worn fedora to rub a grimy sleeve across his sweaty forehead. "I knew we could outrun it."

"Gaia," Krysty Wroth breathed, her sentient crimson hair tightening protectively about her lovely face, "we're lucky it found the elevator shaft to fall down."

"Gren helped," Jak Lauren said. The slim, snowy-haired albino teen walked across the chamber and sat on one of the disks set into the floor.

"Grens always help," J.B. commented.

Keeping a close watch on the door behind them,

Dean Cawdor scowled and said nothing, but shifted the grip on his Browning Hi-Power pistol as if in preparation for an attack.

"Do you think it can get through the door?" Dr. Mildred Wyeth asked anxiously, shifting her backpack of medical supplies on her shoulders.

"The thermal inversion gradient of the armaglass portal is not precisely known," Doc Tanner replied, taking his usual spot on the floor. "But as this establishment was theoretically designed to be nuke-proof, therefore, I would extrapolate that the defensive yield potential is—"

"Door!" Jak barked, pointing past Ryan.

Spinning, Ryan saw that the access door to the control room was slowly bulging inward, distending like the bloated belly of a starving man, horribly straining at the resilient alloy framework. The reek of sulfur hit them as yellow steam spurted around the edges and the walls on either side began to glow warmly. Then a wave of dry heat washed over the group, stinging their eyes and searing exposed flesh.

"By the Three Kennedys!" Doc intoned, pulling out his huge LeMat pistol for no sane reason. "The lava is here!"

"Everybody sit down!" Ryan ordered, starting to close the door to the mat-trans unit. But he was unable to remove his gaze from the terrible scene outside. Although stretching like warm taffy, the trembling door to the control room was still in place. The walls on either side, however, were turning orange from the volcanic heat.

"Soon yellow, then white," Krysty warned,

sweat dripping off her chin. "Then it'll soften and melt away."

Loosening the collar of his jacket, J.B. agreed. "We'll be long gone by then. Got a minute yet, mebbe two."

As he spoke, the glowing walls beyond the chamber shattered in a crackling explosion, the remaining chunks peeling away like a flower blossoming to the sun, and white-hot lava began to thickly pump into the control room.

Beyond the yellowish haze they could see only an endless plain of reddish flames.

Once Ryan saw that all of the companions were properly seated on the floor, he slammed the door shut, triggering the jump mechanism, and quickly went to sit beside Krysty. Immediately, the usual mist filled the chamber, engulfing the seven friends, sparks forming around them like newborn stars.

Drawing his 9 mm SIG-Sauer pistol, Ryan could just barely see the deadly lava flow inexorably rising higher and higher, moving toward them, the locked door standing ludicrously upright in the lambent field of molten stone. If the mat-trans unit failed to work because of damage from the lava, then he'd use the pistol. First on Krysty, then on the others and himself. It'd be a lot quicker than burning alive. He glanced at her and saw she already had her own .38-caliber Smith & Wesson revolver out and was looking at him. They shared a moment of understanding more intimate than any embrace.

Then a great surge of power filled their bodies from within as a subsonic hum tore them apart. The universe yawned wide as all eternity. Instantly, they embarked on a subelectronic journey toward an unknown destination, possibly into the great abyss itself.

Well over one century old, the predark mattertrans chambers sent travelers randomly to other units, the secret of their precise control lost forever.

As always, during the time the friends were unconscious, hallucinations filled their minds, idyllic dreams and mad visions, phantasms of old enemies, bloody battles and sexual fantasies. But on this journey the visions died before being truly formed. Suddenly, solid flooring was beneath Ryan's back, and he was reeling a bit from the usual aftershocks of being instantly transferred to a new destination.

As the mist began to thin, Ryan lay still, a pounding headache momentarily clouding his vision. The masking clouds of mist were unusually thick this time. Or was it the sulfur fumes? The awful heat of the lava seemed still to be with them, and he tried to force breath into his heaving chest. Hot, he was so hot, and needed to draw a lungful of air. But he seemed unable to pull atmosphere inside his aching body. Was this another of the hallucinations? He had never dreamed of arriving before. Had they gone anywhere? Or where they still reduced to electronic signals pulsing along the hidden network of the worldwide web of mat-trans units yet to arrive? Perhaps never to arrive. Fireblast, there were times that he hated these bastard machines.

Slowly, the mists dissipated, but his vision was still oddly obscured. Squinting his good eye, Ryan saw the others working their mouths as if trying to draw air into their lungs.

Krysty was on her hands and knees. "Can't…
breathe," she gasped, her prehensile hair hanging
limply, as if the living strands of crimson were unconscious. Her chest rose and fell unnaturally as she
tried to gather air.

Jak had managed to get to his feet and leaned
weakly against one of the armaglass walls. He began to drip sweat, black stains spreading over his
camou-colored vest. J.B. was on his stomach, his
beloved fedora bunched in a white-knuckled hand.
Gasping, Mildred was tearing at the crew neck of
her T-shirt, desperate to get restrictive clothing
away from her throat. His ebony swordstick lying
at his feet, Doc grimaced as if in the grip of an
invisible fist squeezing the very life out of him.
Clutching the Browning to his chest, Dean stood
stock-still, as if dead and ready to topple over.

Clearly, there was no more time to wait. Ryan
had to know if they were safe or should chance
another jump immediately. Summoning strength,
the one-eyed man forced himself to step out of the
jump unit, half expecting his feet to vanish into fiery
ash. But his worn combat boots thumped onto a
solid floor. There was no lava. The black-walled
chamber was empty except for them. Thankfully,
they had jumped to a different redoubt. Yet the heat
was still here, cooking them to death.

Ryan hawked to clear his dry throat. "Something's wrong," he managed to croak.

"Jump now," Mildred gasped. "Heat's going to
kill us."

Ryan shook his head. "Can't until we know for
sure that the other redoubt is gone. If we jump back

before the volcano melts the chamber completely, we fry.''

"I say thee, nay, Agamemnon,'' Doc gasped. "Trepidation is unnecessary. We are quite safe.''

"Bullshit,'' Dean coughed.

"A useful enough organic by-product of domesticated bovines, but not a correct summation in this particular instance, young Dean,'' Doc said, pausing between the words. "This roasting is merely…'' He swallowed. "From the residual…heat that jumped with us. See?'' He pointed a bony finger downward. There lay several large lumps of glowing orange rock among them, radiating a fierce heat like miniature blast furnaces.

"The old coot is right,'' Mildred gasped. "The lava came along with us.''

"Some. It seems as if our timing has exceeded our quotient of luck by the nth factor.''

"Come on out,'' Ryan ordered, "I can feel the redoubt's life support starting to pump in cool air.'' Then his stomach rebelled and he doubled over to retch loudly in the corner. Jump sickness almost always affected some of the companions, but usually Doc and Jak.

The friends staggered to their feet or pushed from the walls, moving as far from the lava as possible. Everybody was pale and holding throbbing heads. Jak sported a bad nosebleed and several of them used the corners of the chamber to vomit. Wordlessly, Mildred extracted a battered canteen from her backpack. Unscrewing the chained cap took two tries, but it finally came free. The physician made a bitter face, then forced herself to take a long swallow.

"Here," she said, handing it to the nearest person. "This should help."

Uncaring if it was poison or whiskey, everybody took a swallow and passed it on to the next.

"I hope it's better than the last batch," Krysty muttered, tilting her head and luxuriating in the cool breeze from the ceiling vents.

Smoothing his rumpled fedora, J.B. glumly signaled agreement. "Gave us the runs for a week."

"That which does not kill us, makes us stronger," Doc said. "Or at least, that's the theory. Occasionally I have found Nietzsche to be a total ass."

However, minds soon cleared and the knotted stomachs eased some. Not much, but some.

"Best mix so far," Ryan stated, handing the empty canteen to Mildred.

The black woman screwed the cap on tight. "Would have been better if I could have found some mint leaves."

Sitting upright, Jak arched an snowy eyebrow. "Not?" he asked.

The physician shook her head. "Orange peels and scrag root. Close enough in taste, but not effect."

"Hope the mat-trans is still okay," Ryan said, studying the floor with its collection of fiercely glowing rocks.

Hawking loudly, Jak spit out an orange lump and watched the spittle sizzle into steam. "Close," he drawled.

"Too damn close," Krysty added.

"But we got the rations. No hunting mutie deer or trading bullets for chickens for a while," Mildred said. "The risk was worth it. We have enough clean food for a couple weeks."

"'Tis a pity, though," Doc boomed, leaning heavily on his swordstick as he got standing. "That storeroom was a cornucopia of food, sufficient vittles for years. Decades!"

"Took all we could," Ryan said gruffly, checking the action on his SIG-Sauer blaster. The pistol was a prized possession, a military police blaster of the finest quality, and its built-in acoustic baffler made the silenced gun no louder than a cough when it fired.

"It's enough," said Dean, touching his vest to ascertain he hadn't lost anything in transit. Having been caught once with no ammo, and damn near getting aced because of it, Dean was grimly determined it would never happen again. Front and back, the entire expanse of a newly acquired leather vest was sewn into tiny pockets to hold individual rounds for his blaster. He was a walking munitions dump, and the weight was awful. However, he doubted if even an arrow could penetrate the thick garment. His father told him he was carrying too much, that speed was as necessary as bullets to stay alive in Deathlands, and he was right. But the lad wasn't yet ready to admit he had overfigured his own strength.

Feeling better by the minute, Ryan walked about the chamber. "Hmm, black walls with silver streaking. We've never been to this redoubt before."

"Beautiful," Mildred said, running fingertips across the smooth almost frictionless surface.

"Could this be D.C.? Some ancient executive redoubt?"

"Mayhap some crazed billionaire's private penthouse," Doc grumbled. "Notice how the excess heat is almost totally dissipated? The life support system is exemplary."

"Not good enough for me," Krysty said, pinching her nose shut. "Hot lava and sulfur mixed with fresh vomit. This place stinks."

"Agreed," Ryan stated, cracking a rare smile. "Let's move out."

He moved to the door, then started to press the handle. Everybody readied weapons as the heavy portal smoothly swung open on silent hinges. However, instead of the usual anteroom on the other side, there was only a seamless expanse of wood, dark and solid as a mountain.

"Blocked off," Ryan said in amazement.

Dean worked the slide of his Browning, chambering a round for immediate use.

"What in hell for?" Mildred asked. "To hide the mat-trans?"

"Seems likely."

Expertly, J.B. ran his callused hands over the wood. "Hmm, not joined beams, but a single piece."

"Big tree," Jak said.

"Paneling," J.B. stated, tapping the material lightly with a knuckle. "Hear that? Thin stuff. No more than a half inch thick. Pretty light armor."

"To keep others out, not us in," Ryan said, holstering his pistol and sliding the Steyr SSG-70 rifle off his shoulder. "Everybody get ready. Triple red."

Moving to the rear of the pack, Mildred eased back the hammer on her Czech-made ZKR .38-caliber target pistol. Loosening one of the many throwing knives in his belt, Jak did the same with his .357 Colt Python revolver.

J.B. placed an ear to the wood and held his breath. Nobody spoke.

Approaching the man, Ryan placed his mouth near his old friend's ear. "People? Sec droid?" he asked softly, easing the off safety of the Steyr. He was down to only a few rounds, but the heavy-caliber bullets would do far more damage to both man or machine than his pistol.

"Clear," J.B. announced, stepping away. "There're no traps I can find, and nothing is moving on the other side."

Mildred grunted. "Then open it."

"Check." Expertly running his hands over the wood, the Armorer knocked experimentally, then scratched here and there.

"Blast hole?" Jak asked, rummaging in his fatigues and withdrawing a half stick of dynamite.

Resting the rifle on his shoulder, Ryan snorted in contempt. "We can kick our way through."

"Not necessary," J.B. replied, probing the edges of the alloy doorframe. "Ah, here we are. Found the catch." The wood slid aside, exposing darkness.

Instantly, everybody moved away from the open doorway, weapons at the ready. For several minutes they stood motionless, patiently waiting, listening hard. When nothing happened, Ryan took the point, moving in low and fast, the pitted barrel of his Steyr sweeping the room, searching for targets. He was flanked by Jak and Krysty, with J.B. and Doc staying as backup at the open door, ready to block it with their bodies if need be. Dean stood off to the side with Mildred, ready to cover the two men should it be necessary.

It took a moment for Ryan's eye to adjust to the dim light. That wasn't good. Usually, the overhead lights came on automatically. Then he saw the ceiling fixtures were completely smashed, every single bulb systematically destroyed.

"But not the tiles alongside," Krysty noted.

"Somebody wanted it dark," Ryan agreed, keeping his blind side toward his companions.

There was a sigh of steel on leather as Jak eased a knife from its sheath. "Ambush?"

"Most likely."

Carefully, the three moved through the mixture of litter that covered the floor of the anteroom. Next, instead of the usual control room, they discovered an office. The furniture was broken, the pieces scattered randomly with broken plastic and glass underfoot everywhere. Bullet holes stitched a wall at chest height. Ryan checked, and sure enough the opposite wall was the same. A firefight had occurred. Over in a corner was the remains of an executive bar, mirror and bottles reduced to glistening shards from a small explosion.

"Plastique," Ryan stated. "Homemade, weak stuff."

"No shrap," Jak added, kicking away some unidentifiable wreckage. "Diversion."

The hairs on the back of Ryan's neck were starting to rise, and he loosened the 9 mm pistol in its belt holster. "Yeah, but a diversion for who? There's nobody here."

"And no bodies."

"Found them," Krysty called out, holstering her pistol and looking at something on the back side of an overturned couch. Jak and Ryan quickly joined her.

There on the dirty floor, locked in each other's arms were two corpses. Human, male, and both long dead. The skin was drum tight over their bones, teeth exposed in the rictus of death. Their hands were locked around each other's throat, fingers buried in the mottled flesh. A pair of knives lay nearby, as did a rusty U.S. Army Colt .45, the slide kicked back showing it was out of ammo. At the base of the wall was a badly rusted Browning Automatic Rifle, its bolt action open and showing it too was out of bullets. The men were dressed in the usual scavenged rags of a dozen different styles, only their boots and the holsters in decent shape. Two bandoliers of empty cartridge loops crisscrossed the chest of the blond man on top, while the bald man on the bottom wore a vest made entirely of rectangular pockets to hold ammo clips for an autofire blaster.

Satisfied, Ryan whistled sharply through his teeth, once long, then short, and the others cautiously walked into the ancient battle room.

"Died killing each other," Mildred said, studying the desiccated corpses. "Been dead four, maybe five weeks. Air system has kept down the smell."

"But not removed it entirely," Doc admonished, sniffing delicately. "I must say, this locale is getting decidedly most pungent."

Loudly blowing his nose into a handkerchief, Jak inspected the bloody residue and barked a laugh. "Don't breathe."

Stoically, Ryan looked around the room. "Nothing much here to fight over. Bar's empty, no weapon cabinet in sight, and they clearly knew nothing about the mat-trans behind the wall. Must have been personal."

"None of their equipment is from standard military stores," J.B. added, lifting the BAR and working the bolt a few times. "So they didn't get it out of storage here. This is old and been patched many times. Seen a lot of work, too. Probably mercies, or coldhearts."

"My question is how did they get inside the redoubt?" Mildred asked, wiping off her hands on her pant leg. "Could the door be down?"

"Must be. No other way in."

Resting the butt of his rifle on his hip, Ryan chewed that over. "So they somehow blasted through the nuke-proof door? Not likely. Somehow, the bastards figured a way to open the door." He paused. "Or worse, they were let in."

"Sleepers?" Dean asked.

"Always a possibility."

Nudging the blond corpse with the silvered toe of her cowboy boot, Krysty frowned, her long crimson hair tightly circling and uncurling about her lovely face. "This is getting worse by the minute. Secret panels, suicide norms, now sleepers? I vote we go."

"Check," Jak said, pocketing a knife from the floor.

"No," Ryan stated, grimacing. "After that trouble we had with Kaa, anything odd with the redoubts warrants a recce."

"I agree," J.B. said, shoving back his fedora and scratching underneath. "I don't care for it, either, but we gotta know. These things are our lifeline."

Jak scowled but didn't voice a differing opinion, and after a bit, Krysty shrugged her acceptance. Mildred remained neutral.

"Lay on, Macduff," Doc said, extending a hand toward the door.

Gingerly, J.B. went to work using flexible tools that slid under the jamb. A loud click made everybody jump, except the Armorer. He beamed a smile and the door swung into the room. Attached to the handle was a simple affair of a old-fashioned pineapple grenade and string.

"Kid's stuff," J.B. said with a grin, snipping the string and pocketing the grenade. The checkered ball and slim activation lever, or "spoon" as it was called in the predark days, was a predark model from one of the world wars, but still deadly.

The corridor in front of the office was dark, and a quick check showed the overheads were also smashed. In the dim light from the mat-trans unit, they could see the standard redoubt map on the wall. This was level five, office and communications. Below them was storage, power and life support. Above them was the barracks, kitchen and hospital, and the top level—unmarked with a designation.

"Stranger and stranger," Ryan said, the muzzle

of the Steyr SSG-70 sweeping back and forth in perfect rhythm to his own single eye. "We'll head for the elevator. One on one coverage, single yard spread. Soft penetration."

"Top floor?" Jak asked, his head tilted forward.

"Check. If there's anybody here, they'll have supplies or people near the exit."

"Make sense."

"Check."

Keeping near the wall, they felt the air move constantly over them in artificial breezes from the ceiling vents. There was no dust or musky smell of mildew.

"This base must have been absolutely airtight until the recent intrusion," Mildred whispered. "Any supplies in the storerooms should be in perfect shape."

"Could be what those two were fighting over," Krysty noted, straining her spirit to sense any danger.

"Triple stupe," Jak snorted, crouched to offer as poor a target as possible. "Share goods and live."

"Wisdom indeed, my young friend," Doc whispered, patting the teenager on the shoulder. "Share and live. The Oracle at Delphi could not have said it better."

The albino teen ignored the compliment and concentrated on the job at hand.

The end of the hallway was completely dark, and there was no way to see if the elevator was there, or the location of the door to the stairwell. Ryan realized there was no gentle breeze from above.

"The ceiling!" he roared, firing the Steyr upward, working the bolt action. The flashes from the muzzle showed a human figure holding a machine gun as he dropped out of the darkness.

Fast and neat, the group split apart, their pistols and rifles barking a staccato reply. The figure jerked at each deadly impact, but he didn't fall or drop his weapon. Oddly, neither did he return fire. Then the impossible happened. Without dropping his rifle, the stranger opened both of his hands as if majestically offering a holy benediction and two heavy black balls landed on the carpeting with soft thuds, breaking apart and releasing their slim handles.

Chapter Two

"Grenades!" J.B. yelled, dropping his Uzi and diving toward the black spheres. Landing hard on his stomach, the Armorer punched out hard with both hands. He scored a double hit, and the charges bounded down the hallway, disappearing into the darkness.

"Three!" he yelled, covering his head with both arms.

"Open your mouths!" Mildred added, dropping fast.

"Two!" J.B. roared.

"One!" Ryan said, closing his eye.

Double explosions blossomed at the end of the hallway, filling the corridor with flame and thunder. Briefly the fireball silhouetted the hanging man, then violent concussions slammed into the group. A searing wave of heat washed over them, closely followed by a rain of broken ceiling tiles and smoking debris. It made Ryan think of an ant in the barrel of a cannon. Somebody cried out in pain, and a rifle discharged.

In rumbling fury, the blast expanded over them and moved down the corridor, smashing lights and slamming aside doors. Glass shattered somewhere, and an alarm began to sound. Partially deafened and battered, Ryan took heart at that. It meant power was still on somewhere in the redoubt, and each passing second brought them closer to safety. He knew a person died in the first few seconds of an explosion or else survived.

Slowly the strident force died away in ragged stages, leaving in its wake a ringing silence with streamers of acidic smoke moving in the air toward the ducts like ghostly fingers.

"Sweet Jesus!" Mildred coughed. "I...I've had fun before and this isn't it!"

Rolling onto his back, J.B. sat upright and worked his jaw a few times to try to pop his ears clear. "Yeah. Close one."

Leaning against the wall, Krysty hawked and spit to clear her throat. "Too damn close!"

"Everybody okay?" Ryan asked, using the rifle to lever himself upright. Fireblast and hell, he'd felt better after torture.

A ragged chorus answered in the affirmative, then a sudden movement in the smoky darkness caused a wild fusillade of blaster fire.

"Cease firing!" Ryan snapped, shouldering his long blaster. "It's just the meat. He isn't alive."

"Not anymore, you mean," Dean corrected, removing the spent clip from his Browning and slamming in a fresh one. He stuffed the exhausted clip into a pocket where it rattled against others.

"No, he never was alive," Mildred said, patting her hands over her body in a quick check for wounds. There were a couple of holes in her shirt, but nothing worse. "Not for us, anyhow."

Whitish smoke drifting past his pale face, Jak was

almost invisible in the dim corridor. "Possum?" He frowned.

"See for yourself," J.B. said, gesturing. Then he froze and touched his bare head. "Damn!" He turned and started down the corridor, scanning the floor.

Blaster in hand, Jak advanced carefully and pulled a match from a pocket. Striking it on his belt, he studied what remained of the hanging man in the tiny flickering light.

"Dead," he pronounced solemnly. "For while." Sharp spikes of rusty metal jutted from a wooden board that pierced the man's body in a dozen places.

Ryan stepped beside the albino teenager. "Nailed in place." He craned his neck to see into the smashed ceiling. The other end of the board was screwed to a truck-door hinge attached to the concrete roof. The match sputtered and died, so Jak struck another and lit a candle stub. Doc and Krysty did the same. In the soft glow of the triple flames, the scene lost its ghostly feel and became merely another killzone, as familiar as their own faces.

Nudging a lump of twisted steel and plastic on the floor, Dean bent and lifted the dropped weapon. "M-16 A-1 carbine," he said.

"Good?" Doc asked.

"No." He tossed the broken weapon aside.

"Yeah, the gren did a good job on him," Ryan agreed. "Like it was supposed to do on us."

"Simple enough trap," said the returning Armorer, clutching his fedora. "When we approached, the chill swung down, and everybody would naturally shoot at him. Then when you put enough holes

in the ropes, he drops the grens and goodbye."
Smoothing out the crumpled brim, he smiled grimly.
"Exactly the sort of thing I'd do."

Blaster in hand, Dean moved to inspect the
corpse. Chunks of the man were missing, his clothes
only rags, and the ropes holding him in place were
burning in spots, allowing an arm to hang freely.
What little remained of his clothes appeared to be
a tan leather jacket, blue jeans and sandals made
from car tires. Only one sandal was still on a foot,
the other, and the foot inside it, were missing.

Pushing aside the homemade tan jacket, Doc un-
covered a picture on the exposed chest of a curved
knife backed by the rising sun. "What is that?"

Jak squinted against the candlelight. "Knife and
sun?"

"Looks like," J.B. said, adjusting his hat to a
proper cant.

"It's not paint," Ryan stated, trying to rub it off
with a thumb. "Can't be a birthmark."

"This is a tattoo," Mildred said knowledgeably.
She brushed fingertips over the cold torn flesh. "A
lost art these days. See the ulcerations and pitting?
It was done with a sharp pencil and machine oil.
Very crude and must have hurt worse than double
hell."

"Some sort of initiation?" Krysty asked.

"Mayhap. And more importantly, very difficult
for an outsider to forge," Doc noted. "Good way
to identify your own people."

"Not exactly a photo ID," Mildred added, inspecting the lividity of the flesh, "but efficient."

"Exactly."

"ID means more than two," J.B. stated, glancing about.

"Yes, there could be a lot," Krysty agreed. Holding her S&W in a steady grip, she dumped the spent cartridges, trained hands pocketing the spent brass and sliding in fresh rounds.

"Wonder if the others had similar marks," Ryan mused, scratching his chin. "If not, they were probably invaders fighting for turf. If so, it was a mutiny."

Doc sighed. "Internecine, the most uncivil of wars." Gently he prodded the corpse with his swordstick, a few more pieces coming off from the movement. "However, it would be rather valuable data to know if we are facing two gangs, or just one."

"I can check," Mildred offered, pulling a flashlight from her med kit. There was a click and a brilliant cone of white light leaped from the device in her hands, illuminating the corridor with unforgiving clarity.

"Go," Ryan commanded.

Mildred nodded. "Be right back." As she hurried away, the circle of light on the hallway walls bobbed until it angled to the right and disappeared. With the departure of the flash, the darkness seemed even more pronounced than before.

"How'd she get batteries?" Dean asked.

"Doesn't need any," Krysty replied. "When you were at school, Mildred saved the life of the captain of a steamboat. He gave her the flash as payment. It doesn't use batteries. Recharges in sunlight."

"Wow."

"Here," Jak said, passing the boy his own candle. "Hold high."

Dean did as requested, and the albino teen carefully rummaged through the pockets of the dead man. There was some twine knotted into a garrote, a big gold coin embossed with an American eagle on one side and a Nazi swastika on the back, a few 5.7 mm cartridges, a Swiss army knife and a plastic butane lighter, the clear plastic reservoir half full of fuel. He pocketed the lighter and offered the rest to the others. Even though they were the wrong caliber for his Browning, Dean took the cartridges and stuffed them into his already bulging vest. He could extract the powder and primer later for his own bullets. Doc accepted the knife. Nobody took the gold.

"Amazing little thing," Doc said, opening and closing the many small blades. "My daughter would have loved this. She so liked gadgets and such." He glanced about, his voice taking on a gentler, slightly confused tone. "My, I wonder where she, Jolyon and her mother are? It has been hours since I saw them last."

Ryan looked at Krysty, and she moved closer to the old man. "They'll be along soon," the redhead said soothingly. "You wait here."

"Yes, of course," he said amiably, pocketing the knife. "I would not want to miss them. We are going for a picnic down by the river."

Just then, a faint light appeared down the corridor.

"Heads up," Ryan said, snapping his rifle into a combat position. The rest assumed a half circle, blasters ready. As if awakening from a long dream,

Doc put his back to the wall and drew the LeMat, the fog of memories clearing from his face.

"Same marks," Mildred announced, switching off her flash when she reached them. "Knife and sun."

His face masked by the moving candle shadows, Ryan frowned deeply. "So it seems that a gang somehow gained entrance into the redoubt and fought each other to the death." He glanced about. "But why? Over what?"

"Armory," Jak said as if that settled the matter.

J.B. agreed. Blasters were life in the Deathlands.

"I don't think so," Ryan disagreed. "These boys have old weapons, nothing new from military storage."

"Reasonable," Doc said, biting a lip. "I would not be surprised to find out there's nothing here of value."

"Yet they fought to the death over something," Dean pointed out.

"Mebbe it was for the redoubt itself," Krysty suggested. "It's a natural fort that no present-day marauders could ever breach by force."

"Which raises the question, how did they get in?" Mildred asked pointedly. "The front door is nuke-proof and locked with a code."

"Let's go find out," said Ryan, clearing the action of his SSG-70. The long blaster made smooth noises of polished steel moving easily over oiled grooves. "Shoot anything that moves, but try and wound if you can."

"Right. We want these assholes alive for questioning."

As the seven moved to the end of the corridor, the candles revealed the elevator was totally destroyed, its metal frame twisted in wild shapes. The ceiling was bare struts and wiring, the tiles gone, and the terrazzo floor was cracked like hot glass dropped into cold water.

The doors to the stairwell were torn apart, but the metal steps on the other side were still intact. Ryan pointed at J.B., Doc and Jak to go down. Then he tapped his bare wrist, flashed five fingers three times and pointed upward. Next he pointed at Krysty, himself, Dean and Mildred. They nodded and the group split apart, three heading downward, four going up as quietly as possible.

Moving along the stairs, Ryan and his people kept to the side of the steps where the metal would be the strongest and least likely to make noise. Old wood might occasionally creak by itself, just adjusting to temperature and moisture. But old metal was silent, until you stepped where age and rust had weakened it; then steel would squeal louder than pigs getting butchered by an amateur.

Pausing at the first landing, they listened intently, but no sounds disturbed the graveyard peace of the redoubt. Satisfied, they moved on. The doorway to the next level stood gaping open, faint light spilling from the hallway beyond. In a two-on-two rotation formation, they proceeded in, Krysty stepping to one side past the door to allow Ryan to pass her. As he went to the wall, Dean came in fast and crouched low on the floor. Mildred centered last and replaced Krysty at the door, covering their rear, as the redheaded glided past Dean. Staying alert, watching one another's backs, they covered the entire floor, prepared for another trap or ambush. This level of the redoubt proved to be the barracks, every door bearing an empty slot for a nameplate. Each small room was equipped with a single bed, closet, desk, sink, shower and rotting corpse. Some were lying in the middle of the floor with bullet wounds in their foreheads, some with arrows through their chests. A body was found in the closet gut-stabbed. Another was sprawled in the hallway, his body almost cut in two by a shotgun blast. But most of the slain were lying peacefully in bed, their throats slashed, the blankets stiff with dried brown blood.

"Nightcreeps," J.B. growled. "Shoes on the floor, blasters under their pillows. These boys were caught by surprise."

"Mostly," Krysty corrected him. "Remember that guy in the hallway."

"Same tattoos," Dean announced, letting a blanket drop back into place. "These were part of the same group."

"Heads up," Ryan said, easing open a closet with the tip of his rifle. Instantly, there was a twang and out shot an arrow. It streaked across the room to slam into the dead man in the bunk. The corpse jerked at the impact, and the Navy SEAL knife in his withered hand dropped to the floor.

"And it seems as if a few knew something was happening," Dean said, "but most didn't."

"The leaders?" Mildred suggested, eyeing the knife without interest. She already had a Green Beret blade.

Grunting assent, Ryan briefly inspected the contents of the closet. Hanging neatly on racks were blue and gold military uniforms, the creases as sharp as razors, the buttons gleaming with polish. "These are Air Force dress uniforms."

Cradling her S&W .38 on a crooked elbow, Krysty furrowed her brow. "But the last couple of rooms held green Army fatigues."

"A combined military base?"

"Never heard of that before, but why not?"

Ryan made no reply, keeping his own counsel.

"Strange there are no women," Dean said.

"Maybe the leaders did the killing," Mildred replied. "It's happened before."

A metallic noise from the hallway made everybody drop behind furniture, and they waited quietly until two sharp short whistles sounded. Leveling his longblaster at the partially closed door, Ryan whistled once long and low. A few seconds later, his call was repeated exactly. They relaxed and stood as J.B., Jak and Doc entered the room.

"Anything? Ryan asked, shouldering the rifle.

"We found the fifth level burned to the walls," J.B. stated. "The sort of damage done by bathtub Molotov cocktails. Very crude stuff, gasoline and soapflakes. The sixth held the armory and storage. That was full of corpses and more traps. I had to cope with two on the stairwell, a trip wire at the door, a gren attached to a light switch and a crossbow hidden in the—"

"Closet?"

"Crapper. You had some of the same, eh?"

Ryan nodded grimly.

"Kitchen was also clean," Doc said, pulling close a chair and checking underneath it before sitting. "There was not so much as a potato peel or eggshell in the larder. Even the cooking oil in the fryers was gone."

"Probably used it in the Molotovs," Ryan stated.

Studying the predark books on a wall shelf, Mildred said absentmindedly, "Peanut's the best." She pulled out a volume, only to put it right back. Damn, only operation manuals full of abort codes. Nothing interesting.

"Any salt?" Krysty asked, resting a boot on an overturned ammo box, its sides streaked with blood.

The elderly man patted a lumpy pocket in his frock coat. "And some spices."

"Mint?" Mildred asked eagerly.

"A pinch."

"Excellent." She looked at Ryan. "Means we won't be losing lunch on the next mat-trans jump."

Removing his wire-rimmed glasses and polishing them on the end of his shirt, J.B. studied the room. "Nightcreeps, eh? What did they think was so bastard precious down here?"

"Redoubt itself," Jak suggested.

"Something's wrong," Ryan announced. "Let's check the top level. That's where we should find our answer."

"Roger."

"Check."

"Sounds good."

"Yes, sir."

"Doc found the second elevator," J.B. said, following his old friend. "It's in the south end. But I can't recommended using it. Too many traps around."

"Take no chances," Ryan said, working the bolt action on the Steyr. "Shoot anything that moves. I'm on point, J.B. at the rear. Let's go."

The friends proceeded carefully upward. The door on the next level proved to be closed and locked, but with brilliant light seeping from underneath the jamb. After listening for a while, J.B. did his usual magic and the door opened with a minimum of fuss. Inside was a standard military changing room with most of the wall lockers standing ajar. They usually would have done a quick search. Many times they'd found amazing and often useful things that others left behind for no apparent reason.

But the search would wait. The ceiling lights were abnormally bright, brutally illuminating the scene before them in monstrous clarity. A single wooden chair sat in the middle of the room, and sitting limply in it was a girl of no more than ten or twelve years. Her head was tilted, her blond hair streaked with red blood, and lying on the floor beside her was a smoking blaster.

Chapter Three

The seven friends advanced into the room, moving slowly as if mired in molasses. They had seen death hundreds of times, but that didn't make finding a dead child any easier.

"Jak, J.B.," Ryan said, jerking his rifle in different directions. The two men moved off to disappear around the standing rows of lockers. They reappeared a second later at the other end of the room, and gave the clear signal.

Dropping her med kit, Mildred knelt beside the girl and took a limp hand in her own. She pressed on the thumbnail and watched the results. "Dead no more than minutes," she announced. "Skin is warm, blood is viscous and lividity isn't present."

"Minutes?"

"Still smoking," Jak said, pointing to the blaster on the floor. Shifting his rifle, Ryan lifted the pistol. "Barrel is warm," he said, cracking the cylinder. It contained six cartridges of assorted makes, one spent shell. "We just missed her."

Holstering her .38 pistol, Krysty cursed bitterly. "That must have been the odd noise we heard before. A gunshot muffled by the floors between us."

"Makes sense."

"Just skin and bones," Doc rumbled, leaning against a closed locker.

"Check her numbers," Ryan suggested.

The physician brushed aside the bloody hair covering the neck. "Yes, her elevens are showing."

Everybody knew what that meant. They saw a lot of it in the nukelands of America. When a person got close to death by starvation, the twin tendons at the back of the neck would begin to stand out prominently. It was the sure sign that death was only days, maybe hours, away.

"There was no food in the kitchen, or in storage," Mildred said. "No food anywhere that we've seen."

Her hair tightened fiercely about her face as Krysty frowned. "Which means the only thing left to consume was—"

"The dead men." Ryan scowled. "That's a choice few of us can make."

"Rather die," Jak spit, setting his jaw. "Near did once."

"Yeah," the Armorer agreed. "A slug in the head sounds mighty good compared to long pig."

"To consume the flesh of another human," Doc said in his rumbling voice, "is a journey into bestiality that most of us simply cannot take, even if our own lives are forfeit."

"Hot pipe!" Dean said loudly, almost startling himself with the fervor of his cry. He moved his shoulders, making his bulky backpack rustle. "And here we are with a freaking ton of MREs only a floor away. Enough food for an army!"

"Life is timing," Ryan stated, resting a hand on

his son's shoulder. "A minute too soon is as bad as a second too late. Remember that."

Bowing her head, Krysty began to say a short prayer to guide the child's spirit into the world beyond this. The others were respectfully quiet, but stayed alert during the brief ceremony. When Krysty was done, Doc make the Christian sign of the cross and muttered something in Latin.

"One girl, twenty or so men," Mildred mused thoughtfully. "The leader's child? A ransom victim?"

"Or the recreation officer," Ryan said. "Mercies who kill their own usually don't waste time with fancy stunts like kidnapping."

"Not a willing one," Krysty snapped. She lifted the girl's stiffening arm. "See the chain marks on the wrist?"

"That's why she didn't make a run for the door," Doc growled, "The coldhearts were bedamned slavers."

A former slave himself, Jak said, "Good they dead."

Mildred stood and shuddered as if emerging from a river of ice. "The girl might have thought we were the others coming back."

"To claim their prize."

"Yes. To either rape her again, or…"

"Eat her?"

"Mebbe both."

"Sweet Jesus."

"So she was what they were fighting over."

"No," Ryan said abruptly, "she wasn't. The prize was much more important than her." He turned to face the second door across the room. "And we'll find it on the other side of that door." Krysty glanced at the closed portal. "How do you know?"

"Just a hunch. I think I know what this base is." Rifle resting on his hip, Ryan loosened the SIG-Sauer pistol in his belt and removed a gren from his pocket. Carefully, he removed the tape holding the spoon in place and put the primed bomb into his coat.

"I'm on point," he said.

"Maybe we should just leave," Mildred suggested.

"No. What's on the other side could be more valuable to us than it was to the coldhearts."

"Why?"

"Because we can use it." Easing open the door, he waited a moment for a reaction, then slipped through, J.B. at his heels, Krysty close behind.

Dean waited for the others to get a bit ahead of him before following. Then on an impulse, he hurried back, retrieved the Ruger from the floor and tucked it into his belt. What he planned to do with the weapon, Dean had no idea. But he felt angered over the girl's death, and was determined to find somebody or something to blame it on and get revenge.

The next room proved to be the top floor of the redoubt, a single cavernous expanse stretching off for hundreds of yards ahead of them. Broken military machines of a dozen different sizes and shapes dotted the floor in rows upon rows. It was the motor pool. Dean's hopes soared at the sight. His father had told him how many were the times they found working APCs or Hummers, some even with caches of stored fuel and ammo. None of the vehicles ever lasted long, but while they did the team rode in style and safety.

Dodging past a row of vehicles he had once heard Mildred refer to as jeeps, Dean slowed and scowled. The rest of the garage resembled a junkyard, with most of the machines in various stages of being totally disassembled: engines taken out, wheels off, axles bare of brakes and bearings, armor sheeting removed entirely, doors gone, weapon mounts empty.

"Fuel pump!" Jak called, and Dean hurried in that direction. The rest of the group was clustered around a stainless-steel pair of pumps set near the massive ruin of an APC. Dean watched as J.B. worked the priming controls and Jak held a hose hopefully over a bucket. Only vapor belched out.

"Did you prime the pump?" Dean asked.

"This type doesn't need it," Ryan said dourly. "No, the storage tanks have already been drained. Too bad."

"Any sign of that fancy condensed fuel?" Doc asked hopefully.

"None."

"Wish to hell I knew what it was," Mildred grumped. "It doesn't have the odor of regular gas or leave a spectrum pattern on water like any normal petroleum product. Yet regular combustion engines run on it for hundreds of miles a gallon. It's something brand-new."

"Not that there's anything here to fuel," Krysty

said bluntly, glancing around. "The place is a machine graveyard. Nothing but bits and pieces remaining."

Turning off the wheezing pump, J.B. removed his fedora and scratched his head. "Which makes no sense. Why rip apart every machine? Were they searching for a special part?"

"Mebbe they had no idea what they were doing," Dean suggested.

"Doesn't appear so," Ryan said, walking over to a tracked vehicle. The hood was completely gone, the engine compartment exposed to the bare overhead lights. "I spotted it as we passed. See? The engine's been removed, but the nuts on the mounting bolts were screwed back on. A trained mechanic does that so as not to lose a nut, not looters."

"Probably taking parts from one to fix another," Krysty observed. "If so, then there could easily be a Hummer intact somewhere in a corner."

Raking fingers through his hair, Ryan exhaled slowly. "Highly doubtful, but we'll check."

"I saw a big canvas lump over there," Dean said, motioning behind them. "Really huge. Could be anything."

"Show us," Ryan said.

Dodging debris on the floor with the agility of youth, Dean retraced his steps. The neat rows of vehicles became a jumbled array, and finally a barricade of metal parked end to end. Clambering over the impromptu wall, Dean disappeared from view.

The others moved quickly, but with far more care, and found an opening in the ring of steel. Here there was a clear section of floor, and partially covered with a large canvas was the biggest tank any of them had ever seen. A tank of unknown design, but apparently in absolutely perfect condition.

"By the Three Kennedys!" Doc whispered.

J.B. swallowed hard. "The mother lode."

The drapes of canvas covered only the front end of the vehicle, the body stretching over twenty yards in length and twice the height of a man.

"Chassis must be from a cargo truck," Ryan said.

"Twice my height," Jak said, a hand reaching into the air.

"Can it fit out the door?" Mildred asked. "I've never seen anything this large that moved under its own power."

"Unless they were total fools, it'll fit," Ryan replied.

"Eighteen wheels," J.B. said, inspecting the wheel well. "Taken off a Hummer. Only needs six to operate."

"Spares," Ryan decided. "Or a diversion for somebody shooting at them."

"Certainly lowers the odds of a sniper choosing the correct tire to blow."

"She should be able to traverse the worst of the Deathlands."

Keeping a watch on the shadows under the ring of vehicles, the friends walked around their incredible find. The rear doors were louvered, the angled slots perfect for shooting at pursuing vehicles. The dull body armor was of an odd dung-colored material that resembled smooth concrete.

"Antiradar composites taken off stealth helicopters," Mildred guessed. "Probably got some reactive armor plating sandwiched between the outside and the steel sheets inside."

"No way of knowing, short of taking the vehicle apart."

"Even the windows are covered with iron bars to keep anything too big from crashing into the hardened glass."

"Somebody expected this to see serious combat."

Dean carefully climbed on the fender, the wide band of spiked steel resembling a porcupine belt. "It's got a missile pod on the roof. No, there's two!"

J.B. ran his hands over a grooved slot on the hull, which entirely ringed the vehicle. "This is to mount Claymore mines and blow away attackers who get too close. We don't have any mines, but I can put something there. Wads of plastique packed with nails and broken glass should do the trick."

"Mebbe it isn't finished," Krysty said. "Let's get this canvas completely off. Somebody gave me a hand." They all joined in to assist her. "Ready, pull!"

The sheet came down in rustling folds, exposing the slanted nose of the war machine. The prow was armed with a set of 75 mm recoilless rifles. Ryan thankfully spotted the vents to allow the blowback gas to leave the interior of the vehicle and not cook the crew after a single shot. There were side-mounted Remington .50-caliber machine guns, and two aft-mounted Vulcan 40 mm cannons, set on swivels for traversing.

"Shit," Jak drawled, making the word two long syllables.

Doc agreed with a dumb nod.

"It's going to be as loud as hell inside when we use those 75 mm rifles," Mildred commented. "Especially both at once."

"If there's any shells for them," J.B. stated. Along the aft part of the hull were racks for motorcycles, but no bikes. Presumably the coldhearts knew where to find some, but that knowledge was lost forever.

"Needs name," Jak said. "Death wagon."

"May I suggest Leviathan," Doc countered. "It is much more appropriate."

Jak snorted. "Got no balls. Death wagon."

"Leviathan," Ryan decided, then relented. "Vote on it."

Leviathan won.

Inspecting underneath, Jak found some Claymore mines mounted on the belly near the exit hatch. Ryan decided to leave them there. It was a good idea to have your escape route mined in case of possible lurkers.

"Almost makes Trader's war wag look like an oxcart."

"It's the biggest find we've made since the redoubts themselves. It must have taken them months, mebbe longer to build this."

"It's why they fought. With this chariot, they could have ruled an empire."

"And after it was done, the question of who got to be the boss became disputed."

"Makes sense."

"The idiots," Mildred snapped. "Sitting on a gold mine and they whizzed in the water."

"Mixed metaphors," Doc said, smiling, "but I agree wholeheartedly."

"Well, it's ours now," Dean stated, beaming. Then his elation faded. "If we can get in."

J.B. looked contemptuous. "With me and Ryan here, in the middle of a machine shop? Please."

"Doors locked," Jak said, rattling a recessed handle.

"Not for long." Smugly, J.B. went to work with his picks and probes. A few minutes passed.

"Well?" Ryan asked impatiently.

"It's unlocked, but not opening," J.B. said through gritted teeth.

"Bolted from the inside?"

"No, just stuck for some reason. Mebbe jammed. Somebody give me a hand, will you?"

Shouldering their weapons, Dean and Jak went to the tool table then joined the Armorer. Dean slid a long screwdriver between the door and the hull, while Jak forced the end of a pry bar into the opposite side of the portal.

"Wish I had leather gloves," J.B. muttered, as he spit on his hands and grabbed the recessed handle again. "Okay, all together on my mark. Ready? One, two, three, pull!"

The three friends groaned in unison, yet the door remained motionless, the hinges creaking loudly. Suddenly, there was a loud snap and the door swung away, the pieces of a pencil tumbling to the floor. The men dropped their tools and grinned in triumph.

"Ha! Just a freaking pencil caught in the hinge."

J.B. laughed, rubbing his hands together. "I thought it would be something simple— Dark night!" The Armorer threw himself backward as animal growls came from within the tank and a misshapen figure stepped into view.

Vaguely, it resembled a large black dog, only its muscular body was covered with overlapping scales in the manner of an armadillo. Its head was outrageously large, the eyes as yellow as a harvest moon. Two writhing tentacles sprang from the shoulders, and a scorpion's tail tipped with a stinger that glistened moistly curled from its rump.

"Hellhound!" Jak yelled, his .357 Magnum blaster booming at the monstrosity. Both rounds missed and ricocheted off the inside of the craft.

Golden foam dripping from its muzzle, the mutie rushed at them with tentacles thrashing. Dean kicked the door, and the metal slab swung closed on the lashing tail. The animal hissed in pain and struggled frantically to get loose. On the floor, J.B. rolled for his Uzi. Leveling his Steyr longblaster, Ryan aimed and fired in one motion. The big rifle boomed louder than artillery in the garage, the heavy-caliber round smashing the beast against the armored hull. Its stinger lashed out for Ryan's face, and the one-eyed man knocked it away just in time with his rifle butt. Jak appeared around the door, boldly shoving his blaster into the hellhound's right eye and pulling the trigger. The creature's head exploded, spraying pale yellow blood and pink brains everywhere.

"Fireblast!" Ryan cursed, levering in a fresh round. "It's got friends!"

Snarling and hissing, two more hellhounds appeared. Mildred and Krysty each hit the largest with their .38 bullets to no effect, and J.B. sprayed both with 9 mm Parabellum rounds. Neither beast seemed adversely affected. Dean blasted another in the right ear with the Ruger, its head slamming back. Yellow blood flowed from the wound, but the beast struck out with tentacles and stinger, the boy diving behind the door again. The other hellhound reached out its tentacles to grab hold of the top of the tank and impossibly flipped upside down, landing on the roof. There was a patter of pads on metal and the mutie was gone.

The other launched itself over J.B. and landed on the worktable next to the cans of fuel. Everybody tracked the beast, but nobody fired.

"Fuck!" Jak cried, his hand trembling from the exertion of not firing.

"If we miss and hit a can, we'll set fire to ourselves!" Mildred roared.

Low and fast, Ryan pulled out his panga and circled to the left. Dropping the LeMat into his coat pocket, Doc drew the sword within his cane and expertly lunged for the snarling beast. The steel blade went straight into its mouth, going deeper and deeper until the muzzle came dangerously near the old man's hand. Both tentacles slashed at him, but missed, the stinger arching in lethal readiness. Mildred shot at the moist barbed tip, missing. Doc shoved again, putting his full weight behind the thrust. The blade sliced in farther, the black lips touching his hand, the jagged teeth an inch away. Then the beast went stock-still as its mottled eyes rolled in their sockets, showing yellow. The tentacles went limp and the creature toppled over amid the tools, knocking some onto the floor.

Coolly, Mildred walked to the thing and put a round directly into its right eye with surgical precision. The head jerked, and blood flowed out of its mouth and ears.

Shoving the corpse to the floor, Doc placed a boot on the thing's face and yanked his sword free. "And thou, wretched boy, that did consort him here, shall with him hence!" he said with a flourish, wiping the blade clean on the animal's black coat. Then as they watched, the fur began to fade to a neutral color of greenish tan.

"Good God!" Doc gasped.

"More!" Krysty shouted, her revolver banging steadily.

Three more hellhounds leaped from the vehicle. But these didn't join the fight. They bounded off into the junkyard, vanishing underneath and amid the endless collection of disassembled vehicles.

"Gaia, we'll never find them out there," Krysty said, her crimson hair flexing as she reloaded her revolver.

"We're not even going to try," Ryan replied. Something moved in the distance, and he fired the rifle at it. There was no yelp or hiss of pain. "Mildred, Dean, sweep the tank, two-man cover. Go!"

The two climbed into the vehicle under the watching blasters of their companions, then moved into the interior, thrusting the ready muzzles of the blasters under seats, into lockers and ammo bins.

"Clear!" Mildred announced with obvious relief.

"There's nowhere anything as large as them could hide."

"And you should see the control panel," Dean added.

"Later. Everybody in the tank!"

"Once inside, we're trapped," Mildred reminded, kneeling in the open hatchway. "And if there's no fuel in the gas tank, we die long and slow."

Ryan glared, his mouth a rigid line. "Five minutes and counting. Dean by me, shoot anything that moves!"

The boy climbed down to take a position beside his father.

"Move people!" Jak shouted, racing to the work-table. Grabbing an armload of tools, he sprinted to the tank and tossed them inside. Doc shrugged off his backpack of supplies and started ferrying over fuel cans two at a time. Mildred grabbed the packs and hauled them into the tank, making room for the next load. "These things are full of something!" the elderly man announced. "Sure hope it is fuel."

"Me, too!"

"What are hellhounds, anyway?" J.B. demanded, dragging over a massive a toolbox. "Muties?"

"Bio weps," Jak replied, hefting a box full of oil cans.

"Escaped after skydark, eh?"

"Guess."

"Nasty buggers."

Wrapping a chain around the rear stanchion of the tank, Krysty asked, "Any weak points beside the eyes and ears?"

Opening a bulky canvas bag, Jak saw it was full

of engine belts and radiator hoses. Mighty useful. He slung it over his shoulder. "Sure. Can't swim."

"Great," J.B. muttered, helping Doc with more gas canisters. The coldhearts had to have raided every fuel tank in the place to get this much gas. There was nearly a hundred gallons. "Can't swim. Just great."

"We're running out of room in here!" Mildred called.

"I'm on it," Krysty shouted as she laid out the chain to the towbar of a jeep and looped it around. She then cinched the locking clamp tight. She stood back. "There. We can drag this along behind. Throw in anything you want."

As the others rushed to obey, something moved in the shadows and Dean cut loose with his Browning Hi-Power, the bullets ricocheting off a steel support.

"Chill! Stop wasting rounds on shadows. We're being stalked," Ryan said, pulling out his silenced 9 mm blaster. "These things are smart. Too bastard smart for my liking. Wait until you actually see something."

"Okay, Dad," Dean said, slamming a fresh clip into the blaster while studying the darkness underneath a Hummer.

Over by the fuel pumps, a steel drum noisily toppled over. Nobody reacted. Then a loud creak sounded from the rafters. Spinning in a gunfighter's crouch, Doc drew and fired his LeMat, the .44 Magnum slug blasting the overhead light into sparking rubbish. Darkness swallowed them, and immediately things began to move in the cluttered ring of military craft around them.

"Shield your eyes!" Mildred shouted from the front of the tank, and lights erupted all over the Leviathan, catching two of the hellhounds standing brazenly in the open. Ryan and Dean both cut loose, but only succeeded in driving the beasts away.

"Last load!" Ryan barked, dropping the Steyr's clip and sliding in a fresh magazine. "Double time!"

Wasting no time in recriminations, everybody climbed inside, dragging packs of supplies and goods. The thick door was pulled closed with a solid, reassuring clang, and Jak drove home the locking bolt.

"Dark night, I hate leaving supplies," J.B. panted, collapsing into a seat.

"Once the dogs are dead, we can loot the place down to the nails in the walls," Ryan told him, his good eye focused out an ob slit. "But first things first. We kill the hounds."

"Anything moving?" Doc asked.

"Not yet."

"Lights on or off?" Mildred asked from the driver's console.

Wearily, Ryan sat down, the cushioned seat feeling sinfully soft. "On for now. Let's catch our breath."

"Take five," Krysty said, dropping her backpack of supplies.

The recessed ceiling lights were bright but not harsh, and Ryan found the inside of the tank surprisingly plush. The coldhearts had to have liked their comfort. There was combat seating for eight in the back, with lockers lining the two walls. Next was a gunnery seat for the left and right Remington .50-calibers, and ammo dumps, nicely full. In the middle was a field surgery unit that Mildred was already examining. Beyond that was a standardized gun rack with a locking bar holding a couple of longblasters in place. Next was a line of general storage lockers with the pile of tools and fuel cans from the garage. He was surprised at how much loot his people had been able to grab in the short period of time allotted. Near the front were more seats, these facing forward instead of inward, then the cockpit with driver's seat and gunner's chair. Ryan walked closer, pausing to note the water tank seemed to be almost full and pleased that the ceiling was high enough he didn't have to bend or stoop. The dashboard was covered with electronic instruments, only half of which he could identify: radar, nightscopes, infrared and a powerful radio. In spite of the luxurious interior, Ryan reminded himself that this was no pleasure craft, but a combat vehicle, a troop carrier with blasters. Nothing more.

"Can we fuel from inside?" Dean asked from the rear of the tank.

"Yes. There's a feeder pipe over by the flamethrower."

"The what?"

"But there's no lav," Mildred continued, loosening her sleeves and rolling them up. "Could get messy if we're in here for any length of time."

"No kitchen either," Krysty remarked, taking

stock of their most recent acquisition. "But at least we can eat these food packs without cooking them."

Moving to the front, Krysty took the gunnery chair and examined the controls. "There are twice as many nuke batteries as needed." She tapped a gauge with a fingernail. "And fully charged."

"We ever get some insulated wiring," Mildred said, "we can connect the spare batteries to the door handles to dissuade invaders."

"Dissuade?" Jak repeated, arching a snowy eyebrow.

"Fry," Doc explained.

"Ah."

"We also have three motors," Ryan stated, studying the complex collection of gauges, indicators and lights. "But we only need two to run this behemoth."

"A spare motor? There's a fine notion."

A thump sounded from outside.

"Company!" Ryan told them, grabbing his blaster. The friends jumped to the gunports, but the dark shapes were already disappearing into the jumble of vehicles.

"Odd they didn't hit the door or a window," Krysty said, watching them go.

"Maybe they weren't trying to get in," Mildred suggested.

J.B. frowned. "They were doing something else."

"Everybody check for damage," Ryan snapped, looking out the front windshield. "Fine over here."

"No damage."

"Hell's bells," Mildred cried, struggling to see

out the starboard blasterport. "There's a tire missing!"

"What? They ate a tire?"

"One is gone, that's for sure. I see a bare rim on the port side."

"Why would animals eat a tire?" Dean asked.

"Not animals," Jak said distinctly. "Bio weps."

Krysty understood immediately. "Freaking things are going to try and ground us. Without tires we can't leave. The belly won't clear the floor. We'll be trapped and eventually have to walk out or die of starvation."

"Same as the coldhearts," Doc said. "Fuck that," Ryan said, returning to the driver's seat. There was no specialized key to start the engines, merely a push button. Setting the choke to the middle, and hoping that was correct, he hit the gas and revved the starter. The diesels rumbled mightily, making the whole vehicle vibrate with the barely confined power of the Detroit engines.

"Atomic batteries to power," Doc muttered softly to himself. "Turbines to speed."

Only Mildred snorted a laugh at the allusion.

"We're out of here," Ryan said, twisting the steering wheel and working the stick shift. With a crash, Leviathan plowed a path through the metal circle, windshields shattering and APCs shoved aside as they headed for the exit.

Chapter Four

As Leviathan started to rumble forward, two hell-hounds darted out of nowhere. They hit the front windshield in unison, and the iron bars shuddered under the double impact. Black muzzles snapped less than a foot from Ryan's face, and he could actually see down their throats. Muscular tentacles wrapped about the protective gridwork, and their front paws clawed at the glass, scratching the resilient surface of the military composite.

Blaster in hand, Krysty started to roll down the side window when she spotted a barbed tail hovering low alongside the door. "Shit! They're waiting for us to try and get them!"

"Hold on!" Ryan growled, and he slammed on the brakes. Tires squealing, the supplies went hurtling forward as the tank screeched to a halt, throwing the dogs off the hood. Instantly, Ryan hit the gas and the massive vehicle surged forward once more. A hellhound hit the spiked front bumper, its bleeding form stuck there caterwauling in pain. The other fell out of sight, but Ryan felt the big vehicle bump over something that crunched.

"The others are backing off," Dean said, watching from an ob slit. "They're...yep, they're gone."

"Flanking us," Jak said, moving to the starboard .50-caliber machine gun. "What's belly height?"

Working the bolt on the port Remington, J.B. said, "Good foot and a half."

"Don't let them get underneath us!" Ryan ordered from the front.

"Check!"

Doc and Mildred rushed to the louvered rear door and shoved the muzzles of their handblasters out the downward slats.

"Hey, Dean!" Krysty called.

Dean glanced at the woman.

"Here, use this!"

The youngster caught the shotgun thrown his way. It was a beauty, a pump-action 12-gauge. The stock was polished walnut and the shoulder strap was lined with spare shells.

Krysty jerked a thumb. "It was in the gunrack. It'll do more damage than your Browning."

Nodding his thanks, the boy pumped the scattergun and shoved the barrel out a slot.

Ahead of them was a large hole in the redoubt wall, a curved opening almost exactly the size and shape of Leviathan. Ryan eased on the gas and slowed for a moment to correct their alignment. They had a clearance of only inches. He had to go in dead center or risk scraping off some of the external equipment. The coldhearts had to have planned to remove the radar and missiles pods before trying this stunt. But that option wasn't available to them now. The bastard hellhounds were much too loyal to their dead masters, and too freaking smart.

"A camel through the eye of a needle," Mildred commented.

"More like two pounds of muck in a one-pound bag," J.B. countered, adjusting his fedora. "If it gets any tighter, we'll need to grease the walls."

"Too bad the lights are working," Krysty said, measuring the tunnel and the girth of the tank with her hands. "Then you could concentrate on their placement on the far wall as a guide."

"Mebbe next time," Ryan said, slowing their speed and thinning their fuel mix. The diesels were sluggish, and needed to warm.

Smoothly engaging the transmission, Ryan backed a yard, then, as slowly as possible, entered the tunnel. Immediately something scraped noisily overhead, and everybody looked up, weapons in hand.

"It's only the radio antenna," J.B. said, relaxing.

"Or the missile holders," Dean added, looking worried.

In the front gunner's chair, Krysty tapped the instrument panel with a knuckle. "Missile pods are on-line and showing green. No damage."

"Yet," Jak said, seeming more glum than usual.

"Luckily, the coldhearts labeled everything in plain English."

"Yeah, lucky."

With a hand on the gearshift, Ryan said nothing but clenched the steering wheel even tighter. Once more the oversized tank rolled ahead at a snail's pace. The scraping continued, sounding louder than before. Then there was a crunch from above, and the tunnel behind them went dead black. Ryan stopped fast.

"We're smashing the lights," J.B. said, listening to the glass shards sprinkle along the sides of the tank.

"Shitfire. We need darkness ahead of us, not in our wake!"

Grimly, Ryan slid the transmission into gear. "Watch for the dogs! Shoot at anything…no, just randomly shoot!"

Dean promptly fired the Mossberg shotgun out the rear doors, paused, then fired again in an irregular pattern.

"Wasteful," Jak grumbled.

"Necessary," the Armorer snapped, adding a .50-caliber burst from the Remington. The big slugs rained along the tunnel, hitting nothing.

Every foot seemed to take an hour. The tension grew thick in the vehicle, but nobody dared to speak, trying their best not to distract Ryan from the delicate task. At the first narrow turn of the zigzagging maze, Ryan jockeyed the tank back and forth, each maneuver gaining him inches until they could make the corner. But the next turn of the antiradiation maze was set impossibly close to the first, and Leviathan resoundingly rubbed against the rough walls, grinding off chunks of the concrete.

Yard by yard, scraping at every turn, Ryan eased the gigantic vehicle through the tunnel until, finally, it cleared the last turn. Now before them was a length of straight tunnel that would take them to a set of massive vanadium-steel doors. The expanse of burnished metal was widely smudged with dark soot in an unusual flowery pattern. The only clean area was a small metallic keypad that twinkled silvery in the headlights.

Ryan released his death grip on the steering wheel and flexed his hands to restore circulation. "Those are black-powder blast marks."

"The coldhearts must have tried to blow their way out," J.B. said from a rear seat.

"Idiots. Those doors are nuke-proof," Mildred scoffed, "and they thought powder was going to open them?"

"Desperate men will try anything," Krysty remarked. "An animal will chew off its own foot to get free from a trap."

"But if they got in," Dean said, "the same code would let them out, right?"

"Yes," replied his father. "Their leader must have got lucky and figured out the access code. When he got chilled fighting over who would own the Leviathan, that was it for everybody."

"They did it to themselves. The damn fools."

"Damn dead fools." Ryan started to unbuckle his safety harness, but Krysty stopped him.

"I'm faster," she said and was out the side door before he could respond.

"Fireblast!" he cried. "Everybody to the ports. Give her cover!"

Ryan hit the controls, turning on every light they had, as blaster barrels extended from every port. Sprinting to the wall, the redhead rapidly punched in the access code, then turned and headed for the tank.

A flurry of blasterfire from the side .50-caliber

machine guns cut loose and the woman crouched low, both hands gripping her S&W revolver. She had no idea what they were shooting at. The blasters were pointed low, the rounds glancing off the concrete wall. Then from under Leviathan came two hellhounds, the nightmare beasts springing straight for her. The crossing streams of heavy slugs caught one and brutally cut it in two. The undamaged animal retreated into the darkness, while the wounded dog writhed grotesquely, still trying to reach Krysty, the tentacles and paws dragging along the bloody hunks of dying flesh. Standing, she kicked the animal out of the way with her silver-tipped boot and scrambled into the safety of the tank.

"Thanks," she said, locking the door tight.

J.B. tipped his hat. Partially hidden by the large pile of supplies in the middle of the vehicle, Mildred flashed a smile. "No prob," she said, patting the boxy breech of the Remington. "Feeds a bit slow, but it's much better than my Czech revolver."

"Here we go," Ryan announced, shifting gears. The massive steel portal had risen into the ceiling with the sound of oiled gears and smooth hydraulics. Brilliant sunshine poured into the tunnel. Ryan accelerated out of the darkness, and the tank was engulfed in a blinding glare. Nothing could be seen through the windows. Then, incredibly, the glass tinted, dimming the light to bearable levels. "Dean, jump out and punch in the code to close the door," Ryan ordered. As the youth did his father's bidding, the rest of the companions covered Dean until he was safely back on board. When the door had finally descended, the entrance to the base was a solid sheet of sand-colored alloy, the squat dome resembling an outcropping of granite. Leviathan was only a short distance away, and the friends found it difficult to pinpoint the entrance.

"Good disguise," Jak stated, sounding impressed.

Shifting sands and bare rock stretched to the horizon, without a single break of withered grass, dead trees or the ancient remains of a sidewalk. As far as they could tell, this was virgin desert, as pristine as before humanity walked erect.

Krysty gave a shiver. "Dead, it's so dead," she said, hugging her shaggy bearskin coat tight as if she were freezing. "There's no life out here I can feel."

"Good," Jak said, idly stropping one of his countless throwing knives on a pocket whetstone.

"Reminds me of the lunar landscape," Mildred commented.

Dean stared at her and began to ask a question, then stopped. He would take her word on the matter. Mildred knew things that were almost impossible for him to believe, but were true nonetheless.

"It does resemble the moon, dear lady, except for those," Doc noted, pointing. In the far distance, gray mountains rose high into the sky, their sides twinkling as if set with a thousand diamonds.

"Now that's interesting," the physician murmured, raising a pair of binocs to her face and pressing them against the tinted composite glass. "Note those rolling hills before the odd mountains? That's atomic landscaping. When the nuke hit, the soil rippled liked a pond when you drop in a stone, then solidified into place.''

Opening the window a crack, Ryan unclipped the rad counter from his collar and held it outside. ''Clean!''

''Same here,'' J.B. said from the starboard machine gun, inspecting his own rad counter. ''Must have been a short half-life bomb that leveled this area. Background is tolerable.''

''So where are we?'' Mildred asked.

Tucking away his rad counter, J.B. reached into his shirt and produced a minisextant. ''Give me five minutes and I can tell you.''

''Anywhere not Chicago is fine by me,'' Doc said succinctly, his face full of memories.

Returning the rad counter to his collar, Ryan closed the window. ''Area seems secure, but don't dawdle, J.B. Everybody else watch for—''

''Incoming,'' Dean cried loudly from the rear doors.

Doc joined him at the louvered slots. ''By the Three Kennedys, those Dantean canines are yet after us!'' Then his expression changed to befuddlement. ''Shades of the great Houdini! Th-they're gone!''

''Ran away?'' Ryan asked pointedly. He was looking in both the sideview mirrors, but couldn't see the mutie dogs.

''No, sir,'' Dean reported, swallowing hard. ''They're just...gone. Sort of, faded away.''

''They turned light tan in color,'' Doc explained, making sure the bolt on the rear doors was secure. ''Exactly the same hue as the sand.''

''Like chameleons?'' Mildred asked, studying the

desert outside. Only the baked sand was visible, but every little puff of wind-driven dust now held hostile intent. "That's why they were black inside the garage, and the dead went neutral in tone. Better cover. Fascinating."

"Deadly," Ryan corrected, swiveling in his chair. "Krysty, anything on that infrared gizmo?"

"Checking," the redhead replied, fumbling with the unfamiliar controls. It took her a few moments to figure out what was where. "No, it's too hot out here. There's a switch here for something called ultraviolet."

Krysty flipped a switch and a vid screen came to life, showing a stark black-and-white view of the landscape. She rotated a tracking ball, and the picture spun to their wake. "Found them! Smack on top of that big sand dune."

"Got them." The Armorer smiled and he hit a switch.

There was a metallic clang, then a roaring noise that built in volume, then quickly faded away. From the side windows and ports, the friends could see a silvery dart riding a column of reddish fire streak away to violently impact on the hilltop. The entire dune vanished in a tremendous explosion, a geyser of sand blowing into the sky for dozens of yards.

"Dead," Jak said, his scarred face twisting into a smile.

Easing on the clutch, Ryan brought the rumbling machine to a gentle halt. "Well?" he asked.

"No," Krysty replied, fine-tuning the controls. "Two figures are running off into the sunset."

"Where? Directly into the sunset, or on a vector?" J.B. snapped.

"Too late," she announced, as the screen went blank. "They're gone."

"Well, we got most of them," Dean said.

"But not all."

J.B. yanked off his hat and smacked it into his hand. "Dark night! Bastard things are harder to kill than a three-headed stickie!"

"And uglier," Jak drawled, testing a knife edge on a thumb. "Least they gone."

"Indeed, sir," Doc agreed vehemently. "And good riddance I say."

Rolling down a window, Ryan let the dry desert wind blow over his face. "No," he said, "it's not good. Until we have two corpses, nobody goes outside this vehicle alone. At least, not until we're far away from here."

"Can't know we're away till we get the coordinates of here," J.B. said, undogging the lock to the side door. "Okay, everybody cover me. I'm gonna find out where we are."

"Scope is clean," Krysty said, fiddling with the contrast. "But you best hurry. I can't scan on every side at once."

"No prob."

Their handblasters primed, Jak and Dean took positions on either side of the open door, grimly watching the landscape for any suspicious movements. Slinging his submachine gun, J.B. reached inside his shirt and pulled out his minisextant. "Just a second," he announced working the device. Focusing the mirrors on the sun, then the horizon, he checked his arcs and counted off the seconds.

"Hmm, 40 minutes 32 seconds longitude, 82 minutes even 30 seconds latitude. If memory serves me right, we're in northwestern Ohio." The Armorer cracked a smile. "Smack in the middle of Salt Fork Lake."

"Lake?" Jak snorted, squinting at the blazing sun and windswept landscape.

"Nuke landscaping," Ryan reminded him, resting both arms on the steering wheel. "Seems to be desert on every side but straight ahead. What are those odd mountains to the east?"

J.B. climbed in and closed the door. "The Alleghenies, extending into West Virginia and Pennsylvania. Can't tell you more. I don't know this section of America."

"As I recall, it was mostly farmland," Doc said, leaning forward in his seat. "Very low-level-priority targets. No military bases or heavy industry. Therefore, the area most likely avoided a major attack."

"Even some is a lot," Krysty commented, her hair moving as if stirred by unfelt winds. "One nuke can ruin your whole damn day."

"Pennsylvania. That means the Amish," Mildred said thoughtfully. "Even in my day they had renounced technology. Lived by muscle power. Their civilization wouldn't collapse."

"Slave muscle?" Ryan asked suspiciously.

"Never! They were good Christian folks," Doc stated. "Hopefully, they still are. We should be able to trade with them."

"Sounds good," decided the one-eyed warrior. Pulling out the choke, he started the Detroit power plants with a low rumble. The gas gauge read just under the full line, and the side gauge read a reserve tank of four hundred gallons completely full. Plus, they had to have another couple of hundred gallons in cans. "J.B., any roads?"

"Nothing on the map. But there's supposed to be a river ahead of us. Always easy traveling there. Even if it's gone, the bed will make us a good road."

"East it is, then." Easing in the clutch and engaging the gears, Ryan brought the vehicle to a forward roll just as a beep sounded from the dashboard. Then another.

"It's the radar," he said, sounding surprised. "Something is coming our way."

"The dogs again?" Mildred asked, moving quickly to a Remington. She snapped the release and opened the breech, laying in a fresh belt of ammo. J.B. did the same on the other side. In an ever-increasing rhythm, the beeps slowly started coming together faster and faster. "No. Not the dogs," Krysty said.

"So, what is it?"

"I don't know," Ryan said, pushing down the gas pedal, Leviathan moving off with increasing speed. "But it's bastard big and coming our way."

"Direct?"

"Sure is."

Resting the Mossberg on a vacant seat, Dean went to the port blasterslot and scrutinized the desert. Only sunbaked desolation was visible. Some clouds in the far distance. Nothing more. "You sure?" he asked.

Dodging an irregular outcrop, Ryan glanced at the glowing green blip on the luminescent screen, which was increasing in size by the second. "Hell, yeah."

"Found it!" Mildred cried, binocs to her face. "At seven o'clock, and moving fast."

"What is it?" Ryan asked, urging more rpm out of the engines. Fight or flight, speed was to their advantage either way. He didn't care what it was, anything that large was trouble.

"Squat, low." Mildred paused, adjusting the focus. "Resembles a tank, but I'm not familiar with the model. Must have been on patrol around the base."

"Waiting for coldhearts," Jak said. "Another Leviathan?"

"No," she retorted. "A real tank. Straight military. Only it is larger, like a Abrams on steroids. It's covered with antennas and dish shapes. But it only has a little cannon."

"That means no range," J.B. stated confidently. "No prob, as long as we keep enough distance."

"What kind of little?" Ryan interrupted. "Short in length, or thin, a small-caliber blaster?"

"What's the difference?" the physician asked.

He stared in the sideview mirror. Nothing in sight yet. "Escape," he told her over the beeping radar.

"Short and fat," J.B. announced. Hat in hand, the Armorer had his face pressed hard against the slot to steady his view against the jostling of the vehicle.

In response, Ryan pressed the accelerator firmly to the floor. The twin diesels roared in barely restrained fury. The quivering needle of the speedometer steadily climbed to forty kph, fifty, sixty, seventy, seventy-five, seventy-six....

Chapter Five

The radar was starting to keen so J.B. turned the machine off. They had been warned, its job was done.

"Could it be," Krysty asked urgently, "an intact Ranger?

"Hope not," Ryan said through gritted teeth.

"What's a Ranger?" Dean asked.

"A predark robot tank, comp-operated, no driver. Never heard of anybody ever stopping one."

Krysty spun her chair and worked the breech on the 75 mm recoilless rifle. It was empty. "Jak, help me find the shells for the rifle!"

"Move it or lose it, people!" Ryan shouted, watching their Hummer of supplies bounce along behind them. Several boxes had already come loose, and they were losing more goods constantly. But there was nothing he could do about that. Supplies and food could be replaced. Not lives.

"If only we had some bastard trees for cover," he snarled to himself. Those strange gray mountains seemed a million miles away, and there was a nuke crater between them. If it was old and cold, it would mean hardly any cover. Exactly what they didn't want. If it was hot, an even worse death awaited them of bleeding sores and coughing out pieces of their lungs. Maybe it was only the dogs pulling a trick, or some coldhearts in a Hummer.

"I do not see anything," Doc announced at the rear doors. "Just sand and... No, wait. There it is."

"Dark night, it's bigger than us!"

"Stop behind a dune and kill the engines," Doc suggested. "Perhaps it is following us by the noise."

"Must be the tracks in the sand."

"No," Krysty said. "It's following our radar!"

"Already off." Ryan cursed.

"Mebbe the guys inside only want to talk or trade," Dean suggested hopefully. "Or we can lure them out and—"

"There's nobody inside it," Ryan said, turning around a dune so quickly that six wheels left the ground. "That thing is fast."

"We are faster," Doc said in false confidence.

"Not by much," Ryan stated grimly.

Krysty looked at the speedometer. "Can't we get any more speed?"

Weaving around rocks and gullies, Ryan checked the console. "We're at the red line."

Krysty glanced in a mirror. The black shape was closer and bigger. "It's not enough."

"I know."

His face pressed hard against the cushioned eyepiece of the periscope, finger lying next to the launch button of the missile pod, J.B. worked the focus and there it was, just as Mildred had described the thing. A squat angular box covered with antennae and with a single, front-mounted cannon. He couldn't ID the caliber of the gun, but it sure didn't seem big enough to damage anything armored like the Leviathan.

"Hey!" Mildred cried. "Its muzzle just glowed in a rainbow pattern."

"Rainbow?" Dean repeated.

"Yes," Mildred said, clearly puzzled. "No explosions or missile launched. Just some pretty colors. There it goes again!"

Handing Krysty a shell from the bin, Jak scowled. "Colors?"

"Brace for impact!" Ryan yelled, twisting the steering wheel hard. Everybody not buckled in was thrown from their seats, and supplies scattered as the ground alongside the Leviathan violently exploded. The armored craft rocked from the concussion.

"It has a laser," Doc gasped, unable to believe his eyes. "The rainbow was the spectrum effect."

J.B scowled. "Laser? Then what exploded?"

"Nothing. That was a thermal cloud from the vaporized sand, or so I would guess," Doc replied.

"Vaporized!"

"Yes."

"Hole's big as a bathtub," Krysty added.

"Laser, schmazer," J.B. said, and he pressed the trigger hard as if he were thrusting a knife into the vitals of a living enemy.

In the sideview mirror, Ryan spied a rustling firebird leap from the rear missile pod to streak away and impact on the turret of the tank with a thunderclap. A fireball blossomed over the machine, obliterating it from view.

"Bull's-eye!" J.B. yelled.

"Hold on," Ryan told him, and he pulled in the choke on the engines. Flooded with fuel, the military diesels revved madly, the console gauge needle going off the scale as the twin 1,250 horse power plants shoved the front wheels of the tank off the ground in its haste to depart.

"Why the rush?" Doc asked, sitting in his seat and calmly crossing his legs. "John Barrymore delivered a mortal blow."

Dean agreed. "We should stop and loot the wreckage."

Concentrating on his driving, Ryan made no reply. As his grinning friends watched, out of the crackling inferno of the blast rolled the ebony tank completely undamaged.

"Dark night, it isn't scratched," J.B. whispered. He took a step from the periscope and almost tripped over a box of spare parts on the floor. "Can't be."

"Rainbow again!" Krysty shouted, and another blast rocked their vehicle.

Ignoring the fight around her, Mildred sat quietly in her chair, studying her watch and counting.

"J.B., launch another missile!" Ryan snapped. "Mebbe it'll work this time! Aim for the laser itself!"

"He can't," Krysty said from the front seat. "The whole control board just went dead. Our rear pod is gone."

"What about the front pod?"

"It can't shoot backward. You want to turn around?"

"Hell, no!"

"My turn," J.B. snapped, cranking the wheel to traverse the rear Vulcan 40 mm cannon. "Jak, Mildred, load me with AP and keep them coming."

"That won't work on a tank," Doc reminded him.

"You got a better plan?"

"Yes, I do." Doc stood, swaying to the motions of the racing vehicle and went to rummage in the wall locker, tossing out ammo boxes and grens as if they were rubbish.

"I saw the empty cases in the garage," he grunted. "So they must be here. They must! They couldn't have used them all against each other."

Ryan watched out of the corner of his vision. He had no idea what the old man was planning and fervently hoped he wasn't off again on a daydream trip to the good old days.

"Twenty-two!" Mildred cried, staring at her watch in triumph. "Yes!"

"What?" Ryan demanded, swerving past the remains of a stone fence. A plastic sign was still in place, but any words had long been abraded off by the windblown sands.

The physician tapped her wrist. "The laser only fires once every twenty-two seconds. I've been timing it."

"Must have to recharge between shots," Krysty said. "Probably why we're still here."

"Mildred, tell me every twenty-one seconds," Ryan ordered.

"Done." She intently studied her watch. "Now!"

Ryan savagely threw the Leviathan to the left. There was no explosion.

"A miss!" J.B. yelled. "It works! You're a genius, Millie."

"This only buys us time," Ryan reminded them. "And not much of that."

"Found it!" Doc cried out in delight, reappearing with a squat tube sealed at both ends and covered with writing. "Now this should do the job."

"We have a bazooka?" Dean asked, a hand braced against the ceiling to keep from falling over.

"A LAW," Doc stated, extending the launch tube. The sights automatically popped up, and the trigger button slid into view. "A light antitank weapon."

"You can't launch a LAW in here," Ryan admonished, skirting a copse of dead trees. "The backwash will fry us!"

"That's why I am going out on the roof."

"What?" Krysty said.

"It is the only way." Doc pulled over a crate and climbed on top, one hand holding the LAW while the other clawed at the ceiling panels. They were easily removed, exposing an internal web of bracings and a veined metal hatch. He undid the latch, and the hatch was almost yanked out of his grip by the wind of their speed.

"Hold on!" Ryan shouted. Leviathan jerked to the left, the right, slowed, spun in a half circle, then lurched forward again. Jak left the ammo bin and moved over to grab Doc's leg and help him stay standing.

"But," Dean began hesitantly, as if afraid of getting an answer, "if the missile doesn't work…"

J.B. answered. "A LAW is meant for tanks. It'll punch straight through solid steel."

"What if its armour is too thick?" Dean asked.

No one had anything to say in response.

Once more, Leviathan bounced over a gully, the boxes and cans tumbling freely about the interior. Jak lost his grip on Doc, and momentarily the elderly man dangled from the roof, his legs kicking to find support.

"Sorry!" Jak gasped, rising from his knees to grab Doc again.

"Hold on tighter, Jak! I need stability!"

J.B. shouted, "Ryan, can you give him a combat stretch?"

"No! We hold still for a second, and that thing'll core us like an apple!"

Counting steadily, Mildred watched as the Ranger bounded into view. "Twenty-one!"

Ryan dodged. The rainbow formed and Leviathan shuddered with sledgehammer force. Doc cried out and everybody heard the whoosh of the light anti-tank weapon launch as he fell to the floor.

"I missed," Doc thundered, climbing to his feet. Frustration distorted his features into a grimace. "It cannot be done. The terrain is too rugged."

"What was that explosion?" Mildred asked, raising her fists and lowering fingers in a steady count. "It sounded a lot louder than the others."

"Our Hummer," Dean announced, looking backward. "It's still there, but the supplies are on fire."

Krysty angled her sideview mirror to see better.

A huge bonfire was trailing the tank, gouts of flame blowing out in wild directions as cans of the condensed fuel ignited. There was a constant barrage of popping sounds as their precious cargo of ammo started cooking off in the growing inferno.

Rushing to the rear blasterport, J.B. cursed bitterly. "We've got plastique in there!" he cried. "The heat won't set it off. Plas burns easy and is as harmless as charcoal. But if a bullet hits a warm block of C-4 just right, the resulting blast will open this thing like a cheap sardine can!"

Dropping his vest of ammo, Dean took a deep breath and then slid aside the locking bolt of the rear door. Cinching his belt tight, the boy shoved the metal portal open. The wind buffeted him, and he grabbed the jamb for support. A chain from their bumper stretched to the bonfire on wheels. The windshield was gone, burning liquid dripped off the side panels, munitions rocketing every way, and fiery orange tongues licking insanely at the sky. Even with the wind coursing around the sides of the tank, the heat reaching them was tremendous.

"Can't see the Ranger!" Dean shouted. "Flames are too thick!"

"Twenty-one!" Mildred called out, and the Hummer blossomed with another detonation of deafening proportions.

"It's still there!"

"Gaia, what in hell are you doing?" Krysty demanded, her crimson hair splaying out in a corona, as the boy stepped onto the motorcycle ramp, one hand clutching the door handle.

"Got to reach the chain and dump the Hummer,"

J.B. shouted, as a bullet zinged past them. "He's the lightest. Doc, grab a seat belt and hold on to me. I'll grab Dean by the waist."

"Me," Jak said, trying to push his way through. "Stronger than Dean."

"But I'm the lightest! Now do as I say!" Dean snapped, for a split second sounding exactly like his father.

"Get back in here!" Ryan commanded at the top of his lungs. "And close that bastard door!"

Dean gestured, "But, Dad, we—"

"Now, boy!"

The door was closed in sullen obedience and locked tight.

"Grab seats!" Ryan growled as he spit on each palm, one hand at a time. "This is going to be rough." Rocking the steering wheel, Leviathan began to fishtail. Again and again, Ryan jerked the wheel as if wrestling with an invisible opponent. The tank brutally swayed, boxes bursting from the storage cabinets. Doc went sprawling, his swordstick nearly impaling its owner. Everybody else desperately clung to their seats. Ryan appeared to be seriously trying to remove the steering wheel, when the ride suddenly smoothed out and the vehicle lunged ahead with renewed speed.

"Trailer's loose," Krysty announced, her ribs aching from the tight safety harness across her chest. "Chain snapped."

"And the Ranger?" Mildred asked, hugging the Remington for support.

"Can't tell," Ryan said, glancing behind. Then he saw the flaming wreckage of the Hummer explode, a million flaming bits spraying everywhere as the indomitable Ranger plowed straight through the conflagration, neither wavering nor slowing.

"Still there," Krysty stated. She made the pronouncement sound as if she had something unclean in her mouth. "There's nothing left between us and it but air."

"Twenty-one!"

His temples throbbing, Ryan danced the heavy Leviathan once more. He couldn't keep this pace forever. His arms were sore from the unaccustomed strain, and every time Mildred called out the mark he damn near jumped out of his skin.

"Any ideas?" he asked.

"Tell you when I get one," Krysty answered, just as steady streams of tracers stitched the air on either side of Leviathan.

"Bracket fire!" J.B. shouted. "Trying to hold us still for a clean kill."

"The hell with that," J.B. said, cranking a handwheel to traverse the starboard 40 mm rapidfire cannon. Jak centered the crosshairs mounted on the end of the stubby barrel on the tank chasing them, flipped the safety with his thumb and pulled the primary trigger. A stuttering line of bright streaks reached out from his weapon and the 40 mm high-explosive shells peppered the enemy nonstop. Lumps of mud were blown away, exposing the gleaming alloy hull underneath.

"Twenty-one!" Mildred shouted.

Ryan grunted with pain as he forced Leviathan to the right, then slowed in a sharply banking curve.

Arcing to the left, he charged forward once more, his face white and sweaty.

"What is it?" Krysty asked, concerned.

"Nothing. I'm okay," he said, his trembling left hand clutching his right biceps. The cramp was getting worse, almost unbearable, but Ryan said nothing.

However, Krysty knew he was lying. Leviathan weighed many tons, and with no power steering the physical strain of combat-driving the colossus was taking its toll on the man. Indomitable warrior that he was, Ryan was clearly becoming exhausted. Decision made, Krysty released her seat belt, but then paused. The bulky radar console stood prominently between them, piles of spent shells from the 40 mm weapon rolling about loose on the floor, and Ryan himself was strapped tight in his seat and jammed behind the wheel. There was no way for her to replace the man without stopping the vehicle and letting him climb out.

Muttering a prayer to the Earth goddess, Krysty reached out a hand and touched the bare skin on his neck. Ryan jerked at the contact. He could hear her humming something soft and soothing. Almost instantly he felt better, more alert, even stronger. The terrible cramp in his arm disappeared as if it had never existed. Releasing him, Krysty dropped into her seat, seemingly exhausted.

The chattering of the Vulcan cannon stopped. "Reload!" Jak demanded, clearing the breech feed. "No armor-piercing. Need antipersonnel!"

J.B. paused at the ammo bin. "Shotgun rounds?"

"Do it!"

"I understand, lad," Doc said, going to the other 40 mm cannon. "Good plan. Let us go for it."

It took both J.B. and Dean to hoist the bulky belt of 40 mm shells into the feeder mechanism of the Vulcan. Jak slammed shut the lid, cocked the hammer bolt and steadied the weapon dead on their pursuer. "On my call," the albino teen shouted. "Slow, stop for a sec!"

Veering past a rain gully, Ryan almost turned at that, but restrained himself. "You gone suicidal?" he demanded.

"Homicidal," Doc corrected, struggling to load the cannon by himself.

Ryan heard the urgency in the teenager's voice and considered the request. Survival was paramount. If Jak had an idea, it was worth a chance.

"Now!" Jak shouted, firing.

Straightening the wheels, Ryan slammed on the brakes.

The nose of Leviathan almost plowed into the ground as it pitched forward. Everything loose inside hurtled to the front, nearly burying Mildred and Krysty. Underneath, the multiple wheels squealed in protest as friction and inertia battled hydraulics. Bucking and shuddering, the mammoth tank ground to a stop in only a couple of dozen yards.

Slowing its pace over the uneven ground, the Ranger paused and leveled its laser straight at them.

Even as Ryan started moving again, Jak expended ammo as if it was limitless. The majority of the shells missed the tank entirely. Then there was a small explosion of glass.

J.B. dropped his jaw. "It worked!"

"Hallelujah!" Doc cried, releasing his hold on the Vulcan.

"Scram!" Jak snapped.

No additional encouragement was needed. Ryan hit the gas and Leviathan rolled away, building speed slowly, but steadily.

"Twenty-one!" Mildred shouted, kicking a hot shell casing away from a can of fuel. If they weren't careful, this bucket would blow up like the *Hindenburg*.

Ryan sent them wildly over the landscape, but nothing detonated. A rainbow-colored searchlight stabbed for a second, illuminating a sand dune in pearlescent beauty, then winked out.

"You smashed the focusing lens."

"Yep," Jak drawled proudly, patting the cannon.

"Was a thousand-to-one shot." J.B. laughed, tilting his hat. "But he did it in under a hundred."

"However," Ryan said, playing with the choke and gas pedal, urging the machine to go faster, "the bastard thing is still after us."

"So?" Dean queried. "What's it going to do? Ram us?"

"Mebbe," Ryan said, smashing through a thicket of dried brown bushes. Damnation, they were leaving the desert. "And two hundred tons of anything hitting us is still the last train west."

"It does not matter if the stone hits the pitcher, or the pitcher hits the stone," Doc said, brandishing his cane. "Either way it is bad for the pitcher."

Rainbow lights poured in through the slots of the rear doors, casting multihued shadows on the interior walls.

"We're faster," Dean offered, squatting low. "It'll never catch up."

"Till we run out of fuel," Dix said. Sitting on the floor, he removed his glasses to rub his face, then replaced them and frowned. "We got a lot, but it's nuke-powered. Been operating for two centuries. Who knows for how much longer it can keep coming?"

"And coming," Jak added. His hand reached out for the Vulcan and dropped away. There was nothing they had, no weapon, blaster or bomb, that could smash the Ranger. It was predark state of the art, and Leviathan was only a skydark Frankenstein, cobbled together from a hundred smaller machines.

"Yeah, we're not free yet," Ryan agreed. "But we're still alive and kicking. Hey, Mildred!"

Belted in, the physician turned, looking out the starboard machine blasterport. "What?"

He jerked his head. "Check Krysty. She's been out for much too long."

Unbuckling, Mildred started wading through the jumble of boxes and cartons covering the floor. The stocky woman had to crawl over the ammo bin for the front 75 mm recoilless before she could reach the redhead. Hands touched the alabaster face, then checked vital signs. "She's okay," the physician announced. "Just fainted. Pulse is strong, breathing regularly, pupils dilated."

Ryan said nothing, but the relief was obvious in his face.

Gently, Mildred dragged the unconscious woman out of the front gunner's chair and buckled her into a vacant passenger seat. Then she clambered into the front and belted herself in place.

"The 75 mm is loaded and ready," she stated, then leaned forward scowling. "Aw hell, look at that!"

Bounding and bucking over the uneven ground, the tank unexpectedly increased in speed as the ride went smooth, their fifteen tires humming softly in unison under the floorboards.

"Fireblast," Ryan spit. "Flat land to the horizon. We can go faster, but so does it."

"Head for those weird gray mountains," J.B. suggested, a hand to the side of his face blocking the colored lights streaming in from the blasterports. Damn that thing's accuracy! "Mebbe we can go places it can't."

"We're smaller and more nimble," Mildred agreed, working the breech mechanism to fire the recoilless. It might be pointing in the wrong direction at present, but a person never knew when that might change.

"Mebbe we can find a bridge it's too big to go across," Dean added. "Or a narrow tunnel"

"Cave," Jak stated, brushing the white hair from his face. His ruby-red eyes stared directly at the reflected laser lights coming in through the chinks of their battered hull. Each spot would have to be repaired later. If they lived.

"Got a better idea," Ryan said, hunching his shoulders. "We're heading for that rad pit."

Nobody spoke, the only sound discernible the gentle humming of the tires.

"Radiation fries electronics. We go in there, the

damn thing wouldn't dare to follow us. Too many transistors and chips. Its main comp would scram." He patted the dashboard. "But we're mostly manual."

"True enough. Radiation destroys advanced electronics as bad as it does flesh," Mildred stated just as rainbow lights washed in through the windows and blasterports. Now that they were traveling straight and true, the Ranger was scoring a hit with every discharge of the unfocused laser.

"But just to be sure, we better turn off everything electric," Ryan continued. "Lights, radio, the works."

"Check." Mildred started flipping switches. The UV screen winked out, the dashboard went dark and the interior lights dimmed to nothingness.

"And what about us?" Dean asked calmly.

"We should be safe. Check the land," Ryan replied. "This is a really old blast crater."

"That does not mean it is not hot," Doc said. "I have seen much older ones still glowing at night!"

"Our composite hull will give some protection," J.B. said hesitantly. "But we've got lots of cracks."

"No, the radiation is too low. We'll be safe," Ryan stated brusquely. The slick, fused soil under their wheels was nearly frictionless; it was worse than driving on ice. Scenes from their awful trek through the arctic flashed through his mind. "But the Ranger won't know that."

"Wouldn't the whitecoats program it to check rad levels?" Dean asked, worried. "Just to be sure?"

"Why? When a nuclear bomb goes off, if the tank survives the EMP wave, it still can't go anywhere near a rad pit for hundreds of years. And no military would plan to leave its equipment alone for that long," Mildred said.

"How about the folks who built the redoubts in the first place?" Dean said in stark candor. Nobody had an answer to that.

As Ryan angled Leviathan into an arroyo, the bottom of the rad pit came directly into view. Barren, featureless land, as level as a skillet, stretched into the distance, with low rolling hills rising in a perfect circle around the rim. Not a stick or a pebble marred the dead perfection, and not even a breeze seemed to disturb the pristine stillness of the hellblasted pit.

There was no time to take a rad count, so Ryan plowed straight into the crater.

"Here it comes!" J.B. said, as the laser rose above the hillock behind them. But before the tank came into view, the short barrel stopped and began to withdraw. "Hey, it's retreating!"

"The trick worked," Dean breathed in relief. Hugging his Mossberg shotgun, the boy slumped in his chair, looking twice his age.

"Advanced technology is so primitive." Doc sighed in contentment.

"Keep going straight," Mildred said, keeping a constant watch on the hilltop. "Don't make your move until we're far, far away from this point."

Ryan gave agreement and continued to pretend he was going to drive through the very heart of the nuke hole.

SLOWING TO a complete halt, the General Electric Ranger Mark IV sat on the lee side of the low hillock reviewing its options with machine speed.

SIG REP DELTA? asked the auxiliary subprocessor, after the main subprocessor didn't respond after the regulation four tries.

The main CDP replied, *Confirm. Nuclear strike zone on record. Scram factor 99. Do not proceed on this course.*

AFFIRMATIVE. QUERY: LAUNCII MISSILE SALVO?

Negative. Supplies depleted, February 14, 2095, 1409 AM.

CONFIRM. QUERY: FLANK ESCAPING ENEMY TANK?

Processing.

QUERY: RETURN TO BASE?

Processing.

QUERY: ABANDON PURSUIT OF TARGET?

Negative. There was a full millisecond pause. *Repairs to the primary weapon system must be performed stat.*

CONFIRM. ACCESSING FIELD REPAIR FILES...HIGHEST PROBABILITY LOCATION FOR SUCCESS IS—THE PEARL IN THE WHEEL.

Accepted. Implement. And the mammoth war machine rumbled off toward the east at its top speed.

Chapter Six

Rifles and handblasters were held tight in sweaty hands as good luck charms as Leviathan rolled over the flat plain of the nuclear crater for miles. In spite of their exhaustion, everyone's face was pressed tight to a window or blasterport, watching for the return of the dreaded predark war machine.

Scanning ahead with binocs, Krysty cursed. "There's a river coming up ahead. If the Ranger tries to circle around and ambush us from the other side, it'll reach the water and be able to see inside the blast crater and track us."

"No, it won't," Ryan decided, twisting the wheel sharply. The tires squealed, as Leviathan banked sharply on a new course. "We're cutting a tangent. By the time it reaches the river, we'll be long gone."

The redhead nodded. "Hopefully."

"It's all we have."

The rippled glass under the wheels gave way to streaks of fused glass, shiny fingers reaching into the sterilized dirt. Acid rain gullies cut miniature ravines across the arid plain. Eventually, the pale dirt darkened in color to a proper brown, with some mutated plants and milkweeds appearing in tiny clumps, fighting for subsistence. Then flecks of true grass were seen, the faint green as incongruous as flowers on the moon amid the rad-blasted vegetation. Then more green grass, thickening to patches, followed by small irregular fields with stumpy bushes and corpses of withered bushes that became copses of mutant trees. The trunks were gnarled and malformed, the branches knotted as if in pain and the fruits hairy pulsating sacks. But even these malformations were a welcome sight after the blighted zone of the rad pit.

"Almost out," Mildred stated, motioning with a hand. "See there! Fields of green grass. Been a while since we saw that."

"East wasn't as bad hit as the west," J.B. said, stubbornly chewing bites off a bar of stale cheese as he manned the starboard Remington. "I don't think the big radstorms ever made it this far."

"Doesn't seem as if the acid rains hit here much, either."

"It's not paradise," Ryan said, feeling the desolation, "but I've seen worse."

A rabbit bolted by them, its six legs hurtling it across the clearing into the safety of the greenery. "Muties don't seem too extreme, either," Krysty observed.

"I noticed."

Sipping a cup of MRE coffee from a battered tin cup, Krysty perked up in her seat as Leviathan crested a low ground swell. "What's that noise?" she demanded.

Ryan slowed their speed. "I've been noticing it for hours. Getting worse."

"Controls say the engines are fine," Mildred announced. She tapped the console with a finger. "If the gauges are working correctly, that is."

"Seems to be coming from underneath us," J.B told them, cupping an ear to listen. "Mebbe there's a branch caught in a wheelwell."

"Could be the tire the hellhounds ate," Dean said, loading his weapon from the cache of rounds in his vest. "You know, the empty rim spinning loose."

Easing out the clutch, Ryan braked the vehicle to stop and pulled the handle to set the tandem brakes, fore and aft. "More reasonable than a branch." He released the seat harness and stood stiffly. Checking his 9 mm pistol, Ryan accepted the flashlight from Mildred, clicking it on once to make sure it was working properly. "Come on, J.B., let's go see what's the prob."

"Right," the Armorer said, grabbing a toolbox and his Uzi.

The two men climbed outside while the rest kept a careful watch. After ascertaining there were no surprises waiting for them below the vehicle, they lay on the grass and slid out of sight.

Walking to the middle of the tank, Krysty undid the bolts and clamps on the belly hatch and lifted it out of the way. "See anything?" she called down.

"Shit, yeah! We got a hole in our transmission!" J.B. shouted. "We've lost all of our gear oil!"

"We catch some shrapnel from the Hummer?" Dean asked through the hole.

His father answered. "No. Apparently, the cold-hearts didn't tighten the draining bolt good enough.

"J.B., check the fill plug to make sure it's okay."

"Doing it," the Armorer answered.

Ryan's face came into view. "Dean, Jak, search for that bastard bolt in our wake," he said. "Mebbe it only came off recently. Should be just behind a big puddle of smelly reddish oil."

"Be right back, Dad," Dean said. The two youths took their weapons and headed off on foot. In the harsh sunlight, Jak blinked harshly and removed an old pair of taped-together sunglasses from a pocket of his camous. Sliding them onto his pale face, the albino blinked red eyes for a moment, then followed after Dean, easily catching up to the hurrying boy.

"How bad is our situation?" Doc asked, who had been sharpening his blade with a whetstone. The sword whispered a sigh as he slid it into its ebony sheath, then locked it into place with a click and a twist. There was no way for an outsider to know it was anything but a walking cane.

"Pretty bad," Krysty replied, her hair coiling and uncoiling nervously. "The gears will burn out in minutes without any lubricant."

"So Leviathan is effectively dead?"

Mildred got out of her seat and started to rummage in a box full of cartons. "Maybe not. We have some spare oil here," she said, lifting a can. "No, this is motor oil. Brake fluid, antifreeze, antijellying. What's that?"

"For diesels," Krysty said. Kneeling by the pile of supplies, she started shifting boxes. "When it gets too cold, the fuel makes a sort of jelly and won't ignite anymore."

"The hell you say."

Laying his cane across an empty seat, Doc joined

them in the task. "More oil, and more again. Do diesels consume a lot of oil?"

"Always," Krysty said, shoving aside an ammo box and a backpack of food. The only boxes left on the floor were clearly fuel and tools. "No transmission fluid here."

"None here, either," Mildred stated, rocking back on her heels. Then she motioned at the wall lockers. "Anybody check in there?"

"Some blankets, a few tools, rope, not much more," Doc answered. "We lost a lot in the Hummer."

"That's trouble," Ryan said from the doorway. He rested a boot on the corrugated floor. "We fixed the leak part. J.B. used a bolt from the knuckle of the dead wheel. Took some effort, but it fit the hole."

"Won't ever come out again," J.B. stated, standing behind the man and using a rag to wipe his hands clean. "But it's in there."

"Is there any substitute we can use?" Krysty asked, lifting a plastic container of hydraulic brake fluid. "Mebbe mix a couple or distill them into something usable?"

"No," Mildred replied. "Not without a full laboratory."

"Yeah," Ryan countered. "We can use regular engine oil."

"But..."

"Yeah, sure," J.B. said, brightening. "That'll do, long as we keep the tranny in low gear, and don't go very fast. That should minimize the frothing."

"Frothing?"

"But we won't be able to shift gears," Ryan added, scratching his unshaven chin. "First, mebbe second, will be it."

"Ryan," Mildred stated, "there's bound to be plenty of transmission fluid in the redoubt. Think we can sneak past the Ranger?"

"Even if we did," Ryan replied, "we'd never make it that far. What do you guess, J.B., ten, mebbe fifteen miles?"

"At most."

Jak and Dean returned, hands empty.

"Zip," the albino teen reported.

"The oil trail was only scattered drops for as far as we could track," Dean added apologetically. "We must have been losing it for a while. Stretched out of sight."

"Shitfire, and we can't go back. The Ranger might be flanking us, and if we're caught walking out in the open…" J.B. made a slicing sound and drew his thumbnail across his throat.

Climbing out of the tank, Krysty raised a pair of binocs to her face and stared into the distance. "I say we go due east," she said. "Those aren't mountains out there, they're skyscrapers. I've been studying them since I woke."

Resting the Mossberg on his shoulder, Dean said, "That doesn't mean they have any garages or repair shops not looted."

"Don't need them," Ryan said, extending a brass sailor's telescope to its full-length and lifting it to his good eye. The thing didn't have half the magnifying power of binocs, but it didn't give him a headache, either. "Any building that tall must have elevators."

"So?"

"The Trader used to drain the hydraulic fluid from the lifters in the basement to use in his tranny and gunswivels."

"How far away do you think?" Doc asked, trying to gauge the distance with his thumb. "Fifteen miles?"

"I'd guess thirty," Ryan replied, compacting the telescope. "Well beyond our estimated maximum."

"So we better prep our packs to go on foot," Krysty said. "Just in case."

"Right."

J.B. started to collect cans of 10W40 motor oil in his arms. "Doc, still got the Swiss army knife?"

Doc displayed his newest possession.

"Need the can opener," the Armorer stated, accepting the multiblade. "Mine's kind of bent. Be right back."

"Want help?" Jak asked, stuffing his long hair into his collar as a prelude to work. He had seen more than enough fools have their heads pulled into working engines because of long hair or loose clothing to know better.

"No," J.B. told him. "This is the easy part. Putting it in."

Jak released his hair. "Okay."

J.B. went out of sight and muffled cursing wafted up from the floor.

Yawning mightily, Ryan rubbed his eye and cracked the vertebrae in his neck. "Somebody else can drive for a while," he announced. "I'm too bastard tired to see straight. And any more of that damn MRE coffee and I'll start pissing black. Got to get some sleep.''

"I'll take over," Mildred offered, sliding into the driver's seat. The steering wheel was too high and she adjusted it downward. "Been driving since I was sixteen. My father had a pickup truck I used to borrow."

"We better get some shut-eye," Ryan said, making a rough bed out of some moth-eaten Army blankets. "It'll take us a while to reach the town, ruins, whatever. Two-hour shifts."

Doc covered a yawn himself. "Ah, the arms of Morpheus claim us all. To visit the land of Nod seems an unparalleled Bacchanalian delight.''

"Done," J.B. reported, stepping into the vehicle and sliding the door closed. "And catching some z's sounds mighty good."

From his prone position, Ryan tossed the man a blanket. J.B. made the catch and laid it on the floor as a cushion.

"Seats are more comfortable," Doc stated, lying lengthwise across several of them, the armrests folded out of the way.

"And then I kiss the floor when I roll over," J.B. said, covering his face with his fedora. "So I might as well start off here."

"I'm fine," Dean said. "Wide awake."

"Me, too," Krysty added. "Just had a nap."

Tightening the harness to fit her smaller frame, Mildred eased the tank into second gear, bypassing first entirely. "Then you two take first watch. Krysty, starboard guns, Dean, port."

"Done."

"Yes, Mildred."

The physician started the twin engines and engaged the clutch. Leviathan lurched as if it had been kicked. Bucking and shaking, it start to roll and soon was moving with a steady rattle at fifteen miles per hour.

"Hardly better than walking," Mildred muttered, making a mental note to herself to watch the pressure and not burn out the clutch. Lord alone knew if they had a spare. Then a thought occurred and she killed the interior lights rear of the machine guns.

"Thanks." Rolling onto his side, Ryan slid his SIG-Sauer under the makeshift pillow and ordered himself to sleep. It worked at first, but every dip and hole jarred him awake again. Privately, he was beginning to regret his wishing for a war wag. Flat tires, bad roads, mechanical breakage, and they made one hell of a target for raiders. Right about now, a mat-trans jump, even with the sickness, was starting to look pretty good.

SEVENTY MILES to the east, a cold wind moaned over the bare stone battlements of a medieval-style tower, the tallest edifice among many such buildings. The design of the granite-block complex with its distant outer walls was primitive, crude, a brute force–approach to architecture. However, platoons of sec men sporting autofire blasters patrolled the heights in grim resolution, hand-rolled cigarettes of local tobacco dangling from their tight-lipped mouths. The smokes offered only a small source of fleeting warmth against the bitter winds that flowed down from the surrounding mountain range like an invisible river of ice.

In the cobblestone courtyards below, ragged slaves pushed ramshackle carts of withered winter vegetables and hauled buckets of muddy water past an ominous array of high wooden gallows. Several of the dangling nooses were occupied by the remains of outlanders. The rotting bodies had been left in full view of all, both as an object lesson to other would-be troublemakers, and to lure in crows for the Citadel larder. No food of any kind was never wasted in Novaville.

Every movement and expression of the shuffling workers was duly scrutinized by fat overseers for any hint of rebellion, their own faces gleaming with health, coiled bullwhips of knotted leather held in callused hands. Dressed in bulky military jackets and predark jumpboots, the guards still shivered from the omnipresent cold and looked eagerly for any excuse from the prisoners to vent their displeasure at this onerous duty.

However, deep inside the labyrinthine bowels of the massive stone Citadel, a beautiful woman rose smiling and naked from a silver bathtub, the soapy water dripping off her long limbs and full breasts. Servants stepped forward with soft towels and began daintily drying off her alabaster skin. Primly, almost absentmindedly, the Lady Ward Amanda Coultier nodded approval at their gentle attention.

Torches of pitch and wood lined the stone block walls, but those were only for emergencies. Chandeliers of electric lights hung from the oak rafters, filling the spacious room with illumination so bright that most visitors to the Citadel of Novaville considered it magic.

"It's a foolish plan," her brother, Richard, said from the other side of a folding lacquered screen. The deputy ward was sounding extremely concerned. "Chances of success are very small."

The heiress to the Citadel ran strong fingers through her long silky hair as a young female slave stroked a soft towel along her inner thighs, then even higher, drying the woman everywhere.

"I agree, dearest brother." She laughed. "There's no need to be so gentle, little one. I am not made of crystal."

The girl bowed. "Yes, Lady Ward." But her administrations became even more careful.

Spreading her arms wide, Amanda allowed the other female slaves to dry her arms and towel her cascading blond hair.

"It won't work," Richard repeated, louder than before.

"Perhaps," Amanda agreed, "but more importantly, would Father approve of me trying?"

There came an unseen sigh from the deputy ward. "Well, yes, of course. Cowards cannot rule a ville. But consider the danger!"

Anger flared in Amanda's face for just a second, distorting the visage of beauty into a feral mask. "Oh, my dearest brother, you know they must die and as quickly as possible. Who better than I to accomplish the task?"

"So when will you leave?" Richard asked. "This

afternoon? Tonight, under cover of darkness?"

"All in good time, brother. All in good time."

RYAN AWOKE to the sound of splashing. Popping a stick of MRE gum into his mouth to remove the sour taste of sleep, he checked out the starboard blasterport. The tank was lumbering across a shallow stream, the water foaming over its fifteen tires. Then he noticed the vehicle had been organized while he slept, the spent shells from the .50-caliber and the rapidfires stuffed into boxes and tucked under seats. The rest of the supplies were piled on seats and strapped into place for ease of access. Everybody else was awake and sitting at their posts.

"Good morning," Doc called out from the driver's seat.

Stretching, Ryan swallowed the gum and returned the greeting. "Where are we?"

"Just a mile or so from the skyscrapers." To Ryan's expression he added, "We thought you needed the rest."

"I did," he agreed, as the smell of breakfast filled the air.

"Go eat," Krysty said, sipping coffee in the gunner's seat. "We already have."

"Thanks." He found J.B. warming some rations in an aluminum frying pan held over a small campfire, made out of what appeared to be slats from a packing crate, the bits of wood stuffed inside a brass 75 mm shell. The shell was shoved through two large wooden slats in a cross pattern, which kept it from tumbling over.

"My idea," J.B. told him. "Jak did the carving."

"Nice job. MRE rations, I see," Ryan said, squatting on his heels.

"Yep, powdered eggs, dehydrated bread, artificial butter, bacon, jerky, coffee, no sugar, the usual crap." J.B. added another sliver of packing crate to the flames. "Doesn't taste bad."

Ryan took a deep breath. "Had worse." Careful not to spill any, he filled a tin cup with pale coffee and stirred in the hundred-year-old artificial cream powder. He took a sip. "No, don't think I have," Ryan corrected, making a face. "But it's warm, and edible."

"If you say so. There's vacuum-packed nutcake for dessert, if you want some."

"Anything that doesn't bite me first," Ryan replied, wolfing his meager share of the fare. Afterward, he used a rag and a canteen to wash the sleep from his face.

Unceremoniously, J.B. shoved the breakfast debris out a window.

Feeling vastly refreshed, Ryan checked his weapons and armed himself properly. "I'll take over, Doc," he told the white-haired gentleman at the wheel.

"Certainly. However, it is too much trouble to start and stop this cumbersome dreadnought," Doc said, undoing the belt. "Grab hold of the wheel, and as I slide out, you squeeze in." The exchange was made without mishap.

Ryan settled into the task, almost enjoying it. Less than an hour later, the soaring skyscrapers were readily visible over the treetops, and Ryan looked for a clear path through the trees to the city beyond.

Locating a breach, he lumbered onto the muddy shore and directed Leviathan along a cracked concrete stretch that angled off in the correct direction. Soon, the burned-out frames of individual homes marked the beginning of the old civilization. Sometimes only a bent stack of chimney stones remained to show where a home had once stood. Wordlessly, they passed the crumbled remains of stores and shops, the glass windows long gone, molding leaves piled high inside.

Then the road became smoother, with more ruined houses appearing until they regularly lined both sides of the street. As Leviathan advanced farther, the buildings looked to be in better condition, until they crossed some railroad tracks and entered a warehouse district. Here the streets were covered with a thick cushion of green ivy that grew along the outside of everything in sight. Odd lumps dotting the street were presumably parked cars. Filling every block, hundreds of green buildings rose six or more stories tall. And standing as sparkling glass giants among these were the skyscrapers, their pinnacles nearly out of sight. The company names on the lintels were readable, but meant nothing.

"How big?" Jak asked, furrowing his brow.

Abandoning her attempt to read a vine-covered movie marquee, Mildred answered, "Thirty stories. Maybe forty. Surely no higher than that."

Jak stared at the woman as if she had clearly gone insane.

"People," he said.

"Oh, population. I don't know. Maybe a hundred thousand."

"I would postulate a neutron bomb," Doc said, and he shuddered.

"I agree," Mildred replied softly. "Damn the fools. God damn them all."

"A what?" Dean asked, unable to look away from the city. So much green! Could the ivy be protecting the city from the terrible effects of the acid rains?

Making sure Leviathan didn't bump into any of the lumps in the street, Ryan said, "The ancient whitecoats had lots of different boomers. I read a long time ago that the worst was the Hellstorm. It set fire to the atmosphere. Second worst was the neutron. It killed people, but didn't damage the buildings or machines."

"Just killed the people?"

"Killed everything alive," Krysty said angrily. "People, bugs, bathroom fungus, anything."

"Except ivy," J.B. added, scowling at the lush plants rustling at their approach. All this green was unnatural.

"How find what we need?" he asked.

"Keep a watch for machine shops and gas stations. If need be, we'll climb down into some elevator shafts. Maintenance department is always in the basement. The oil from the hydraulic pumps will do fine for the transmission."

"Excellent."

"I wonder why this city has not been occupied," Doc remarked. "These buildings are in perfect condition."

"Impossible to defend." Krysty pointed with her gun barrel. "Too many windows."

"Rad is clear," J.B. told them, checking his counter.

Leviathan proceeded slowly toward the center of the wide street, the ivy crushing softly under the military tires. Most of the store signs were impossible to read, either covered by the plants or damaged by minor rust. The few they could decipher weren't helpful—clothing stores with mannequins in the windows, pizza parlors, bookstores with white rectangles displayed, the covers bleached from decades of exposure to sunlight.

"No people in sight, or any sign of them," Ryan said. He turned to Krysty. "You feel anything?"

Krysty shook her head. "No norms or muties, but there's something alive out there."

"Mebbe the ivy?" Dean suggested.

She was tolerant. "That's just a plant."

"Not exactly," Doc stated. "Ivy isn't a separate crop such as stalks of corn, or groves of apples. Ivy grows together into a single homogenous plant."

"Covering a whole city?"

"The old coot is right for a change," Mildred said. "If nobody's here to prune it, why not? Stuff's more resilient than kudzu, or even horseradish."

"Mebbe," Krysty said, sounding unsure.

Ignoring the side streets and alleys, Ryan kept traveling through the main thoroughfares of the downtown area. A few of the smaller buildings were no more than squarish mounds of ivy, the millions of pointy leaves covering whatever edifice of humanity had once stood proudly at that location. The normal hard angles of corners and sharp outlines of the city were pleasantly softened by the living blanket.

"What's that place?" Dean asked, gesturing.

"Which?" Ryan asked.

"There. The only building not covered by the ivy."

"Odd that the plants don't grow there," his father admitted.

Doc said, "I do not see any charred residue, so it was not burned away."

"Not trimmed," Jak added. "Edges not smooth."

"Millie, why wouldn't plants grow there?" J.B. asked.

Meticulously, Mildred counted on her fingers. "Gas leak, radiation sources inside, microwave leakage, toxic waste, excessive salt concentrates or maybe acid spills."

Ryan let Leviathan move on. He wanted nothing to do with any of that stuff. If ivy didn't go there, they didn't want to, either.

"From the air, this place must seem to be wild country," Krysty observed. "Wait, there's a parking garage!"

Studying the gate, Ryan didn't slow. "Cars only. Wrong transmission fluid. We need trucks."

"Dark night!" J.B. yelled, pressing his face to the window. "There it is!"

"Public works? Sanitation department?" Dean asked.

"Auto store?" Jak asked.

"The Ranger," J.B. said softly, as if it could hear

him through the composite hull. He jerked a thumb. "Next street over."

"Gaia save us," Krysty prayed, hauling out the binocs and scanning the area. "And we're a sitting duck."

"Mebbe we could get inside that garage," Dean suggested hopefully. "Hide in there."

Ryan vetoed that idea. "If it's got infrared, as it almost surely does, it'll find us in a minute."

"Rather face the machine out here anyway," J.B. said, going to the starboard Remington and working the bolt. It engaged with a loud snap. "Besides, we can always make a run for it on foot."

"How could it have found us?" Doc demanded. "The radar is off, and the river should have muddled our tires tracks."

"Fuck!"

Turning in the direction Jak was facing, the friends saw the Ranger crest a corner and stop dead in its tracks before the facade of a one-hour vision center. Instantly, every dish antenna and radar array the war machine boasted spun madly and froze, pointing straight toward Leviathan. It almost seemed as surprised to see them as they were it.

"Swap seats," Ryan ordered, freeing his harness.

As he left the driver's seat, the Ranger's main cannon shifted aim and once more the crawling Leviathan was bathed in the harmless light show.

In sudden understanding, Mildred cursed. "God's blood, it's parked in front of an optometrist's office. The damn thing is here to repair the focusing lens!"

Taking the gunner's chair, Ryan quickly activated the front missile pod and tracking system. "Angle us more," he snapped. "I need a clear shot backward!"

"So there *is* somebody inside that thing!" Krysty remarked, correcting their course. "I knew it wasn't just a comp!"

"Who cares?" J.B. grabbed his satchel of explosives and moved for the exit. "Come on! We'll climb on top while it's standing still and blow open the hatch."

Ryan flipped the main sequence control to salvo and hit the launch button. Leviathan bucked six times as the remaining rockets from the pod streaked away on fiery tails, smoky contrails filling the air.

"Those won't penetrate tank armor!" Mildred told him.

"Don't have to," Ryan said, staring hard at the enemy tank.

"Krysty, keep moving! Head for an alley!" The woman did as requested, although she had no idea why.

Again, the Ranger pumped out gigawatts of rainbows at the crawling Leviathan as the half dozen Air Force missiles streaked past the tank and punched through the big picture windows of the tall brick building standing on the corner—the one without any ivy. Smoke and glass vomited into the intersection, a maelstrom of chaos masking the Ranger from their view.

"You missed!"

"Now!" Ryan ordered, raising a clenched fist. "Go!"

Krysty yanked the wheel hard about, and Leviathan casually rolled toward an alleyway several yards away.

"We're not going to make it!" she shouted over the grinding gears.

"Got to! No time to escape on foot!"

The Ranger fired again and started toward them when a much larger explosion rattled the building to its foundation. Fireballs blew out of every ground-floor window, then the side of the structure became canted, angling dangerously as more detonations shook the building again and again, ripping apart the inner walls.

Smoke washed over the street, the squat body of the tank barely visible through the swirling clouds.

"Here it comes!" Ryan shouted as a gigantic shadow engulfed both machines.

Acting on impulse, Dean put a stream of 40 mm shells into the street directly in front of the Ranger. The HE rounds blew apart the ivy and asphalt, chewing a gaping pit in the concrete foundation. Shifting treads, the Ranger dodged the blasthole just as the building finished its brief journey downward. The whole world seemed to jump as the irresistible force met the immovable object with disastrous results. The robotic tank disappeared as countless tons of brick and concrete deafeningly crashed onto the street. Windows shattered from the thunderous concussion as the smashed road buckled and sank. In every direction, sidewalks splintered, cracks racing off like crazed lightning bolts. Telephone poles toppled, as dirty water erupted from a score of burst hydrants.

Debris pummeled the back end of Leviathan as

the craft was shoved forward into the alley. Standing on the brakes, Krysty managed to bring the tank to a halt just as they were completely enveloped by the swirling dust storm.

The rumbling of the crash echoed throughout the dead city, reverberating along the concrete canyons. Then an eerie stillness descended, filling the void with a ringing silence louder than any possible detonation.

Getting stiffly off the floor, the friends checked to make sure none was injured, then grabbed weapons and headed for the door. Half climbing, half falling out of Leviathan, they stood beside the vehicle and stared dumbfounded at the broken building lying sideways in the street, blocking the mouth of the alley.

"Missed us by feet," J.B. whispered, respectfully removing his fedora.

Doc made the sign of the cross, and somebody else said amen. Dean started forward, and Ryan grabbed his arm, stopping the boy.

"Careful. The ground is still shaky."

Accepting the wisdom, the group waited a few minutes, closely watching for any additional destruction from the endless little aftershock quakes caused by the titanic pounding. All around them, the bedraggled fields of ivy were shaking madly, waves of agitation moving out over the city like ripples in a pond.

Minutes passed, and finally Ryan permitted himself a satisfactory grunt. "Sounds like it's over."

"I certainly hope so," Mildred said, licking dry lips.

"Hot pipe, I never saw anything like that!" Dean gushed.

"Not want again," Jak said, scrutinizing the sideways building.

Beaming delight, Doc patted Ryan on the back. "That was inspired, my dear Ryan. Inspired! A tactic from *The Art of War,* perhaps? Or the ruminations of Julius Caesar?"

Ryan looked at the man with no amusement. "You never swatted a fly?" he asked simply.

Doc opened his mouth, then closed it with a snap. "I stand corrected," he said, bowing. "It was genius born, not borrowed."

"Good shooting," Krysty said to Ryan.

He shrugged. "Kind of hard to miss a stationary building."

Muffled detonations sounded from within the collapsed structure and with a grinding screech, the middle of the skyscraper tumbled apart, sending another plume of dust into the murky sky.

"Is there enough room for us to get out?" Krysty asked, studying the mouth of the alley.

"Sure, plenty," Mildred said confidently.

J.B. started for the street, both hands tight on the strap of his bag full of explosives. "More important, let's go make sure the bastard thing really is dead."

And that was when the ivy attacked.

Chapter Seven

Vines lashed out from every direction. Ryan dodged and only got a stinging gash across his cheek. His Steyr was leveled in a second, firing into the thrashing ivy. Movement out of the corner of his good eye made the man spin, firing instinctively. The plants were crawling over Leviathan, wrapping around the wheels and covering the windows in a thick protective blanket of living green.

Cursing, Jak fired his .357 Magnum, blowing off the leaves covering the door latch. But try as he might, the hatch couldn't open. "Jammed! Ivy in the hinges!"

"Why is it attacking?"

"We dropped a building on it!"

Turning in a circle, J.B. sprayed his Uzi in a figure-eight pattern, not sure what to aim at. "How the fuck do you kill a plant this big?"

"Flamethrower!" Doc shouted, his pistol holstered, his sword out and moving. The slashing steel blade sliced a clear space around them, but more ivy filled in the spot almost instantly. "We have got to get inside! Use the flamethrower!"

"Dean," Ryan shouted. "The can!"

The boy lifted the container of fuel in his hand and threw it at the side hatch of Leviathan. The canister was still airborne when Mildred blasted it with her revolver. The fuel detonated, fire spreading over the side of the craft, and the ivy retreated.

Together, the group grabbed the door. Forcing it open, they piled inside and slammed the hatch shut. A single tendril of ivy stabbing for Mildred was cut in two and fell to the floor, quivering.

"Dark night," J.B. heaved, a thermite gren primed in his left hand, his index finger in the ring. "No wonder nobody has ever looted this place!"

"Not deserted," Jak agreed, a dark spot on his arm spreading outward, a thin trickle of blood appearing on his wrist.

Crushing the vine under her boot, Mildred grabbed her kit and ripped open the teenager's shirt. "Just a flesh wound," she declared. "Nothing serious."

"Poison?" Jak asked, ready for the worst.

She wrapped a white bandage made from a naval officer's class A uniform around his forearm. "No sign of it," the physician said, splitting the end with her teeth and tying it off in a fast field dressing. "I'd say you're clear."

"Everybody else okay?" Ryan queried, sliding shells into J.B.'s M-4000 scattergun.

"I thought..." Dean started again. "Where's Krysty?"

Startled, Ryan jerked his head around. One glance told him that she wasn't in the tank with them. Rushing to a blasterport, the one-eyed man blew away the outside greenery with a single discharge and looked frantically at the alleyway. Ivy was everywhere, thickening by the second like an incoming tide.

"Second floor!" Doc cried, standing at the rooftop periscope.

Ryan turned and found her, dangling from the grip of the mutie plant twenty feet in the air. Her .38 discharged once, pointing at nothing in particular. Then she was hauled over the rooftop and gone.

"Combat positions," Ryan ordered, striding past his friends and sliding into the driver's seat. "We're going after her!"

Nobody spoke. They just obeyed, knowing that seconds counted if they wanted the woman back alive.

Callused hands darting over the controls, Ryan primed the flamethrower pump, set the spray for maximum and hit the switch. It was a design similar to the flamer used by the Trader in War Wag One. Orange hell hosed outward from their roof and the windshield cleared of the plants, giving them a clear view of the rustling green alley. Ryan lowered the angle and washed the craft itself with burning gasoline. Waves of heat flooded in through the blasterports, and a thin wavering lance of flame reached inside from the rear louvers, hovering in midair to stretch toward a startled Jak before dying away.

The ivy retreated. Already in gear, the freed Leviathan lurched into motion and started to crawl away at its pitiful top speed.

"Watch for her," Ryan said, fighting to retain control of the vehicle as it bumped over the mutant plant. "It must be taking her somewhere. When it sets her down, we do a recce and snatch."

"Sure as hell going to try," J.B. said, scanning the sky. "But where could it be taking her?"

"And us," Mildred added softly. She wondered if the plant wanted just the redhead, or if it was only using her to pull them someplace special. Cheese on a string.

"A rooftop," Doc said, bare sword in hand. "The heart, head, whatever, of the plant will be on the roof."

"Plants need sunlight," Jak agreed.

"But they feed from the roots!"

Feed. Ryan felt ice fill his veins, but forced the word out of his head. Thoughts like that would only muddle his thinking. This was a time for quick action. He could consider the danger later, after he had her back safe and sound.

"What's our missile status?" Mildred asked, sliding into the front gunner's chair and hitting switches.

"None," Doc replied, loading a fresh belt of shells into the Vulcan 40 mm cannon. "We have several of the LAWs left, but they're armor piercing. No napalm or AP rounds."

"Useless against this," Mildred stormed.

Pumping the clutch and working the choke, Ryan maneuvered Leviathan past the roof of the toppled building lying shattered in the street. "What about the 75s?" he asked, putting a burst of flame before them. The wiggling ivy crisped into ash, the rest fleeing to a safe distance. For a while.

"Willy Peter and AP both."

"Excellent."

Dean was confused, then remembered Willy Peter was oldtalk for white phosphorus. The chemical burned at a thousand degrees and water only made it hotter. Killed nearly anything.

"Fuel level?" Ryan demanded. The building on the corner over which Krysty had disappeared was a clothing store with something unreadable on sale for half price. A flexible iron grating covered the big windows as protection against thieves in the night. Unfortunately, Ryan wasn't sure the slow-moving tank could get through any of those.

"Half full," Mildred answered, checking a dial. "Goddamn flamethrower eats gas like crazy."

"You kill, we'll fill," J.B. told her, unscrewing the internal feeder pipe to the gasoline tanks. Without being asked, Dean arrived with two of the twenty-gallon cans from the lockers.

"Reg or condensed?"

"One of each."

"Hot damn. Any more?"

"Six or so."

"Keep them coming!"

A soft blastershot sounded from their left.

Moving along the littered streets, Leviathan rolled over lumps and assorted junk, crushing everything underneath them. Vines shot out at crazy angles, the slim tendrils going through the iron grid to lash at the windows. But the resilient glass stopped any further invasion. Ryan gave them a touch of flame, and the killer leaves retreated.

Another shot, softer than the others.

"Everybody quiet!" Ryan ordered, killing the engines.

Silence reigned, except for the soft rustling of the mutie plant all around them. There was another gunshot and the shattering of glass.

"There!" Mildred shouted, pointing. "Seems to be coming from that furniture store by the vacant lot!" The yard was strewed with ancient wreckage and assorted rubbish completely unidentifiable.

"A furniture store?" Dean asked, lugging over two more cans.

"The second mistake," Ryan growled fiercely. "J.B., prep a satchel charge, the biggest you have. Set it for five minutes."

"Can do. Diversion?"

"Yeah. A furniture store means a loading dock big enough for Leviathan to get through to the cellar."

"Cellar?" Dean queried, pausing in emptying another gas can into the access pipe.

"That's where plants feed," Ryan reminded him grimly. "The roots."

Ramming a timing pencil into a block of C-4, J.B. tied shut the canvas sack full of plastique and moved to the roof hatch. Cradling his hurt arm, Jak was there, the locking bolt already thrown.

"Throw!" Jak shouted, as the tank lurched to the right and started into an ivy-infested alley.

Flames washed over the craft once more and as they went into the alley, Doc flipped back the hatch and J.B. heaved out the satchel. But as quickly as Jak slammed shut the hatch again, a dozen vines wiggled in and struck out at anything near them. Boots and knives finished off the invaders.

"Hellhounds, robot tanks, killer ivy." J.B. cursed, crushing a vine as if it were a cigarette butt. "Damn the day we ever opened that redoubt!"

"A Pandora's box for sure," Doc said, skewering a vine and splitting it lengthwise. "But as with the Grecian myth, we still have hope."

"And blasters."

"There it is," Ryan said, trying not to shout his impatience over the sluggish advance of their craft. He could outwalk this bastard thing going uphill! A wooden gate barring the end of the alley offered no resistance. Relentlessly, he drove the tank straight through a heap of bones and bent motorcycles piled toward the rear of the store.

Brick stairs led to a door, and alongside was an inclined ramp going to a loading dock, the three big doors made of hinged steel planks banded together with rivets. Pulsating waves of ivy coated everything.

"Center door," Mildred said.

Ryan headed for the middle as the twin 75 mm recoilless rifles spoke in unison, the shells detonating on the loading dock, blowing the sheet metal into rubbish. Mildred lowered the angle and fired again, blasting off the jagged metal strips that edged the entrance to the cellar. She knew their military tires were tough, but there was no sense asking for flats when speed was what they needed most. A few remaining strips of steel jutted or dangled from the smoking entranceway, but Ryan paid them no heed and plowed the juggernaut through. The headlights came on automatically as darkness engulfed the vehicle.

The inside of the building was a jungle, vines as thick as cables festooning the walls and ceiling. More bones, hundreds of them, thousands, littered the leafy floor, and fat cocoons hung in clusters like bunches of grapes. A curtain of ivy formed a solid barrier across the room effectively hiding anything beyond the expanse of moving greenery.

Dean poured the last canister of extra fuel into the pipe and screwed the cap on tight. "Done," he announced.

Starring at the morass before them, something deep inside Ryan demanded that he lead the recce into the building. It took a force of will stronger than Ryan knew he had to counter that. He was the best driver, and already behind the wheel. It was his task to stay here, direct the rescue and protect Leviathan. What was the point of saving his lover if there was nothing for her to come back to but ivy-infested wreckage?

Ignorant of the man's private struggle, J.B. took the M-4000 from the rack behind the driver's seat and walked to the port-side hatch. "This going to be nasty, people," he said softly. "We got to get hard, move fast."

"John." Mildred spoke with feeling, pausing in the work of sliding fresh shells into the 75 mm rifles. Their gaze met, but neither spoke. Sometime words weren't enough.

A boom shook the entire structure, smoke appearing over the leafy rooftop. The plants went mad, ripping apart rubbish and smashing random debris.

"Go!" Ryan ordered, clearing a path ahead of the tank.

"Welcome to hell," J.B. shouted, as he shoved open the door, firing the 12-gauge and the Uzi. Clumps of ivy were shredded into mulch, and he jumped to the soft floor.

Two quick shots, followed by silence.

"That's six," Dean said, joining the Armorer. "She's out. But why two at once?"

"To tell us she's not going anywhere else."

Exhaling sharply, the boy understood, his combat face returning, making him appear years older. "Check. We better move."

"Nyah, I say thee, hold, Pericles," Doc said, jumping to the ground, his arms full of fuel canisters. Dropping one at their feet, he tossed another deeper into the loading dock, and the next farther still.

"What're you doing?" J.B. demanded to the elderly man. "Those are empty."

"Aren't they?" Dean asked, furious for missing so many.

Doc grinned, displaying his oddly perfect white teeth. "Ah, but how can the plants know that?"

Sure enough, the ivy on the ground wiggled away, exposing bare concrete. Doc reappeared with more empties, and the three friends threw them in as far as they could. The plants went mad, damaging themselves to get away. The few spilled drops of gasoline on the spouts of the aluminum cans were more than sufficient to show that these were the same type of deadly containers used before.

"I thought they would remember," Doc said, going back inside. "I shall get more!"

The process was repeated and the curtain of green parted as if by magic. Beyond was a line of waiting humans. The men braced for an attack, but these weren't guards. Some were naked, a few in filthy rags. The group stood there, men, a woman and an infant child no more than a newborn, their heads and limbs oddly placed. Using the binocs, Mildred distorted her face in vile disgust. Ryan grabbed his binocs and noted the raw terror in their rolling eyes, the flecks of foam on pale lips. And where clothing didn't cover them, tendrils of the ivy were clearly visible lining their bodies, the roots embedded into the living flesh.

"They're a shield!" Mildred shouted.

"Probably thinks we won't kill our own kind," Ryan said without emotion. "Mistake three. By the looks of things, they're already dead. Jak, fire."

Angling the big vented barrel forward, the teenager cut loose with the side-mounted .50-caliber machine gun, the heavy slugs from the Remington tearing the people into shreds. Their bodies jerked about madly, red blood splattering the leafy walls in a grisly spray.

They could see that the filaments of the ivy reached everywhere inside the prisoners, extruding from every pore, every opening.

"By the Three Kennedys," Doc gasped.

"Not prisoners," Dean spit, pumping the Mossberg. "Puppets."

"Find her," Ryan commanded over the external

PA system. There was a tone in his voice none of them had ever heard before. ''Find her!''

Ryan's hands were white on the steering wheel as he put more fuel onto the writhing plants, scorching a path through the unholy puppets.

Grabbing the last of the empty gas cans, J.B. and Doc were close behind as Dean took off. Ryan stared after them, as he sent a fresh spray from the flamethrower across the ceiling of the dock as a protective umbrella. As the burning liquid flowed onto the cocoons, the pods burst open, spilling out desiccated bodies dried of every possible nutrient fluid. They blazed like seasoned cordwood.

As the three friends passed the crumpled puppets, the headlights of Leviathan grew faint, but the conflagration gave them ample light to see. Warily, they proceeded deeper into the lush hell of the store. Abundant plants covered the floor, walls and ceiling, dainty reddish flowers decorating the thick growth. Broaching the parted curtain, they tossed more cans ahead of them and continued. The ivy whipped away.

Reaching the interior, they could see there was no second or third level to the building; the floors had been removed and a great hole reached upward to the glass skylight. Below was a slanted pit in the floor. Without hesitation, they scrambled down the incline.

''Roof and cellar,'' Doc noted, his sword slashing as steadily as a harvest reaper. ''No sign of her clothes,'' J.B. said, which was neither good or bad. It meant she was still alive, or they weren't near her yet.

Dean said nothing, keeping careful count of his shells. Once he got past the halfway mark, he would have to decide to keep going, or retreat. Neither sounded good.

The three walked on into the leafy hell. Bones crunched underfoot, many of them fresh. More than once, vines tried to close off their avenue of escape, or drop from overhead. But the friends expected those ploys and their combined firepower blasted apart the killer plants. And the fuel cans kept a series of clear spots free from any leafy entanglements. Escape wasn't a problem yet.

"It's aware we're here," J.B. said, resetting the glasses on his nose.

Grunting with the effort, Doc tossed a fuel can ahead of them. It landed a few yards away on a pile of leaves, which quickly became bare floor.

"That is it," he said, drawing the LeMat. "End of the line."

J.B. glanced behind them, the faint headlights of the distant Leviathan and the burning plants giving off an unearthly illumination. Demonic shadows danced on the ivy, adding to the malevolent ambience.

"Hate to say this," J.B. observed, "but if we can't see, we can't fight."

"A little ways more," Dean insisted, stepping around a lump of equipment that resembled a U.S. Army portable flamethrower, the pressurized tanks broken and smashed to junk. They weren't the first in here.

"To the last can," J.B. said, straining to see in

the dim light. His imagination was running wild, seeing attacks from every direction. And the heat!

"Yes," Doc wheezed, coughing from the smoke. "No farther."

More cocoons were found, time reducing them to only tatters of fibrous material. Inside one was the rusting remains of what resembled military power armor, a skeleton grinning behind the Kevlar faceplate.

"Ivy did that?" J.B. whispered, shocked.

Dean whirled. "No!" he shouted, firing twice.

Black bugs boiled out of the foliage, scuttling along the walls and ceilings, insects as big as a loaf of bread, and each wiggling on the end of a pulsating green vine.

"Dark night!" J.B. yelled, his shotgun blasting apart the closest insects.

The companions cut loose with their weapons, moving carefully over the vine-encrusted floor to form a defensive circle. Another wave of insects crawled into view, as a third descended the walls in sheets. Blasters discharged in every direction. J.B. used both of his grens to devastating effect, but more bugs advanced, endless waves, their pincers snapping a hideous cacophony.

Then bright white light flooded the area, and Leviathan appeared at the top of the pit. As it crushed and scraped a path, the vehicle's heavy engines rumbled. It began plowing along the tunnel, an overhead stream of fire heralding its ponderous advance. Ivy and insects disintegrated under the barrage of antipersonnel rounds from the 75 mm recoilless rifles.

Bracketed by pyrotechnic death, the three companions stood their ground and fought without pause until the insects unexpectedly closed their pincers and stopped fighting. The recce team killed dozens more until they realized the bugs had ceased to move. Then the ivy parted on the left wall and a mass of vines thrust out a human figure in tattered clothing.

"Thank Gaia, it's you!" Krysty coughed, stumbling into the hazy light. "I was wrapped in some sort of cocoon and it just…let me go."

"We won?" Dean asked, his face a mask of doubt. They were still in the womb, surrounded on every side. "It gave up?"

"Mebbe," J.B growled. "Or this is another trap." He grabbed the woman's arms, holding them tight. "Doc, check her!"

Without hesitation, the old man ran his hands over her body. "I am sorry, my dear, but this search must be conducted." Doc managed to hide his embarrassment at the rude examination, especially since Krysty's clothing had been slashed to ribbons. However, regardless of his discomfort, their survival depended on the search.

"She is clean," Doc stated in relief. "There is no ivy."

J.B. lowered his weapons. "Good. Let's go."

"I do apologize, madam," Doc added, offering Krysty his frock coat. "But if you had seen what we have—"

"I did," the redhead replied, wrapping the long garment around her shoulders. "Those…others are everywhere in here. If I hadn't already shot my last bullet, I would have used it on myself after seeing those poor bastards.''

"Our thoughts exactly," J.B. said, herding her toward Leviathan.

Krysty paused. "Is there any chance we can help them?"

J.B. shook his head.

"Kill them?" she pleaded.

"Good lady, perhaps we should discuss it in safer surroundings," Doc suggested, pointedly looking around.

Understanding, she moved faster, placing her feet carefully amid the collection of brass cartridges that covered the floor.

"Watch out," Dean cried, shoving the woman aside as a burning clump fell from the ceiling to land atop of one of the empty gas containers.

Krysty jumped at the sight and started to run for Leviathan. The others followed in less haste, knowing there was no real danger of an explosion.

The abandoned canister nosily expanded under the heat, and the ivy retracted farther. Then the cap banged off as the thin fumes inside cooked, but nothing else happened. The whole building full of ivy went deathly still, and the bugs scurried out of sight. In seconds, the humans were alone in the headlights of the tank.

"Oh, hell," J.B. whispered.

In slow majesty, a misshapen figure began to rise from the Stygian blackness of the irregular hole in the floor, something so dark it was as if light falling into it was consumed. It was a blackness so great it was clearly visible, highlighted by the ebony expanse of the underground cavern.

Scrambling from her seat, Mildred raced to reach the hatch.

"Everybody, on the double," Ryan ordered calmly over the external PA system. "We've got company coming."

Picking their way through the destruction, the friends rushed to comply. Mildred hastily threw the lock and shoved aside the door. The others piled in haphazardly.

"In," Dean said, slamming the hatch.

After briefly checking to see that Krysty was alive, Ryan shoved the tank into reverse and pressed the pedal to the floor. The twin diesels roared as the huge vehicle lumbered backward through the burning jungle of the furniture store.

Mildred threw the lock on the armored door and glanced out the front windshield. The gnarled thing in the pit was ascending steadily, and the bug-covered walls started to wildly chitter in frenzied discord, like a crowd cheering the arrival of its ruler. "The recoilless isn't going to do much damage to that thing," she stated bluntly. "And we're out of missiles."

"We'll use what we got," Ryan said, pausing for a second as the Leviathan bounded over the line of corpses. "Mebbe everything at once will do the job."

Buttoning the frock coat, Krysty turned. "J.B., give me a satchel charge."

The Armorer spread his hands. "Used our last as a diversion to get past the plants."

She pointed in the corner. "Then what's that?"

"Bag of grens."

Crossing the bucking floor, Krysty grabbed the bag and glanced inside. "High explosive?"

"Mixed."

"Great. We got any more?"

"No, that's the lot."

"They'll have to do then," she said grimly.

"Bag of grens won't stop that monster," J.B. stated, jerking a thumb.

Way ahead of the others, Doc was already pulling down the access ladder to the roof hatch.

"Oh, yes, it will," the woman said.

She turned to Jak and held up a hand. "Cut me."

The teenager furrowed his brow, then slashed out with a leaf-blade knife. Blood welled from the shallow gash across her palm reaching from heel to thumb. Smearing the blood over the bag, she tossed it to Doc. Making the catch, he reached inside and pulled the ring on a random gren, then flipped the bag out of the opening and slammed shut the hatch. It landed behind them on the soft ivy covering.

The ebony creature was still coming out of its dank hole. The body seemed endless, as if the inside of a long tunnel had been made into living flesh, its black chitin shining like armor in the light of the burning dead. Its visage was a gnarled twisted mix of bug and man, if such a hellish combination was possible. Huge segmented eyes stared with hostile intent at the tank.

"Payback time," Krysty said, staring back at the colossus.

The thing almost stalked past the tiny parcel when

the lumpy head gaped its irregular slash of a mouth just enough for an ivy-covered tongue to lick up the bloody morsel and swallow it whole.

As Leviathan burst out of the greenery and onto the loading dock, the pulsating head of the nightmare suddenly bulged outward and burst apart like rotting fruit, the separating pieces spraying out streams of pale pink ichor. The body writhed in agony, black chitin peeling away as searing gouts of chemical hell blossomed out from the mottled flesh of its yawning gullet. The whole length of the sectioned body convulsed out of control, smashing walls and making bricks rain from the sides of the already weakened building. Violently split down the middle, the vivisected mutie limply slumped to the ground twice. A pupilless eye burst from the impact, as shrapnel holes in the other eye pumped out a river of pink that spread on the floor and seeped into the sewer grating.

The ivy thrashed mindlessly, slicing apart its dead master in bestial frenzy. Leafy tendrils sank deep into the headless corpse, the vines pulsating as they pumped the thin ichor from the dead creature back into its huge trembling corpse.

Mildred worked the arming bolt on the 75 mm rifle.

Ryan stopped her. "No need to waste ammo," he said, turning Leviathan around to drive forward again. "That's as dead as anything gets."

"The bigger they are, the harder they fall," J.B. pronounced, wiping sweat off the brow of his fedora.

"That is the unmitigated truth, my dear John Barrymore,'' Doc added, wrinkling his nose. The stench coming from the devastation was almost beyond words. Roasting sewage was the closest he could approximate.

''Goodbye and good riddance,'' Mildred muttered.

Reaching the freedom of the streets, Ryan turned in his seat. ''Krysty?'' he asked softly.

Squatting in front of the medical locker, the redhead didn't stop tending to the wound in her hand. ''Let's get out of this bastard pesthole,'' she growled.

Chapter Eight

At an inexorable pace, Leviathan crawled from the furniture store along the main street. Their hearts still pounding, everybody stood post at a blasterport, weapons primed and ready, but nothing barred their path.

Mildred watched in the mirrors as the leafy building shook once more, then broke into pieces. With the flood of fresh air, flames rose from the tumbling sections, frying the vines, while the writhing bugs popped into green ichor. A thick plume of smoke rose into the mottled sky, the intense heat of the conflagration causing the classic mushroom shape to form above the city.

Mildred and Doc were unperturbed by the sight. Both knew any sufficiently hot ground-level combustion yielded a mushroom cloud. The rest of the friends simply scowled at the legendary sign of destruction.

"Six o'clock," J.B. said, pulling the bolt on his Uzi.

"What now?" Ryan barked irritably.

Standing brazenly on the roof of a diner was a young man in leather clothes and an elderly woman in a ragged housedress. Green vines fringed their limbs, and the puppets watched as Leviathan drove slowly away.

"Must be more than one of those things," Ryan stated.

Doc agreed. "Ascertaining if we are truly departing."

A rifle discharged inside the tank, and Ryan saw Dean standing at a blasterport with his Steyr SSG-70.

"Notch to the left," Ryan suggested. "Adjust for wind."

Nodding, the boy expertly worked the bolt and shot again. He hit both puppets, the hollowpoint rounds punching neat holes in their faces, but completely removing the back of their skulls. Gushing blood from the titanic wounds, the bodies stiffly turned and walked into the shadows.

"Waste ammo," Jak said dourly.

"Removing sentries," J.B. replied. "Protecting our retreat."

The boy removed the clip from the longblaster and thumbed in fresh cartridges. "That's not why I did it."

"Yeah, we know," Ryan said, feeling oddly proud of his son. Even though he hated to admit the fact, sometimes in this brutal struggle for life you had to waste a precious bullet just to be able to call yourself a human being.

They turned onto a side street, the center of the road a bare dirt median, dotted with dead trees, and no sign of the ivy anywhere. The buildings were in an advanced state of decay, some only piles of masonry to show where once stood mighty edifices attesting to the power of man over nature.

"Ah, the suburbs," Doc stated, wiping his sword blade clean. "We can relax, I think."

His 9 mm Uzi pressed to a cheek, J.B. looked out a blasterport. "I'll relax when this muck-eating rad pit is far behind us."

"Which way?" Mildred asked, as a swarm of the big black bugs, without any vines attached, scuttled out of a sewer grating and took off to the south. "Never mind, follow them. They should know the shortest route out of here."

"When in doubt," Ryan agreed, "follow the escaping prisoners."

Unfolding a small plastic sheet, J.B. checked his pocket map. "Nothing much to the south. No more towns worth mentioning, no flatland for farms."

Jak cracked open an ammo box and started reloading his revolver. "Bottom land best. Hill for taters."

J.B. refolded the map. "If you say so."

"Isn't there a redoubt we've already been to in northern Virginia?" Krysty asked, from the rear of the tank. The redhead was nearly finished getting dressed in a khaki jumpsuit she found in a locker.

"J.B., how far away is the redoubt?" Ryan asked.

"King's Bay? Roughly 120 miles."

"Mildred, can we make it?"

"I'm not sure," the physician replied, studying a gauge. "Fuel levels are less than half."

"Anything closer?"

The map was scrutinized. "Nope."

"Then it's our best bet." Ryan worked the choke,

trying to thin the mixture of fuel and air. "We've been on the run since we got out of that bastard Ohio redoubt. Mebbe we can find some supplies along the way, but we know there's fuel in long storage at Virginia. Then we can rest and decide what to do next."

"Fine by me," Doc said, accepting his frock coat from Krysty.

Ryan glanced at Krysty as she took the front seat vacated by Mildred. There was no need for him to ask; he already knew her opinion on the matter.

"So let's roll," Mildred said, sitting next to J.B. "The sooner we're out of here, the better."

TWISTING THE GRIPS on the handlebars, Lady Ward Amanda of Novaville Citadel angled her camou-painted BMW motorcycle off the dusty highway and followed the off-ramp to the old rest station. The parking lot was carved out of the side of a low hill, like a slice taken from an apple. The rusted remains of a hundred predark cars and even more trucks of assorted sizes filled the parking lot to overflowing, forming a maze of rotting tires and lopsided chassis and empty windshields. Under a sagging awning of dead fluorescent lights and bird nests, stands of fuel pumps fronted a squat white building whose dirt-smeared windows and dead neon offered cold beer and chili on sale, both reduced to dust long ago.

As silent as the wind, she rode the huge bike through the labyrinth of wrecks ever mindful of the sharp metal shards that reached out for unwary travelers like thirsty daggers. A single scratch from a rusty nail could kill these days. First every muscle went sore, then your mouth clamped shut, then came the tremors, the sweats and death. She blocked the memory of that terrible day in the Citadel when the healer's axe fell upon her father, the ward himself. The chems did exist, white powders and tiny pills, but they were rare beyond words and fetched the owner's weight in bullets, or a full season of food.

Stopping the BMW motorcycle near the pumps, Amanda killed the 200 cc engine. The vibration between her thighs ceasing was the only sign the motor had ceased to function. Unlike so many other motorcycles, the BMW wasn't driven by a sprocket and chain assembly, but possessed a multigear transmission like a car. It was as quiet as a whisper, perfect transport for a recce.

Kicking down the stand, Amanda stepped off and drew her Thompson machine gun from its cradle on the handlebars. The tommy gun was heavy and long, but was chambered in .22-caliber rounds and carried six hundred shots in a massive cheesewheel clip. As a spray-'n'-pray for enemies hidden in the bushes, or for onrushing crowds of muties, it was an excellent weapon. For max penetration, Amanda carried a pristine blue-steel Desert Eagle .50-caliber autoloader on her hip.

Releasing the chin strap, Amanda removed her camou helmet and glanced carefully around, searching for any signs others might have been here recently—a cig butt on the ground, the faint smell of gasoline or maryjane in the air, fresh urine stains on the white walls. But the area seemed clear. Good. Not many travelers were aware that a supply of fuel remained in the deep underground tanks. However, the Sons of the Knife *did* know about it, and this was a major refueling spot for them. The bikers challenged her ville's right to loot the Wheel, and they, too, were on her agenda today.

Resting the helmet on the handlebars, Amanda set the alarm, palmed the key into a pocket, then got a siphon hose and a fuel can from her saddlebags. She had plenty, but wanted full tanks for the next leg of her journey. It was only twenty more miles to the Wheel, and there she would try to deal with the driver of the huge tank that protected the ivy-coated city. The massive war machine was often seen traversing the streets of the Wheel in perfect safety. But if anybody dared to enter the city limits, they were never heard from again. Clearly, the tank commander ruthlessly ruled the predark ruins and had no intention of sharing the unimaginable wealth stored in its warehouses and skyscrapers. Her face burned with fury at the thought that her father's leg might have been saved if only her sec men could have reached the medicines in the hospital downtown. With only whiskey mixed with jolt to dull the pain, it was a miracle her father had survived. But that was why she was here. Where commoners failed, the barons had to succeed. She would cut a deal with the driver, marry him if necessary, or die trying to kill him. Whatever happened, the Wheel would belong to Novaville, and then the whole mountain range.

Unzipping her leather jacket a few inches to ease the stifling heat, Amanda walked slowly, listening to the world around her. Cicadas chirped in the tall weeds, and a stingwing shot through the darkening sky overhead, chasing a smaller bird. Feathers and blood sprayed from the impact as the needle-thin beak of the stingwing stabbed its victim. She smiled. Feasting on a fresh kill, the stingwing wouldn't bother her. In spite of her bravado at court, Amanda didn't want to be outside the ville walls. However, while large groups were always attacked by the Knives, solos often snuck by without hindrance. Alone was her best bet for success.

Stepping by the pumps, she moved to the white snack bar and found a couple of doors marked for both sexes. She eased open each with the Thompson, and found only autumn-leaves yellow papers and a newly dead squirrel, a prisoner of the inner swing door. Grabbing the rodent by its tail, she stuffed dinner into her pocket and continued with the inspection.

Inside the building, tables had been piled into a makeshift barricade, bullet holes dotting the Formica surfaces. But there was nobody behind the counter. However, off in the corner she found the remains of a campfire, norm bones mixed with mutie skulls in the cold ashes. The muties had to have chased some norms to this place. The men had staged a last-ditch fight and the stickies got them anyway, afterward eating norm and mutie corpses alike. Amanda spit on the corpses. Norm fools! She was glad they were dead, and hoped it wasn't quick or painless. Giving muties flame this close to the fuel dump, were they insane?

The kitchen and freezer were empty, as were the offices and video games room. The squat machines painted with gay colors had died the microsecond electrical power was lost. Satisfied she was alone, the heiress to the Citadel went outside the snack bar and around back. Searching the ground, she found faint yellow lines and a blue striped area for some sort of wheeled transport, and beyond that, a couple of flat metal disks set into the concrete on the ground—the access lids for the underground storage tanks. Oddly, all three contained gasoline, and nobody had ever been able to satisfactorily explain why the station would have three different storage tanks for the exact same thing. Safety wasn't an issue, because if one tank detonated, surely the others would ignite also. Fuel was fuel. It didn't come in calibers the way bullets did. What worked in one engine worked in another. The predark world was full of such inexplicable mysteries. Maybe that was why it fell—simple foolishness.

Kneeling on the asphalt, she tried to unscrew a lid but was unable to make it budge, and the others proved equally resistant. Laying down her gun, she used both hands to strain against the accumulation of rust, almost busting a knuckle as the lid came free. Sucking on the minor wound, she slid the heavy steel disk aside.

Inside the round depression was the main feeder pipe, two valves, a button that did nothing these days and the vent hole. That was what she wanted. The hole had been plugged with a piece of cork long ago to prevent evaporation and save every drop of the juice. Wiggling out the cork, Amanda dropped in the hose until she heard a splash. Making sure the other end was in the canister before starting, she worked the hand pump in smooth strokes, nice and easy. In a few minutes, the container was full. She neatly returned everything to its original position, awkwardly jockeying the heavy metal lid back into place.

Capping the canister, she reached for her weapon and a blur struck the Thompson, sending it skittering into the weeds. Spitting a curse, she drew the Eagle and fell backward against the snack bar. That had been an arrow!

Controlling her breathing, she studied the weeds and wreckage. Nothing was in sight. A sound made her jump, and the woman raced for her bike. Damn her stupidity! Stickies she could handle by the dozen, and stingwings and grumblers were common problems. But an arrow meant people. Could be throwbacks, technophobes, rad worshipers, or worse, the Sons of the Knife. If that rabble got their filthy hands on a lady of the blood, daughter of the ward himself...

As the blonde turned the corner, a black shape hit her in the face. Amanda had to have blacked out for a second for she awoke lying on the ground, surrounded by them. She screamed, knowing full well that nobody could hear, and the pack was upon her, ripping and tearing like wild animals.

LEVIATHAN'S FIFTEEN wheels hummed steadily as the vehicle rolled along the road. Once past the suburbs, Ryan found a highway in good shape. The concrete was relatively smooth, and there were few potholes. As was to be expected, the road had no signposts, so they could only guess it was the Route

65 on J.B.'s map and hope for the best. Most of the day went by in unaccustomed quiet, as the friends cleaned and reloaded their weapons, then consumed another meal of the starchy MREs.

"Ryan, need stop," Jak said.

Taking another swallow of the U.S. Army coffee, Ryan asked, "What for?"

"Pee."

"Could use a visit to the bushes myself," Mildred admitted.

"Sure, but wait till we reach a stream," Ryan said, draining the cup. "That way the water will wash away our traces from any predators."

"Long as it's not too long," J.B. grumbled, sliding his hat over his face and crossing his arms. Soon, soft snoring sounded.

"Hey! Check over there!" Krysty cried from the front seat. She pointed to their right. "A highway rest stop."

"It appears to be in good condition," Doc announced, wiping his chin clean with a moist towelette.

"And check those trucks!"

J.B. jerked upright and shoved his fedora into position at the same time. "Trucks?"

"Dozens of them," Ryan said, placing his tin cup on the dashboard into a small recess that seemed made for the purpose. "Exactly what we need. Leviathan's chassis is built on a civilian truck frame."

"Even if the transmissions were drained," J.B. said, "a few drops would remain on the gears, and over the years flow to the bottom. We get a couple of spoonfuls from each, and we got us a working tank again.''

''Get hard, people,'' Ryan said, checking the SIG-Sauer in his belt. ''What we've thought of, so will others. This is a natural place for an ambush.''

As weapons were primed, Ryan took the tank out of gear and silently rolled down the gentle incline onto the oil-stained concrete apron, easing the craft to a halt between a couple of tractor trailer combos. The closest was a refrigerator unit, its belly hung with liquid air tanks to chill the cargo. The next was a flatbed fenced with wooden slats.

''For hauling livestock,'' Doc stated, opening the cylinder of his .44 LeMat and making sure the copper nipples for the percussion charges were firmly in place. ''There appear to be pig bones in there.''

''I've never seen so many cars and trucks,'' Dean ventured, his lips moving as he tried to count.

''Might even be gas in the storage tanks,'' J.B. said, stuffing tools into his clothes. ''Dean, check and see if we have a hose to use as a siphon, will you?''

''Sure,'' the lad replied, and he was in the center locker rooting about. ''Found one!''

''How long?''

''Ten, twelve yards.''

''More than enough.''

''Hilltop is clean,'' Krysty said, putting aside her binocs. ''If there are sentries or snipers, they're too well hidden for me to find.''

''Trucks seem okay,'' Mildred added, sweeping her vision over the rusting assemblage of vehicles.

"Lots of rats, some stingwings, but no sign of inhabitants."

Reluctantly killing the engines, Ryan set the brakes and spun his chair. "This bothers me," he said bluntly. "One of the first lessons the Trader ever taught me was, anything that seems too good to be true, *is* too good to be true."

"Leave?" Jak asked pointedly. "Or hard and fast?"

Ryan slung his Steyr over a shoulder. "As if we were under attack. J.B., get the juice and nothing else. No side trips. Our fuel is okay for now. Mildred, help him stay on that goal. Doc and Krysty, guard duty. Dean and I will do a fast perimeter recce for any trouble."

"Hey," Jak drawled. Magnum in hand, he was crouched by the door, his long snowy hair masking his pale features.

Resting the stock of his Steyr on a hip, Ryan stared at the teenager. "How's the arm?"

Sheepishly, the teenager flexed his shoulder. "Sore," he admitted.

"That's why you're on sentry duty. Stay inside, no matter what happens out here. You remember the codes?"

"Yeah," he said and took his position at the driver's seat. "Roger, Adam, Charles."

"Right. Stay sharp."

"Codes?" Dean asked, sliding on his bulky vest.

"When you're on sentry," explained Ryan. "You stay hidden, doors locked. Gives us an edge having a secret member of the group."

"So if trouble comes," J.B. added, "shoot high and we duck."

"What if somebody drags one of you over with a knife to the throat and says you're the key?" Dean asked.

Ryan looked at the boy. "That's where the codes come into use. In a situation like that, we would have more information than the sentry, so he would follow our lead."

"Meaning?"

"If any of us calls the sentry Roger, then he gets the hell out and leaves us. Roger means run."

"Gotcha."

"Adam means let us in, but kill whoever we're with."

"Adam is an ambush, check."

"Charlie means it's clear."

"And if you use his real name?"

Ryan stared at his son hard. "That means they broke us, kill everybody, including us, and do a Roger."

The boy nodded.

"Let's get moving," Krysty said, jacking the Ruger for action. She didn't really care for automatics. You had to load and unload the clips every damn night, or else the springs would weaken and they'd jam, usually when you needed them the most, unlike a revolver, which could stay loaded for decades and still function perfectly in combat. But it would do until she got a replacement revolver.

Removing his panga from its sheath on his belt, Ryan tucked the blade into his boot. "Stay alert, people."

Easing open the side hatch, J.B. and his Uzi waited for something to happen. Cicadas faintly chirped in the weeds. When nothing else occurred, he stepped down and moved aside, the stubby barrel of the submachine gun sweeping for targets. The others closely followed, spreading out so as not to offer a potential sniper a group shot. Doc was the last out. Jak then closed and bolted the door.

"Get busy," Ryan ordered, crouched low. "Hit and git. We'll be back in ten."

"Understood," Mildred said, her .38 Czech target pistol held in an expert tournament-style grip. "Ten and counting."

Moving stealthily through the jumble of trucks, the two Cawdors disappeared behind an oil tanker, its cylindrical body rusted full of holes. The weeds waved at their passing, then went still.

Going to his hands and knees, J.B. inspected the refrigerator truck next to them. "Hey, beginners' luck. Tranny has no holes. Here's hoping." Lying flat, he rolled underneath, and there were some metallic bangs and muffled curses. A few seconds later he rolled out, his face streaked with grease.

"Get any?" Doc asked, cradling the LeMat in his arms. He and Mildred were standing back to back, just far enough from each other that a dropped net wouldn't get them both. Lessons learned hard were long remembered.

"About half a cup," J.B. said, sloshing the canteen with his bleeding hand. "A few more of these and we're back in business."

"Excellent."

Agreeing, J.B. checked under the flatbed. "Dark night, the whole undercarriage is gone on this one."

"No engine here at all," Mildred said, looking into the empty engine compartment of a garbage truck.

"The next one is flat on the ground," Doc noted.

"Let's try the bulldog," J.B. decided, and they moved on to a Mack cement mixer with an apple tree growing out of its top hole.

"I'M ON POINT," Ryan stated as the others went out of sight. "Single file, yard spread. Don't shoot unless you have to."

Dean acknowledged, his Mossberg held smartly at quarter arms.

Loose grit and windblown gravel on the concrete apron made every step crunch as father and son walked through the collection of wrecks. Dean was fascinated by the sights. It was the exact opposite of the redoubt. Those vehicles had been in perfect shape, deliberately disassembled by mechanics. These were merely rusting hulks abandoned by their owners.

Dean had never known there were so many different types of transports in the predark world. He was more used to rebuilt military vehicles, designed strictly for utility. These civilian trucks came in a hundred faded colors, some with leather seats, others with silhouettes of women on the mud flaps. And the cars were even more outrageous. Some had fringe, fuzzy cubes hanging from rearview mirrors, or huge birds painted on the hoods. There wasn't a sign of a single weapon mount or armor plating.

Cresting a rotting pile of tires, Ryan held up a hand and closed his fingers into a fist. The boy froze. Faintly, they could hear the slapping sounds of flesh on flesh, low laughter and muffled gasps of pain. Ryan circled his fist and pointed to the left. Running on his toes, Dean went to the wall of the white building, hugging the Mossberg. His father joined him, and they both stole a peek around the corner.

There were five of them, four men clustered around a naked blond woman. The men were dressed in biker togs—leather jackets, ripped denims and boots. Each had his fly unzipped and was fully exposed. The sobbing woman was on her hands and knees, a sweaty biker pushing into her face, another eagerly pumping behind her. The others were laughing and whipped her with their belts, leaving huge red welts. Her breasts jerked at every violation and a steady trickle of blood flowed from her thighs. Nearby, a gleaming white tooth lay on the ground next to a pile of torn clothing.

Having seen enough, Ryan and Dean pulled out of sight.

Estimating the distance as twenty yards, Dean tightened the choke on the Mossberg to the minimum, the soft clicks sounding louder than fireworks in the whispering quiet.

"Let's go," Ryan whispered.

"And circle round," Dean said, sliding a spare shotgun shell into his mouth for a fast reload. "Okay."

"No. I mean leave. Go back to the others."

The boy removed the shell. "We don't need any help. We can take them."

"Son, we're not going to help her."

Dean stared at his father. Ryan took the boy by the arm and pulled him farther from the corner.

"Our first concern," Ryan stated sternly, "is staying alive. After that, fixing the tank and getting out of here. They'll be busy with her for hours, mebbe more. Once we're mobile, we can decide to risk returning to shoot them through the blasterports. Never risk your life for a stranger."

"But—"

"Never."

The discussion finished, Ryan turned to go. Dean started to follow, but unbidden, a picture of the young girl in the redoubt flooded into his mind, the smoking gun at her feet, the torn dress on her skinny body. Red anger filled Dean's vision as he grimly stepped into the clear, raised his shotgun and fired. The spray of double-aught buck completely removed a biker's head above his leather collar. The other men registered shock as the decapitated corpse thrust his hips one last time, then collapsed on top of the woman.

"Fireblast!" Ryan cursed, triggering his Steyr twice at the bikers as he joined his son. The SSG-70 boomed louder than doomsday as the titanic rounds caught a man smack in the chest. Spinning, arms flailing, he collided with the others and the three went down in a tangle. Shooting with every step, father and son moved fast and in seconds the battle was finished.

"Damn fool," Ryan growled, checking the bodies for any sign of life. "We were lucky. Four to two, even with the element of surprise, are terrible odds. Why'd you do it? Why?"

"Had to," Dean said, kneeling beside the woman and helping her to stand.

"Th-th-a-ank you," she mumbled past puffy lips. Dean grabbed a shirt off the pile of clothes and offered it to her. The woman gratefully took the garment and weakly pulled it on. The shirt barely covered her loins, but it would have to do. The rest of her clothes were slashed to pieces.

A movement caught Ryan's attention, and he found a biker still breathing, so he slit the rapist's throat with his panga. Cleaning the blade on the man's shirt, the one-eyed man noticed a colorful tattoo on the dead man's chest, a knife stabbing the sun. Exactly the same as the coldhearts from the Ohio redoubt.

Chapter Nine

Different styles of car seats lined both of the long metal walls. Resting on some bricks, a small block V-8 engine, gutted of all moving parts, served as a cookstove, with some chicory browning in a low pan. Mixed with burned bread crumbs, it made crude frontier coffee that was better than nothing, but not by much. A wide rack for longblasters stood in the corner, two bolt-action Browning rifles and a semiauto M-1 carbine rested there. Ammo boxes were stacked neatly on an iron shelf. A couple of poorly cured animal-skin rugs were on the metal floor, the fur coming off in patches. Brittle yellow centerfolds adorned the ceiling.

"Holy shit!" Monk cried out from his vantage point on a stool near a peephole in the wall. A lit cig dropped from his lips. "I don't believe it!"

"What?" Long Tom asked. Reclining in a bucket seat, the man was paring his fingernails with a bowie knife. "Are they done already? Can we have her now?"

"I want her bike," Renny rumbled. More than seven feet tall, the giant sat on the back seat of a car, as no regular single seat could accommodate him. A screwdriver was nearly lost in his hands as he delicately worked on a carburetor.

The fat redhead almost sputtered in his hurry. "They more than done. A couple of walkers just aced Bob and his boys!"

All work stopped.

"Balls." Long Tom smirked, rising from his seat.

Fumbling with a new cig, Monk moved aside. "See for yourself."

Ignoring the stool, Long Tom bent to the peephole, then spit a virulent curse. "Damnation, it's true! Walkers got the quim and Bob's eating dirt."

"Must be kin come to the rescue," Monk stated, cracking his knuckles nervously.

At the gun rack, Long Tom grabbed a Browning and worked the bolt. He tossed it to Monk and took the M-1 carbine for himself.

Renny stood, his shaved skull brushing against the high ceiling. "Don't know, don't care," he said. "It's killin' time."

"Yeah, bastards deserve to die for what they did to Bob," Monk said, checking his weapon. Exhaling a stream of white smoke, he then added, "Hell, everybody deserves to die."

"Amen," Renny intoned, shouldering his weapon. "Let's go tell the boss."

WITH THE STEYR up and ready, Ryan walked around the white building with Dean and the blonde close behind. The boy had his Mossberg clenched in one hand, and an arm around the waist of the partially clad woman. Her legs trembled from the exertion of walking and she stumbled constantly.

"Wait," the woman whispered, slowing. "The gas, my weapons…must…have them…."

"We're not going back," Ryan replied, listening for the sounds of motorcycles. "You want to, fine. But you go alone."

"Then stop...at my bike."

"Where is it?" he asked brusquely, his good eye squinting against the setting sun.

She pointed. "Near the pumps...front of building."

"We pass it on our way," Dean told his father.

But Ryan was already moving in that direction. There was nobody in sight. Quiet ruled, except for the cicadas. "Clear," he announced.

Pushing herself free from Dean, the woman fell more than walked to her BMW motorcycle. Quickly, she made sure the motorcycle was in functioning shape, then pulled a MAC 10 from her saddlebag, worked the bolt and slung it over a shoulder. She took tallow from a med kit and put it on her eye and lips, then used her torn shirt to wipe away the blood and semen between her legs. Only then did she retrieve clothes from the other bag and clumsily dress in a khaki shirt and denim pants. Apparently, she had no spare underwear, or boots.

Gingerly, the woman climbed aboard the motorcycle. Sliding aside a trick panel in the heavily cushioned seat, she pulled out a key and started the engine. Only a nearly invisible vibration in the motor and wisps of exhaust from the camou-colored tailpipes showed the bike was running. She sat there for a moment, as if absorbing strength from the machine.

A stick cracked amid the foremost line of deteriorating cars, Dean and Ryan pivoted in combat stances, but the cicadas never stopped their chirping.

"You have clothes, blaster and bike," Ryan said. "That's enough. Time to go, miss."

"Lady," she said, a faint lisp caused by a missing tooth marring her words. She rubbed her mouth with a hand, and it came away streaked with blood. "I am Amanda Coultier, Lady Ward of Novaville, heiress to the Citadel.

"After my brother, naturally," she added almost as an afterthought.

The Cawdors didn't reply.

"And you are?" Amanda prompted impatiently.

"Ryan."

"Dean."

"Why the rush?" Amanda asked innocently, playing for information. How much did they know of what was going on in the valley? "Those men are dead."

"Wrong," Ryan said. "They were part of a gang, and more could be coming."

She glanced sideways. "So, you have heard about the Sons of the Knife?"

The lie came easy because it was partially true. "Yeah."

"Come then," she said, moving to the tip of the cushioned seat. "It'll be a squeeze, but we can all fit on my bike. After what you did, it's the least I can do, and my bike is much faster than walking. Hop on."

Dean started forward, but Ryan stopped him. "We have our own transport."

"Really. Then may I travel with you for a

ways?'' she asked. "For protection, until I'm closer to my ville.''

"How do you know we're going that way?'' Dean asked suspiciously. Beautiful or not, he was getting a bad feeling from this woman. She was amazingly clean in a world of scabs and dirt, and yet behaved like a gaudy slut. It was confusing. Dean decided to take his father's lead in the matter.

Amanda laughed, a golden sound of distant bells. "The road has only two directions, and you've already been to the Wheel.''

"Wheel?''

"The city.''

As they started off, Amanda asked, "By the way, can my bike fit inside your truck?''

Ryan didn't correct the guess. "You can ride alongside.''

She smiled demurely, as if a hostess offering a guest a sweetmeat, and fluttered a hand. "And what if after my ordeal I'm too weak to ride?''

"Tough,'' Dean said, continuing through the weeds. He was liking this woman less and less by the word.

Amanda sat there for a minute. The two outlanders kept walking away as if she were no more than a common quiff. It was outrageous! Men and women died to be with her, killed kin to lie with her, and they turned their backs? Wordlessly, she stepped off the bike and pushed it across the concrete apron and into the rustling morass of dry weeds and rotting tires.

She was hard-pressed to keep with them. They moved as fast as panthers, pausing for nothing and never looking backward to keep track of her progress.

"A ville ruler," Ryan said, "off by herself?"

"I'm on a mission," she replied curtly. "I stopped here for gas, relaxed my guard for just a second and they jumped. Never got off a shot."

"Not wise to ride solo," Dean told her. "Everybody gets tired, and tired is dead."

"Or worse," Amanda agreed, pulling hair over the left side of her face to hide the bruising. "They hadn't started on me yet. Not really. And if they knew who I was…"

"Not friendly neighbors?"

"Sworn enemies. They stalk this road and rob travelers of goods and life. A major priority was to see if I could find a way to deal with them."

"Deal?" Dean asked.

"Kill."

A lone woman tackle a whole gang? Dean said nothing, but it raised his suspicions.

"What was the other part?" Ryan asked, half listening to her, but closely watching the shadows under the vehicles around them. Time was pressing, but he knew it was better to get her story while she still felt gratitude toward them. Soon enough pragmatism would return. This section of Deathlands wasn't hard-hit by either radiation or the acid rains. So it seemed as if every madman and mutie had run here to claim new territory. He needed to know what was what, so they could get out intact.

She could think of no reason to lie, so told them the truth. They had saved her life. "I left the ville to try and sneak into the Wheel and deal with the problem of the tank commander who rules the city.''

"Kill," Dean said.

Amanda switched off the bike. "No. Negotiate a treaty, pay him off, seduce him, marry if needs be. Anything to bring peace between the Wheel and Novaville.''

Knowing the info was totally wrong, Ryan said nothing, waiting to see if she would volunteer any additional data.

"Well, it's dead," Dean stated, a touch of pride in his voice. "Wasn't a norm or a mutie, but a machine, and we killed the thing. That is, my father dropped a building on it." He pantomimed the event for her. "Smashed flatter than dust.''

Turning toward them, Amanda tugged on her collar, exposing a great wealth of cleavage.

Unmoved by the display, Ryan thought the seduction tactic odd for a woman who had just been brutally assaulted.

Dean swallowed hard.

"Interesting, if true," Amanda said softly. "And, yes, I can see by the expression in your face, sir, that it is true. The Beast of the Wheel is no more?''

"You could say that, yes." Then Ryan added, "Although whether a machine can truly die is beyond me. But it will never work again. That's for bastard sure.''

"Excellent," the blonde purred excitedly. "Indeed, more than excellent. Superb. Then you can claim a triple reward from my father, the ward. First for rescuing me, another for killing the Beast and for slaying six of the Sons.''

"Fine. Always need supplies," Ryan said.

"And what would you wish?" she asked with a smile. "Name it. Perhaps a ville, with servants and a thousand acres of land?"

"Had a bigger spread than that already," Ryan said gruffly. "Left it behind."

"Really?" She seemed surprised, and regarded him more closely. "You are from a barony?"

Ryan scowled. "Was."

Amanda demurred. She wasn't quite sure how to handle this situation. These were unusual people. They helped a strange woman in distress, yet didn't take her themselves, even when she offered. The conclusion was obvious. They had women of their own, which meant there was more than just the two of them. Perhaps an entire ville, or a roving band.

Past the trucks, she could see they were nearing the ramp that led to the roadway. From here it would be simplicity to start her bike and roar away. But she had no wish to leave their presence. Not yet. If they had truly slain the Beast of the Wheel, they were a force to be reckoned with.

Stopping amid the last row of vehicles, Ryan whistled twice, then proceeded.

Amanda gasped as an enormous tank came into view, its curved hull bristling with weapons. Standing alongside the behemoth was an old man in a frock coat holding a cane, and a stocky black woman with hair resembling snakes, blasters in their hands. On the ground, a pair of legs stuck out from underneath the armored chassis.

"The beast!" Amanda screamed, drawing her weapon.

"No!" Dean cried.

Diving for cover, Doc and Mildred went into the weeds as the MAC-10 sprayed bullets across the hull. As the legs on the ground retracted fully under the vehicle, Ryan knocked the machine pistol out of the woman's grip with the stock of the Steyr. Her blaster fell with a clatter, and Dean put his foot on top.

"What are you doing?" she screamed. "That is the Beast! It has murdered hundreds of my people!"

"This is our tank."

"Yours?"

"Everybody okay?" Dean called out, picking up the MAC-10, never taking his sight off the so-called lady.

Mildred and Doc rose from the weeds, both of their weapons pointed straight toward the barefoot beauty.

Ryan opened and closed his hand twice in the all-clear signal. "And how is Charles?"

"Charles is fine," Mildred said, responding correctly. Neither of them relaxed, but their barrels were no longer pointed directly at the blonde on the bike.

Arm in a sling, Jak appeared in the doorway. "We fine, too."

"Good, and how are the—" Ryan started to say repairs, but looked at the furious woman. "How is the hunt going? Find those snake eggs yet?"

"Nearly," J.B. said from under the vehicle. "And I gather we have a guest?"

"Guest? Prisoner, you lying scum!" Amanda spit

in unbridled fury. "So you are the masters of the Beast! "

Ryan shook his head. "This is another vehicle."

"You lie!"

"Why?" Dean asked.

"As a trick to get the ransom!" she stormed. "Or to get past the ville defenses and kill my people. But it won't work! You'll get nothing from me. I'll never talk!"

His patience clearly at an end, Ryan's face got hard, so Dean asked quickly, "What do you know of the Beast? Do we resemble the craft in any way?"

Confused, Amanda paused, conflicting emotions playing across her bruised face. "Well, no," she admitted hesitantly. "Not really. It is known to have metal treads and you have wheels."

"Anything else?"

She studied the vehicle closely. Its dull gray hull was battered and damaged, the radio antenna only a short nub, something metallic had melted on the rooftop, rivulets of cooled steel dangling down like silvery icicles, and there were scorch marks where burning fluids had washed over the vehicle from stem to stern. The reports of her spies told how nothing seemed to mark the mirror black hull of the Beast.

"Your craft, although large, is much too small," Amanda said, moving toward the open door. It promptly closed. "And where is the blaster with the light that kills?"

"We don't have one," Ryan replied gruffly. "Be nice if we did."

The cicadas stooped singing.

"Infrared shows ten incoming," Krysty called over the PA system.

Everybody turned and lifted their blasters a split second before the roar of engines. Then the front line of trucks shook as a wave of motorcycles bounded over them in tight formation. The bikes hit the ground hard, but the leather clad riders stayed on, yelling a battle cry and revving the engines to full throttle.

"Yee-haw!" screamed a bearded man, a blaster in his free hand, long hair flying in the wind. "Found them!"

"Run them down!" cried a tall man with a gap-toothed smile.

"Don't kill the slut!" added another, wielding an ax.

"Kill everybody!" a bald giant corrected.

Dean tossed the blonde her MAC-10, as he turned and fired twice with the Mossberg. He hit nothing, the reports only causing a flurry of return fire from the cavorting bikes.

Putting his back to Leviathan, J.B. cut loose with the Uzi, chasing the wild bikers. "Damn bikers are harder to hit than bees!"

"J.B.!" Ryan snapped, quickly exchanging the Steyr for the Armorer's M-4000 shotgun. "Fix the tranny!"

"In the middle of a fight?"

"We may have to evac!"

Accepting the logic, J.B. slung his machine gun and crawled under Leviathan, dragging the canteen of precious hydraulic fluid after him. A shot zinged off the concrete near his boots, nearly puncturing the canteen, and he was gone from sight.

"Look at that! They're running away!" a biker cried, swinging around for another pass. "Hiding like babies!"

"Let's make them dance!" yelled a snaggle-toothed rider, shooting a sawed-off shotgun. The left barrel failed to discharge, but the right boomed, showering pellets into the ground near Ryan, who neither flinched nor paused as he loaded his own crowd sweeper. As the biker roared by, the one eyed man fired, blowing off the man's arm at the elbow. Howling in agony, the rider went down, blood gushing from the ragged stump.

Drawing his .357 Magnum Colt Python, Jak assumed a firing stance. Holding the big bore blaster steady with two hands, he tracked a target and fired once. A biker's helmet exploded off his head leaving the man stunned but undamaged.

"I got the mutie!" a fat redheaded man shouted, brandishing a Thompson submachine gun with a huge cheesewheel clip, and he hosed a stream of bullets at the pale teenager. Jak's pantleg fluttered as a slug came lethally close. The albino teen fired again, and the man's face was removed in chunks. The riderless bike raced off, hit the severed arm, bounced and flipped into the air to crash resoundingly on the dirty concrete.

Bypassing the white-haired killer, the rest of the bikers concentrated on the open hatchway of Leviathan. A round slammed into an ammo locker next to Krysty at the starboard Remington. Her hair flattening in response, the redhead spun and fanned her

Ruger at the motorcycle riders rushing straight toward her.

"They're trying to get in!" Mildred yelled, her .38 banging away, the rounds hitting with surgical precision. The bikers recoiled from the impacts, but didn't fall. "Some of them have flak jackets!"

"Then consider me Baldar on the bridge!" Doc said. He shoved Mildred inside, slamming shut the door while firing his LeMat from the hip. "None shall pass!"

Splitting apart, the pack swerved away the closed hull, darting between the individual defenders. A biker made a pass at Doc with a length of chain that smashed onto the hull with sledgehammer force. The elderly man nimbly ducked and the LeMat boomed, the muzzle-flame almost reaching the laughing biker. The motorcycle kept going, but the rider flew off and crashed through the window of a rusty car.

Segmented into slices, Mildred's angry face appeared in the louvered slots of a blasterport. "Baldar, my ass! This isn't Asgard, you old coot! Get inside! I'll give cover with the Remington!"

"Can't risk them getting in," Krysty said as the military diesels started. "And if one gren bounces into the ammo bin, this tin can is history!" Then she killed the engine when a squawk of pain came from J.B. under the floor.

A scraggly woman in a sleeveless T-shirt expertly flipped her bike onto its rear wheel and charged for Ryan. With the engine giving her protective cover, he had no choice but to dive out of the way. The studded wheels spun past his head, missing by an inch. From the prone position, he triggered the SIG-Sauer upward and removed most of the biker's throat with a single well-placed shot. She tumbled sideways and got caught angled in the spinning spokes of her wheels. The results were colorful.

Through a blasterport, Mildred fired twice, making an obscenely fat biker stagger, but not fall off. Dean blew the tires off another two-wheeler and the machine crashed into the end of a truck, the bike going underneath, the rider hitting it dead on. Blood sprayed out from the impact, and the limp body slid down the metal wall, leaving a horrid trail of teeth and eyes.

Leathering his gun, Ryan unlimbered the Steyr and worked the bolt. Area effect wasn't doing the job. Time for big punch.

A sputtering chatter announced that Krysty was operating the Remington on full-auto, the .50-caliber rounds chewing the ground as she hosed men and machines with high-caliber death. Two woofed into pyres. Mildred added the firepower of the port Remington, but the rest wheeled crazily about in a knot of confusion, making it impossible for them to get a clear shot.

Crouching behind her motorcycle, Amanda was hosing the lines of trucks and cars endlessly with her MAC-10 as if bullets were free. When the machine pistol stopped, she dropped a clip and reloaded in a heartbeat. She didn't appear to be doing any damage to the bikers, but if there was anybody hiding in the ruins, they would have been insane to chance rising into view.

Slowing his chopper, a beefy biker with a crew

cut pulled something from within his jacket and tossed it at them.

"Gren!" Jak shouted, fanning his Magnum.

As the ball arched into the sky, Dean tracked it with his Mossberg, patiently waiting. As the gren reached the apex of its arch and slowed, he fired. The charge detonated, slapping them with a powerful concussion.

"Hot pipe! If that had been AP," he cried, dropping the exhausted shotgun and drawing his Browning Hi-Power blaster, "the shrapnel would have aced the lot of us!"

Every blaster spit flame at the muscular biker, but he turned tail and took off into the distance.

"Excellent, one less to fight," Doc rumbled, his back to the tank for protection, the LeMat .44 booming at the attackers. Ricochets zinged off the composite armor hull and the man flinched as a line of blood appeared along his cheek.

"Unless he's going for more grens," Ryan grunted. "That's what I'd do." His Steyr SSG-70 blasted hot lead death at a giant biker who was raising a spiked baseball bat. The big steel-jacketed slug went clean through the man, wounding a bald rider behind him in the chest. Cawdor shot again, and missed. "There's too many, and they're too bastard fast! Let's finish this now!"

Struggling to regroup, the remaining bikers retaliated with their machine pistols, hosing the tank. Somebody inside the vehicle touched off the rear 40 mm cannon, adding their destructive bid to the battle zone. Blood pooled around burning wreckage. Jagged pieces of wrecked bikes covered the concrete and threatened to trip the friends at every step, and the bikers maintained a constant fusillade of incoming rounds.

Ryan shouldered his longblaster and drew the SIG-Sauer. The silenced 9 mm pistol coughed and a motorcycle fuel tank burst, covering a biker with gasoline that ignited as it dripped upon the hot engine. Running amok, the human torch screamed at the top of his lungs. His companions wheeled uncaring past the torch, and then mercifully his ammo cooked off and killed him.

Inside Leviathan, Krysty rammed AP shells into the front 75 mm recoilless rifles. "J.B., how you doing?" she yelled at the floor. The big blasters couldn't traverse or swivel, only elevate. But if the bikers got stupid and slowed in front of the tank, they would never know what hit them. "J.B.?" she repeated. "Hey, J.B.!"

There was no answer.

Leaving the Vulcan, Mildred moved to the closed hatch in the floor, not daring to open it for fear of who might be on the other side. "John, you okay?"

Silence.

Outside, a black dart riding a column of flame streaked past Leviathan to violently impact on the distant highway, concrete and asphalt forming a geyser.

"They got a bazooka!" Dean shouted.

Backtracking the most likely trajectory, Ryan saw a distant figure crouching on top of a truck, a long tube in his or her hands. The one-eyed man forced the sounds of battle from his mind, concentrating on the task at hand. Closing a hatch on the end of the long tube, the figure stood and raised it to his or her shoulder. Ryan instantly emptied the SIG-Sauer, riding the bucking 9 mm rounds into a tight cluster. For a moment, the figure seemed unaffected, then took a step backward, dropped the weapon and tumbled off the truck.

"Not anymore," he announced, ramming a fresh clip into the blaster. In that part of any warrior's mind that remained cool during any battle, Ryan noted it was his last loaded clip. Fifteen shots, and he'd have to grab something off the ground. There was a sawed-off nearby, but he didn't trust the ammo.

Suddenly, a riderless motorcycle soared over a pile of rubble, flying straight for the motionless Leviathan. A sputtering fuse dangled from its lumpy saddlebags.

"Kamikaze!" Amanda yelled, the recovered Thompson chattering nonstop in her grip.

Weapons tracked the airborne assailant and the booby-trapped bike detonated into a fireball, shrapnel raining on the prow of the tank. A handlebar and seat slammed off the iron bar grid, as a red-hot piston smacked into the hardened windshield, sending out cracks but not quite bursting through.

"Not want us whole anymore," Jak said, reloading his blaster without looking. Snapping the cylinder shut, he took off at a run. "Get bazooka. Cover!"

"Go!" Dean said, ramming in a fresh clip.

Careening over the bodies of their fallen comrades, the bikers stubbornly maintained the attack on the tank. One of the tires went flat, then another.

Brutally, Leviathan was pounded under a hail of bullets and grens as the hull was ruthlessly probed for a weak spot.

Crouching behind the smoking ruin of a dead bike for cover, Ryan watched the motorcycles circle the tank like coyotes closing on a wounded animal. They were outgunned and outmanned at this point, but refused to leave. He could feel it in his bones. The Sons of the Knife had something more planned.

Safely masked by the clouds of smoke in front of Leviathan, the gang stopped for a second, a scruffy fellow passing out packs of grayish clay to the others—shaped charges of C-4.

A horn beeped and the bikers turned to see a beautiful redhead in the driver's seat behind the cracked windshield just as the twin 75 mm rifles spoke in unison. The volcanic hellstorm of AP shotgun rounds blew the attackers off their bikes. Reduced to mincemeat, unrecognizable chunks flew everywhere and the riddled two-wheelers spun away as engines burst into flames, and fuel tanks exploded.

Wary of shrapnel, the friends converged on the sight and did a clean sweep of the wounded survivors. In seconds it was done. The bikers lay sprawled on the ground, pumping out their lives into the weeds.

Holstering his 9 mm blaster, Ryan reviewed the battle zone as he reloaded the empty clip of his Steyr from the loose rounds in his pocket. Four tires on Leviathan were only rubbery tatters, and the tank was listing to starboard some, but nothing serious. Spent brass covered the ground, making walking treacherous. Acrid smoke from the burning bikes was probably the only thing keeping the stingwings away from the mangled bodies. He could see them circling overhead, waiting for the first opportunity to begin their feeding frenzy.

Retrieving the shotgun, Ryan knocked on the side of the hull with the stock. "Hey, J.B.! You alive?"

A greasy hand came into view, and the hatless Armorer crawled out. Struggling to his feet, J.B. dusted himself off with dirty hands. "Well, it's done. We have a working transmission again."

"What took so damn long?" Ryan asked in concern.

"Where the hell's my hat?" J.B. demanded.

It was found and returned, basically intact. The Armorer straightened the rumpled brim and pulled his fedora into its accustomed locale. "What took so long? You ever try a repair job in the dark, upside down, with bullets flying by?

"Besides," he added, hitching his belt, "I had to take care of something in case we got captured by those rad-licking scums."

With a clank, the bolt on the side hatch was released and the hatch slid aside, revealing Mildred, med kit in hand. "Anybody hurt?" she asked, exiting carefully.

"Just them," Ryan said, ramming home the clip.

She surveyed the carnage. "Better them than us. But still a waste of life." Mildred hopped to the ground, then walked over and handed Doc a foil pack containing a moistened towelette from an MRE pack.

"Clean that cut," she ordered. "Don't want an infection, do you?"

Doc accepted the towelette with a grateful nod.

Busy working the bolt of her Thompson to clear a round jammed in the ejector, Amanda jerked up her head at those words and openly stared at the stocky black woman.

A sharp whistle came from the weeds. Ryan answered, and Jak returned with a stovepipe-style bazooka in his grip, and a canvas sack of bulky rockets slung over a shoulder. He deposited the booty inside Leviathan.

"How did they find us?" Dean demanded, sitting on the step of the tank. Even though it was partially depleted, his ammo vest weighed a ton. He was bone tired, but had no intention of showing the fact. "Been following us, or what?"

Ryan rested the butt of the longblaster on his hip.

"I think they live here," Ryan said, studying the bullet-riddled vehicles of the rest stop. The destruction was widespread.

"Lived," Doc corrected, tossing away the soiled towelette. He winced slightly as the air hit the alcohol in the scrape. "Past tense, my dear Ryan. Past tense."

"In ruins?" Jak asked.

"Sure. Fuel in the underground tanks, spare parts by the ton and plenty of space to hide lots of folks inside the bigger trucks."

Wheeling over her BMW, Amanda said, "That makes sense. That way, they could safely hide and decide who they'll hit and who can pass."

"Decide?" Dean repeated, reclaiming his Mossberg. A swipe of a cloth removed some human remains from the barrel. "Why wouldn't they hit everyone who stopped?"

"If they ambushed everybody, soon nobody would stop here, and what's the point?"

"Gotcha."

"Yes, very clever," Amanda stated, kicking down the stand.

"Hey, Ryan. What about those bikes?" Mildred asked, indicating several of the more intact motorcycles. "Couple of them seem in good shape."

"Might make fine scouting craft," Krysty added, stepping into view, "and good escape wags."

"We could strap them to the outside of Leviathan," Dean suggested, rising wearily, ready to do his share of the work. "We have the mounts."

"So we do," Ryan said, running a callused hand over the stands installed by the coldhearts from the redoubt. "Okay. We'll use the drive chains of the busted cycles to secure the serviceable bikes."

"Doc, Jak, guard duty," Krysty said. "I'll be on the infrared."

The decision made, two functioning motorcycles were firmly attached to the hull of the tank. Afterward, the friends rooted among the dead, salvaging weapons, ammo, an ax, a can opener, a precious set of binocs only slightly warped and a ring of brass keys.

"Could come in handy," J.B. said, pocketing the keys.

"What for?" Mildred asked. "We don't even know what they unlock."

"Might be something good, might be nothing.

But a set of keys always makes fine bait in a booby trap.''

Resting against her BMW, Amanda watched their proceedings with a disinterested air. Her gaze, though, kept darting to the interior of Leviathan. Krysty noticed her attraction and moved between the stranger and the dashboard console. Curiosity was natural, but she got an odd feeling about the blonde. The woman had clearly been badly beaten. Purplish bruises were slowly appearing all over her body, especially the thighs, and there was a prominent tooth missing. Krysty could guess exactly what kind of trouble Ryan and Dean had rescued her from. Yet the blonde wasn't angry or humiliated as any normal person should have been. She almost seemed amused. Even pleased.

"Achilles, don these, for the world knows your plight," Doc said, handing Dean a pair of leather boots.

The youngster tried them on, delightedly finding the footgear to be a near-perfect fit. "Bit large," he commented, standing and stamping his feet.

"You'll grow into them," Ryan said, his expression belying the stern tone.

"Wait a moment," Amanda said, going to her saddlebags. "I have something here that might work better than those."

A warning tingle flared through every nerve, and Krysty drew the .38 Ruger, but Doc and Jak were between her and the woman. Both of the blonde's hands were out of sight inside the bags doing something.

"Ryan!" Krysty yelled. "Something's wrong! Stop her!"

But before anybody could react, an intense hissing sound came from the motorcycle. Nothing was visible, but Doc and Dean toppled limply to the ground. Scowling, Ryan managed to pull his handblaster when he also folded.

"It's gas!" Mildred cried, drawing her .38 blaster. But the weapon fell from nerveless hands and she slumped as if dead.

Drawing a knife, Jak held his breath and backed away, but he also folded. Over the loud hissing, Amanda laughed contemptuously as J.B. tried to fire the Uzi and failed, crumbling as if every bone in his body were dissolved. Even though she had a clear shot, Krysty dropped her pistol and tried to shut the door when blackness swallowed her whole.

lumps while were floating over the destructive
angle. Memory chips triggered to identify the antiradiation and the servomotors were operating at
speed. The optics flickered then came fully into
clarity and the remaining intact cameras fed the
aboveground input by the direct control line. The sensors built up from black to gray as the computer tried
to make sense of it all.

Chapter Ten

Blackness. Total and complete. The dead silence
was broken only by the echo of a drip striking water, then a creak of straining metal and a rumble of
collapsing stonework. A brief flicker of greenish
light shattered the dark, then a second flicker. There
was the soft high-pitched whine of accumulators releasing stored power and servomotors revving to operational speeds.

In agonizing slowness, circuits grew warm, then
solder cracked and wires parted. Fat sparks crawled
like neon spiders over the shattered transistors, broken chips, smashed relays and cracked motherboard
of the General Electric Ranger Mark IV before its
auxiliary CDPs flared into microsecond life again.
The autorepair systems strained against the electronic and physical damage. Reserve power flowed
from the nuke batteries past pulverized circuit
boards and along the very alloy framework of the
annihilated tank until finally reaching relays and in-
candescent bus bars. Most of the sensors were off-
line, some completely dead. The few still working
indicated impossible things, so the diagnostic systems promptly disconnected the malfunctioning el-
ements. But the remaining handful registered that
water rich with decaying leaves and faint traces of

human waste were flowing over the decimated vehicle. Memory chips struggled to identify the environment, and the answer came soon enough: a sewer. The Ranger was in a city sewer. High probability: driven through the street and into the underground pipes by the force from above. The circuits had no solid data on what was the generating factor of the crushing blow, but from the concrete dust, glass splinters, broken bricks and such, it postulated a falling building.

Then alarms sounded. Trace levels of gallium, arsenic and selenium were found in the muddy water. Subprocessors indicated very high probabilities that there were computers in the structure above the Ranger. If the repair droids could only reach those, the machine could get back on-line. Once more, the autorepair systems tried valiantly to function, and failed. They tried again, and failed again.

Searching for an answer to the repair problem, complex arrays of sophisticated Thinking Wires surged with stored bytes, and virtual-reality monitors flashed random data, blueprints and schematics. A hundred thousand miscellaneous files were opened and read as the diagnostic software searched for the correct command prefixes. Stored bits of conversation and recorded visuals had to be listened to endlessly as the search continued at the speed of light. One file was heard a thousand times before the loop could be severed and the work continued.

Sluggishly, the main data processor of the Ranger came awake. A soft ethereal glow began to tint the dark as a series of small submonitors came to life. Each showed the view around the hull from a different direction, including directly behind and straight above. No details, only brown. Secret codes and complex commands started to scroll on the arced array of virtual screens, and the gloom wildly strobed with the combined pyrotechnic effect. Cybernetic relays slid into position, superconductor bus bars hummed alive and a torrent of fresh electricity from miniature nuke batteries flooded deactivated circuits with a massive infusion of power.

Instantly, a subcomputer ran a full diagnostic. Blueprints and electronic diagrams scrolled across every monitor in furious study. The probability of success was 8.9 percent. Good enough. It was smashed to pieces, with most of its computers destroyed, and circuits dead, but the Ranger had gone into many battles with a lower probability and emerged victorious.

A primary circuit sparked and nothing happened. A secondary was tried and a solenoid thumped, but the tiny hatch it was connected to refused to open, the metal buckled into an impossible condition. When the computer realized the truth, it bypassed the escape hatch and sent a hundred crablike drones out through the cracks in the hull. Clambering through the bricks and wreckage, most of the drones stepped on a loose piece of masonry and were subsequently crushed under an avalanche of debris. The remaining handful climbed over their fallen units, continuing ever upward into the tangle of glass and carpeting and out of visual range.

Time passed slowly, then the drones radioed with important news. In the ruins above were smashed computers of superior technology than those on-board the Ranger. Generations better. There were fax machines for wiring, TV remote controls for infrared relays, video games loaded with integrated chips and microwave beamers inside kitchen ovens. The inventory went on for hours: rare metals from office copiers, fiber optics from phone lines, Plexiglas windows, optical lenses from security cameras, titanium steel from the building itself, electric motors in escalators, hydraulic pumps from the elevators, endless coaxial cable from VCRs, cooling units from refrigerators and air conditioners, and low-power civilian lasers from countless CD stereos and office printers.

Snipping bits and pieces from this and that, the handful of drones first repaired the rest of the broken droids. Dozens, then hundreds of the little machines started to ferry ton after ton of processed materials to the smashed tank. Hours passed in frantic activity as the sewer walls were shored up to prevent any further collapse onto the tank. Then primary power was restored, and miniature lasers began to weld the hull solid as hydraulic pumps forced warped sections closed.

Scurrying drones covered the tank, banging on treads and rewiring command boards. The world was at war, with millions of American lives depending upon the operational efficiency of the robotic guardian. Soon, the Ranger would be on-line and combat ready, with its invisibility shield and polycyclic laser fully restored. Then the machine would hunt down the unauthorized intruders who stole valuable military supplies from redoubt 549.

The carrier wave of their badly shielded radio gave off an easily traceable signature.

But the Ranger wouldn't try to capture the thieves again. They had illegally resisted with lethal force and the Mark IV was programmed to learn from mistakes. This time, it would simply kill them on sight.

Chapter Eleven

Drip, drip, drip. The noise was maddening, neither slowing nor increasing in tempo. It was as regular as clockwork.

The laughing woman, Amanda, filled Ryan's vision and he put a bullet through her face. A neat hole punching in her forehead, the blood flowing out to drip-drip-drip to the ground. But the woman neither stopped laughing nor fell. Ryan shot again with his massive revolver. Pieces of her clothing were blown away, her seminude body punctured in a dozen places, but the great volume of welling blood still only dripped in that single maddening beat.

"Fire!" he shouted, and Leviathan's main cannon boomed, blowing her into a dozen pieces. The steaming chunks hit the ground and oozed, in perfect unison, a chorus of blood.

Ryan stared at her with both eyes, shaking his fists in silent rage as he began to feel the world dissolve. The sound of the drip continued unabated, but the images left his vision and he awakened in a large dark room, his hands manacled to the cold stone wall above him.

As his eye became accustomed to the dim light, Ryan saw the rest of his people were chained to the wall to his right. In surging waves of recollection, he remembered the fight on the highway, the bikers, then Amanda gassing his crew, their bodies dropping to the ground as if dead. But it was worse than that; now they were her prisoners. A glance at his clothes said he had been thoroughly searched, everything, not just his weapons, gone except for the clothes themselves. Even the spent shell casings.

The rest of the companions were shackled alongside him. Everybody seemed alive, chests rising and falling, so Ryan turned his attention to the chains. They were inordinately thick, like a tow chain for a boat anchor. The links were clean and oily with not a sign of rust or corrosion. The bolt they looped through was in equally good condition, and not sunk into the mortar between the stone blocks, but directly into the granite.

He noticed a door on the far side of the room, squat and massive, banded with iron. It was a tough barrier, but the lock appeared to be an old-fashioned turnkey. J.B. could probably pick that in a minute. Once they were off the wall.

To the left were four grilled openings, only blackness visible beyond. But the bars were spotless, the handles gleaming not from constant use, but from being highly polished, with faint traces of wax still in the seam where the brass handle joined to the steel door frame. Damn, but the place was clean.

A collection of chains and ropes hung above a grated drain in the center of the windowless room. That boded ill, evoking images of tortured souls bleeding into the sewer. The drain was very large, nearly a foot across, but still too small for even

Dean to crawl through. A trickle of water flowed into the grating, and Ryan backtracked it to a neatly coiled garden hose hanging from a shining brass wall mount, the nozzle steadily dripping water. The source of his torment.

The one-eyed man licked dry lips, then turned his head away. Staring and wishing would only make his thirst worse. Concentrate on the problem at hand. Recon, then escape. Revenge, if possible.

"Bitch," he muttered aloud, the tendons of his arms standing out as he pulled against the chains with all of his strength. They didn't give.

"I have to agree," Krysty murmured, rattling her chains. "So, she got all of us, eh?"

"And all of our stuff. We've been searched by pros."

Krysty gazed at her misbuttoned shirt. "I know."

Doc came awake with a sour expression.

"Bloody hell" he rumbled. "Captives of the lady ward, I surmise."

"Everybody okay?" Krysty asked, her hair coiling tightly. "I have a terrible sense of suffering."

"Yeah, fine."

"Not bleeding," Jak said, his tumbling hair almost completely masking his face.

"I am undamaged," Doc said. "Merely acrimonious."

Dean looked upward. "If that means pissed off, count me in."

"Whatever that gas was, it moved like lighting," Ryan said. "Must be predark military stuff."

"I don't know of any knockout gas that can strike with that kind of speed. Nerve gas, yes, but nothing that merely incapacitates," Mildred said. She smacked her lips and looked longingly at the dripping water, then sighed.

Suddenly, Ryan understood what it was there for, and chalked up another point against the blond bitch.

"No wonder she wanted her bike so badly," Dean said. "I thought it was so she could escape from us."

"If only," J.B. grumped, probing the inside of his mouth. "Damn, they got my lockpick." Then he wiggled his body around. "Not a thing in my pockets. Bet she took the lint."

"No sign of your hat, either," Mildred added.

"Tell me about it."

"Call if guards approach," Doc said, and bracing his long legs against the wall, he tried to force his thin wrists out of the manacles. Sweat broke out on his brow, and tendons stood out on his arms. A line of blood flowed down his wrists and into his sleeve. For a moment, Ryan thought it was going to work, then with an explosion of breath, Doc stopped his exertions.

"Negative," he growled. "They have been adjusted for my size."

"Get close?" Jak asked.

"No."

Dean lifted his boots off the floor and jerked downward with his full weight. The chains shook from the effort, but the boy's hands stayed inside the cuffs. Placing his feet back on the floor, this time, he bent his knees and jumped into the air, to cry out as his fall was arrested by the shackles.

"That was stupe," Krysty commented. "You could have busted a bone."

"I was trying to," Dean told her. "Break a few fingers, and the cuff will slide right off."

"Good try," Ryan said, his gaze moving back and forth across the room. "But save it till we know more. Something is odd here."

"Yes, it's the damnedest thing," Mildred muttered, sniffing the air. "But if this was a torture chamber, it's cleaner than most hospitals."

Massaging his wrists, Doc agreed. "A condition that logically makes no sense. Having this grotesque locale disgusting with rotting corpses and such is a good way to soften up a victim's resolve. It would make it much easier to get the information the person wanted."

Ryan frowned. "Or mebbe she wants her victims comfortable, so they last longer. Lots of folks get their jollies slicing and dicing for no other reason than to hear the red music."

"Yes, an intriguing puzzle."

"Not like puzzles," Jak stated. Hawking loudly, he spit on his manacles and tried to wiggle his own hands free, to no success.

"The ward won't tolerate no dirt," a gruff voice said from the darkness. "No, sir. Litter is a slap. Rust gets ya whipped, and so on."

Ryan went cold inside, frantically searching for the telltale feeling of cold fingers stroking his brain. He had just been wondering why everything was so bastard clean down here. But try as he might, there was no sensation of a mutie reading his thoughts.

"Everybody says the same thing first time down here, eh?" Ryan stated.

"Yep. Don't recognize your voices. What block ya from? Nine? Ten? Or is ya farmers from Detail?"

"Outlanders from beyond the desert," Krysty replied, staring directly at the cell as if she could see into the lightless interior.

There came a guttural laugh. "Ha! Good story. Nothing out there but the Beast, and folks who like to eat folks. Or so I hear."

"Also some vines and bugs that eat damn near anything," Ryan commented. "But on the most part you're correct."

"Eh?" asked the voice. "You really from outside?"

"Yeah."

"What happened? Got caught trying to steal food from the guards?"

"We rescued a woman who called herself Amanda, and got this as a reward." Ryan shook his chains.

"Blond woman, big chest, green eyes?"

"You know her, then."

"Yes. I do." He paused. "This the truth?"

"As sure as death," Ryan stated.

"Who are you anyway?" Krysty asked. "Another traveler?"

"Prisoner 224474," the voice stated. "But my friends call me Shard."

Ryan looked at Krysty, and she nodded. The other was a prisoner, and not a guard or sec man trying to fool them. With her okay, the companions introduced themselves.

"So, is that blond bitch actually in charge here?" J.B. asked, "or just some gaudy slut hired to tease in the customers?"

Chains rattled, and a disheveled face appeared at the bars. The hair was long and tied back with rag strips, the beard was full, but squared off. His clothes were old and patched a thousand times, but painfully clean. "Never say that to her face, or you'll get the twisters, right on the spot."

"Twisters?" Jak repeated.

Shard shuddered.

Probably thumbscrews, Ryan realized, or something similarly medieval. Maybe electric drills. "Sounds bad," he said. "Ville run by real coldhearts, eh?"

"They got names?" J.B. asked.

"Our lord and leader is the Ward Coultier," Shard seemed to be reciting by route. "But his children speak for him—Lady Ward Amanda and Deputy Ward Richard. Heirs to the Citadel. Ain't personally heard the old ward talk for years. Some say he's dead, some say worse."

"And the kids?"

"Bad ones. Hurt for no reason but the liking of it."

"And this is their torture chamber."

"They call it Times Square."

"Just like in prison," Ryan said. Then he looked around. "Shard, have you ever been outside?"

"Sure, I was out last spring for good behavior.

No, it was the spring before that. Mostly I work in the mills and coal mine.''

"Coal mine?" J.B. asked.

Shard stomped the floor. "We're on top of it. Goes down deep. Straight to hell, some say. I don't know about such things, but I can swing a pick with the best of them.''

"I can tell you're a powerful man," Krysty said, offering a sweet smile. It was clear that Ryan wanted some information from the wreck, and flattery was the only way to bribe Shard at present.

"Shard," Ryan said slowly and distinctly, "you want to escape?''

"Don't!" Shard thrust a hand out between the bars of his cell as if trying to reach Ryan and close his mouth by force. "Don't never say that word again! They give you to the fat man and his dogs!''

"But—''

"Never say that word!''

"It's what we're going to do," Ryan continued, with as much conviction as he could muster. "With or without your help.''

Shaking his head, Shard placed both hands over his ears.

"If you want to come along, then talk to us. Describe the outside.''

"Better yet," J.B. said, "we'll tell you. There's a big courtyard in front, and the whole place is surrounded by high stone walls, topped with spikes.''

"To keep the muties out," Dean continued.

"And everybody else in," Mildred added.

"Beyond which is..." Krysty prompted.

"Farms," Shard said, looking about nervously.

He scratched his beard and spoke fast. "And our town. After that, it's rad pits and muties. Forever and ever, all the way to the boiling sea."

"The town is called what, Detail?" Ryan guessed.

Shard stared. "How'd you know?"

"By Gadfrey, this is a prison," Doc said, understanding at last. "Or perhaps a federal penitentiary. Fascinating. I had never before considered the fact that a prison, designed to keep people in, was by necessity well designed to also keep people out. High stone walls lined with guard towers, one single massive armored door, facilities for hundreds, maybe thousands of prisoners, hospital, library, machine shops, kitchens, morgue. Yes, a prison makes a natural fort."

Mildred frowned. "After skydark, the warden proclaimed himself ruler and used the prisoners as slave labor to make the place self-sufficient."

"And the town is called Detail," Dean said slowly, as if working out the problem as he spoke. "Like in a work detail."

"No help there," J.B. groused. "Not out of a whole city bred from folks who keep their heads low and always obey orders."

"Sheep," Jak snorted.

"The carrot," Ryan corrected, "to the stick of the twisters."

Shard shrugged and said nothing.

Unexpectedly, brilliant lights crashed upon them from the ceiling.

"Electric lights!" Doc gasped.

"Wait," Mildred said, tilting her head. The last

in line, she leaned toward the closed door. "I hear footsteps, a lot of them coming our way."

"Stay loose, people," Ryan ordered. "Krysty, sense them out and give me clues to follow. I'll do the talking."

"Oh, now, don't you folks worry none," Shard stated with a broken smile. "They're not coming to lesson you none. Not on your first day."

"So we're okay?" Dean asked, furrowing his brow.

Shard's smile faded. "No, lad. You're not, and be sure about it. But nothing will happen to you today, is all. Nothing to your body, that is. But we're in for a show."

"What kind of a show?" Ryan asked.

"Like nothing this side of hell," Shard stated, retreating into his cell. "And you gotta watch, or else they'll make ya."

"Make us how?" Mildred asked. "Whip us?"

"Don't ask. You don't want to know."

The marching became audible, then stopped. The stout door was loudly unlocked, and a group of people entered the room. One man was naked except for an array of chains. He could barely shuffle under the tremendous load. Surrounding the prisoner were a dozen men in flowing white robes, and one obscenely fat bald man wearing only a loincloth and biker boots. A pack of dogs milled about him, barking and snarling at the prisoner, but never leaving their master's side. The chained man was dragged to the center of the room and hauled into the air above the drain.

"Baldy is a eunuch," Mildred muttered, contorting her features.

"That bad?" Dean asked.

"Torquemada specialized in using them," Doc said, gritting his teeth. "Mostly because they have a special perverse pleasure in torturing normal men."

His hairless head shining under the bright lights, the eunuch waddled over to Ryan and smiled. "Welcome to Novaville. I am Eugene. This is your first lesson in obedience," he said in a girlish voice. "Watch everything that happens, but don't look away. Vomit, if you wish, scream whenever you like, but you will and must watch. It has been ordered so." The fat man drew a small curved blade from inside his clothing. "If necessary, I'll remove your eyelids. But all must watch."

"No problem," Ryan said, forcing a smile. "Mebbe we like to see a good show."

The eunuch seemed taken aback. He stared openly at the one-eye warrior, worked his mouth a few times, then waddled away, casting suspicious glances at Ryan over his pudgy shoulder.

"Students," Eugene said, spreading his fat arms dramatically wide, as an assistant opened a box of surgical instruments. "Pay close attention and watch what I do, and why."

The slavering dogs were chained before the terrified prisoner as portable braziers full of hot coals were fanned to flaming life.

"I'm only a thief," the captive cried. "I already gave back the food! There's nothing more I can tell you!"

Eugene smiled as a white-hot iron was pressed to the prisoner's side, and he piteously screamed.

Forcing himself not to turn away, Ryan knew the captive wouldn't be feeling that pain yet. The pain was so intense with burning like that, a person's nerves simply shut down for a while, unable to handle the overload. But when the flesh cooled, then agony would come. However, Ryan doubted the prisoner would still be alive then. And if he was, the minor pain of a branding wouldn't be noticed.

"Nothing can save you, thief." Eugene smirked, pulling shiny steel pliers into view and snapping them in the air. "Because we don't want you. You don't have anything we need. You're merely an object here, a thing for the students to practice on. A demonstration to show the valuable inmates what will happen to them if they decide not to talk."

Laboring for breath, the prisoner somehow managed to spit at his obese tormentor.

The eunuch laughed shrilly and wiped his face clean with a forearm. "Excellent, you still resist." He leaned in close. "I might just enjoy this. They usually die so fast I haven't the time for a little fun."

Krysty glanced at Ryan and softly rattled her chains. Ryan sadly shook his head. He knew she could summon more than enough strength to break free of even these iron bounds, but afterward she'd pass out from the effort. This wasn't the time or the place for them to risk fighting to escape. The poor bastard was on his own.

"Let us begin," the fat man whispered, kissing a

scalpel. The crowd of students closed around the hanging man and the screaming started in earnest.

THE BLOATED INSECT sat just below her eye, its body pulsating slightly as it sucked the blood out from underneath her skin. Judging the swelling and discoloring were reduced sufficiently, Amanda ever so gently plucked the leech from her cheek and dropped it to the floor. Sated with blood from the bruise, the bulging bug scuttled away for the molding. Standing, she deliberately crushed the insect, her left shoe leaving a red print for a few steps as she crossed the room to embrace her brother.

"You did well, my sister," whispered the deputy ward hoarsely, running a hand softly along the golden waves of her hair. Richard gathered a fistful and inhaled the perfume. "Oh yes, very well indeed. The Beast and the Sons, both gone." The man couldn't take his sight off her. In a white dress and with flowers in her hair, she seemed an angel.

"From heaven," Richard said aloud.

"There are no more obstacles. The Wheel is ours to loot, beloved," she said, her bruised cheeks dimpling. He held out his arms, and they kissed, bodies pressed tightly together, loins aching for what couldn't be.

"Was it terrible?" he asked. "Did they assault you? Beat you, strip you naked and use you as a common gaudy girl?"

"Yes. Oh, yes. The Sons of the Knife did. Four of them at the same time."

The deputy ward moaned. "How I wish I could have seen."

"You will, dear brother, you will," Amanda promised deep in her throat.

"And the prisoners downstairs in the school?"

Unexpectedly, Amanda broke away from him. "No," she snapped, crossing her arms over her chest. "They did not."

"Impossible!"

"Fact. I practically threw myself into the arms of their leader, and then his young son."

"Perhaps they can't," Richard started, hitching the leather belt about his trim waist. He was adorned in delicately embroidered livery, a red velvet cape with a topaz silk shirt and mauve satin pants. But two big autoloading blasters rode their accustomed places at his hips, the checkered grips worn from use. "Some men from the Deathlands are no longer able to enjoy the pleasures of the flesh."

"Then again, father and son, perhaps they…" He left the possibility open.

She shook her head. "I don't think so."

"The more fools they, then," he growled, stepping in close.

Demurely, she placed both hands against his chest, holding the man at bay. "No, sweet brother. We can't, must not. It's immoral. Illegal!"

"Yes," he said, his hands traveling freely over her form, the white cloth tearing in spots. "We must not. Forbidden."

Amanda grabbed a fistful of hair at his temple and pulled him away. He stared at her like an animal, his face flushed red. "Not until Father is dead, and you are leader," she brutally reminded him. "The maker of laws. Not until then!"

Reluctantly, the deputy ward released his sister and took a step away from her. "Yes, agreed. Of course. Now if you will excuse me..." Turning on a heel, he left the room, his shoulders hunched as if carrying an invisible load.

Amanda watched him go, amused at how childish men were. Give them a treat, then a slap, and they danced like puppets. Once the fool was baron, soon she would become his wife, then the sole, widowed, ruler of Novaville.

"Captain of the guard!" she called out, crossing the bedroom to a predark nightstand and mirror. The sheet of glass was nearly intact, only the tiniest chip in a corner marring its silvered perfection. Even her best servants hadn't been able to patch glass, and many had died trying.

"Captain!" Amanda repeated, taking a seat.

An elderly man bustled into view from behind the curtains of a doorway. "Yes, my lady?" he said, groveling dutifully. "How can I serve you this morning?"

She said nothing for a minute, studying herself in the mirror, letting the man sweat out her displeasure. But Amanda had no plans to debase the elderly fool today. There were more important matters to attend to. "Find me a female servant of good health and my age."

"Certainly, my lady." He bowed.

"Make sure she has good teeth," Amanda said, tonguing the inside of her mouth, then grinning to display her broken smile. "And bring pliers."

Chapter Twelve

The door closed with an echoing boom. The spotlessly clean walls were now splattered with gore, and a ragged thing of mostly bones hung from the ropes above the clogged grating. In the corner, the water hose was still neatly coiled, completely unused.

"God almighty, that was a bad one," Shard said from his cell, a tremor breaking his voice. He leaned his forehead against the bars and closed his eyes at last. "They must really want you folks."

"They have our vehicle," Ryan told him, his stomach an aching empty void, the sour taste of bile in his mouth. The stink in the dungeon was beyond describing. "But they don't know how to operate and maintain the equipment."

"Radar is pretty much magic in these fine days of clubs and arrows," Doc said. The elderly man leaned against the cold stone wall. "I thought I was going mad a few times, and actually wished I would slip away to another time."

"Me, too," Jak stated. The albino teen was staring at the floor, concentrating on his breathing. "Killed before. Lots times. But nothing like…that."

"It was pathological," Mildred uttered in barely

controlled fury. "Madness! That eunuch is a sadist of the highest order."

Finished with a prayer for the dead, Krysty asked, "When will they be returning? For us."

"Tomorrow. We sleep with the mess tonight," Shard said, slumping to the hard floor. "Then in the morning we gotta clean it up, and you go see the ward."

In spite of himself, Ryan admired the technique. This would soften the minds of most people. The dead man's screams and pleas for death were still ringing in his ears. But his friends had seen worse. "J.B., let's get out of here."

Slipping off a boot, J.B. wriggled out of his sock and groped about in the vomit on the floor. "Good thing barfing was allowed. I was afraid we'd have to wait till it worked its way out my other end."

"What did you swallow?" Mildred asked, perking up. "A lockpick?"

"Yep. While the bikers were attacking. I figured it couldn't hurt."

"Good thinking."

Stubby toes worked in the slime. "Dark night, it's too slippery. I can't get a grip."

Dean hawked and spit, hitting the tiny sliver of steel amid the semidigested military rations.

"Good shot," Ryan said, watching the door. "J.B., try again."

"What's the hurry?" Shard asked, gripping the bars. "We're here for the night."

"The sooner we leave, the more distance we can get between us and this bastard pesthole."

"Got it," J.B. announced, lifting the pick into

view. Groaning with the strain, he raised his leg inch by inch, higher and higher. ''Can't hold on much longer— Shit!''

The lockpick tumbled from his grasp, spinning for the floor. It bounced once and Krysty kicked it gently with her cowboy boot. The steel probe lofted high and landed flat in Jak's outstretched palm. He wiped it dry on his shirt and tossed it to J.B. The Armorer made the catch easily and started on his manacles. A second later, there was a click and the cuff fell off. Less than a minute later, the other companions were freed.

Removing the cuffs from the end of his chain, Ryan slid the links through the retaining bolt, then wrapped the length around his fist, leaving a good foot dangling loose. Jak and Krysty followed the example. It was a crude bludgeon, but better than nothing.

Dean stumbled to the water hose, refraining from glancing at the hanging corpse, and washed off the vomit with lukewarm water. Doc joined him in the ablutions, then drank deeply in greedy drafts.

Keeping near the walls to avoid the puddles, Krysty and J.B. hurried to the door. Listening intently, he undid the lock when she gave the okay.

''Hey,'' Shard whispered, hope brightening his features. ''What about me?''

J.B. checked with Ryan. He nodded, and the Armorer started over to unlock the cell door. ''The more the better.''

Shuffling into the dungeon, Shard stood upright. Even in his bare feet, he towered over the tall Doc Tanner.

"Know the way to the armory?" Ryan asked, holding the loose end of the chain to keep it from jangling.

"Armory?"

"Where they keep the blasters."

"Oh, the hack room. But you can't get in. There are always guards."

"How many, and how are they armed?" Ryan asked. "Any backup? Vid cams? Booby traps?"

"Tell us everything," Krysty urged.

THE DOOR SWUNG aside on oiled hinges. Stepping into the hallway, the friends saw that torches on the walls illuminated a hallway. A barred window was deeply set into a thick wall to their left, and a long curving corridor stretched to the right.

"It's night," Krysty said, looking out the window. "Stars are out. Close to midnight, I'd say."

"Good," Mildred said, scowling. "Maybe most of them will be asleep."

"Guards work in shifts," J.B. reminded her. "There's always somebody on duty."

"Too bad for him," Jak said, swinging his heavy chain once around in a deadly circle. It smacked into his palm with a dull thud.

"Why are we in a tower," Ryan asked, "and not underground?"

"Why no guards?" J.B. asked suspiciously.

Jak snorted. "Same reason. Smell."

Doc inhaled and gagged. "By the Three Kennedys, this place stinks worse than an abattoir. No wonder nobody wants sentry duty."

"Odors rise. Stink up the whole place."

"No need anyway," Shard said. "Nobody has ever...you know, before."

"Escaped," Ryan said sternly. "The word is *escaped*. Get used to it."

A plush red carpet ran down the center of the hallway and around the curve out of sight.

Walking carefully between the wall and the carpet, Krysty kept fidgeting. "There's a bad feel to this place," she whispered.

"Many have gone to school," Shard said, shuffling along in his bare feet. "Stone may be dead, but it holds the screams of the dying."

"Not feasible," Doc retorted.

"Foolishness," Mildred stated.

"Yes," Krysty said, her hair moving in concert with her consternation. "You're correct. Gaia is here only because of us. This is an unholy place."

Ryan kept his own counsel on the matter, paying close attention to the possibility of spyholes, or other hidden guards.

The rug ended at the top of three flights of stairs, leading down to a large foyer.

"Don't touch the banister," Shard directed.

"Why?" Ryan demanded, a hand hovering above the wood railing.

"Never seen any of the sec men or the heirs do it," he replied. "And they don't let servants. So mebbe it's old and will fall over."

"Or booby-trapped," J.B. said.

Slowly, they proceeded down. The staircase led into the main hall, a cavernous room with vaulted ceilings. Muttering voices, garbled by distance, sounded somewhere. Feeling incredibly vulnerable, the companions stood in the hall, ready to flee or fight. That decision had been made in the aerial dungeon. They would fight to the death before letting the fat man get hold of them.

"Well?" Ryan demanded, looking at Shard.

"We go right toward the branching corridor." He lowered his voice. "No talking. We'll be near the barracks room."

Ryan frowned and took the point position. Krysty was backup, Jak at the rear position.

As they entered the hall proper, the torches were replaced by electric lights in chandeliers. A roaring fireplace threw out waves of heat. A sleeping dog lay prone on a bearskin rug before the crackling flames, its hind legs moving as it chased imaginary quarry. Ryan moved quickly and swung his chain once to build speed, then struck. The dog jerked at the impact, then went totally still. Mildred and Doc rolled the dog in the rug and shoved it against the wall behind a chair.

The friends moved through an arched doorway and faced twin doors. Rising to twice the height of Ryan, and made out of polished ironwood with huge hinges, the portals had bronze knockers bigger than barrel hoops. A very normal-appearing lock was visible at key height.

Ryan raised a hand and closed it into a fist. Everybody halted. He motioned at the doors to Shard, and the man vehemently shook his head and pointed onward.

"That leads to the servants' quarters," Shard said, glancing about nervously. "Hack room is around the corner, past the kitchen."

J.B. checked the lock, but indicated he couldn't see through the keyhole. Doc tapped his wrist, and Krysty agreed.

Ryan felt something was wrong, but couldn't put his finger on the problem, so reluctantly continued onward, deeper into the prison. A long hallway of doors stretched before them and the companions proceeded as quietly as possible. A woman's laughter rose from the other side of a door, followed by a slap, and the sound of sobbing. From another came the steady sound of a whip striking bare flesh. Snoring from another, the sound of enthusiastic sex, more snoring.

At the end of the corridor was a T-shaped intersection, and Shard pointed to the right. Dropping to his belly, Ryan risked a fast look around the corner.

"Two men with blasters near the door," he whispered to the others. "Big boys, but they look bored."

"Haven't seen enough action," J.B. commented. "After a few decades of protecting your own from nothing, a man gets sloppy."

"Gets dead," Jak corrected, cracking his knuckles. "I'll get."

Ryan stopped him. "With what, the chain? They have blasters. You'll never get close enough."

"You got better?" Jak asked pointedly.

"What we need is a diversion," Doc said. "Catch them unawares."

"I'm fast," Dean offered.

Mildred gazed at the youngster. "Are you good enough with your hands to kill two in silence?"

"No."

"Me either, so don't feel bad."

Kneeling, Ryan studied the floor. "J.B., you got blood on your boots."

The Armorer blinked. "So?"

Ryan handed Doc his chain. The old man accepted the weapon and expertly wrapped it around his gnarled fist. Removing his patch, Ryan exposed the puckered hole underneath. Yanking a button off Jak's shirt, he wrapped it in piece of white cloth from Shard. Stooping over, Ryan rubbed a finger along the sole of J.B.'s boot and smeared the blood on his face in a line from his socket to his collar.

"Be careful," Shard said, pulling his head back from the corner. "I recognize them both. The little one is Hamilton. They call him the Hammer of the Citadel. Be careful, he's dangerous."

"What about the big guy with all the muscles. A mutie?"

"Just very large. But Roy is no danger. Has the mind of a child. Stronger than a mule, but he isn't right in the head."

"Would have thought it would be the other way around," Ryan said. Wetting the blood on his face with spit, he managed to get it nice and runny. "Perhaps that is why they always work together."

"I don't know."

"How do I look?" asked Cawdor.

"Awful," Krysty said.

"Perfect," J.B. added.

Rumpling his clothes and tousling his hair, Ryan lurched around the corner.

"H-Hammer...he-help me," he stammered,

keeping his ghastly face in plain view. A runnel of blood drooled out of the empty socket.

Pistols snapped out of holsters, then the guards gasped in horror and lowered the muzzles.

"What happened!" the big man asked.

"Fell...stairs..." Pitifully, Ryan stretched out the hand holding his blood-covered fake eye. Hammer scowled and stepped out of reach while Roy came closer. Ryan tripped past the big guard and lunged forward, ramming the edge of his hand into Hammer's throat. Gargling in pain, the guard tried to level his pistol, but Ryan hit him again and seized the blaster, slamming the weapon backward into the face of Roy. The big man stumbled back, his mouth a bloody ruin. Viciously, Ryan clubbed both until they dropped, then used his boots until all movement stopped.

The dying men were still bleeding as the rest of the companions slid round the corner. Krysty took Roy's pistol and looped his ammo belt over a shoulder. Mildred searched their pockets and found nothing useful. Lockpick out, J.B. went straight to the unmarked door.

"Doesn't say hack room," Dean said, his clenched fists posed in a boxing stance.

"Would you advertise where the blasters were kept if you were baron?" his father asked, replacing his patch.

"Today, the Hammer fell," Shard said, sounding very pleased. "That settles many debts." He smiled.

"Footsteps, coming this way," Mildred said softly, positioned near the intersection.

"Hurry up with that lock," Ryan snapped.

J.B. shoved the handle with a twist and the door swung open. Ryan eased in fast, the stolen revolver leading the way.

"Clear," he whispered brusquely, and the rest piled inside, dragging the dead men with them.

The room was small, a single electric bulb hanging from a chain. But the stone walls were lined with gun racks, most holding rows of pistols, the butts jutting outward. Everybody grabbed some and boxes of ammo. Several of the rifle racks were empty. Only a few held some old Enfields, Brownings and Remington .22 Explorers, the weapons held in place by a stout locking bar. J.B. headed straight for it.

A bookcase was full of different types of knives, some badly rusted, others razor sharp in oiled leather sheaths. Jak started weeding the good from the bad. Countless wooden crates covered the floor, the tops nailed tight. Doc started to open them haphazardly. A couple of big oak barrels stood by themselves in corners, a clear space around them, indicating explosives.

Dean pried off a lid. "Black powder," he said, and moved on to search elsewhere.

Wandering in a circle, Shard couldn't believe his eyes. "I've never seen so many blasters in my life," he gushed uncontrollably. "There's enough here for every prisoner in the whole ville."

"Now there's an idea," Mildred said, stuffing her pockets with loose bullets.

Ryan tossed the man a Browning rifle. "Here's one of your own. Know how to use it?"

With clumsy hands, Shard worked the bolt, peering inside the slide to check the stacked clip of .38 long rounds. "I've seen enough runaways slain," he stated grimly, levering a round into the chamber.

"Good, then you know to shoot for the body, not the head."

"Head wound would kill quicker, no?"

"And it's tougher to hit, even for somebody trained. Shoot for the belly, that's your best bet."

Shard slung a belt of cartridges over his neck. "As you say."

"No autofires, no grenades," Doc reported, shouldering a Browning Automatic Rifle.

"Must have them elsewhere," Ryan said, rejecting an Enfield and taking a BAR. "Too bad."

All conversation stopped as footsteps sounded outside the hack room. Someone asked somebody else about the blood on the floor. The door latch rattled, then stopped and the steps moved away quickly.

"Time to go," Ryan said, tucking a knife into his boot.

"Any fuses?" Doc asked, closing a revolver and tucking it into his belt. His frock coat bulged with ammo boxes, and another revolver.

J.B. nudged a roll of what resembled gray string on the floor. "Sure, lots. Why?"

"Diversion. Just in case."

"Good idea," Ryan said, filling his pockets with live rounds. "J.B., give us…say, twenty minutes."

Cutting off a length of the fuse, J.B. held it to the light bulb until it caught. He counted as it sizzled into ash.

"Three seconds for a foot," he said, impressed. "Smooth burn."

"Too fast," Jak said, searching his clothes for somewhere to hide another blade.

"Better drape it over the gun racks for maximum length," Krysty suggested.

Agreeing, J.B. started to wrap the fuse around his arm to measure the length, but soon ran out. "We have ten minutes," he said, tucking the end into a barrel of black powder. "Then it's boom."

Ryan slung a Winchester rifle over a shoulder. "Ready?" he asked, a big-bore Browning resting in a combat grip. "J.B., light her up."

The Armorer pressed the end of the fuse against the light bulb and it caught immediately. Dropping the gray twine on the floor, he made sure it didn't loop over itself and cut their time short. Ten minutes was barely enough to get away as it was.

Jak eased open the door, and Doc checked outside. When he announced it was clear, they regrouped in the hallway. J.B. locked the door.

Krysty then shoved in a knife blade and snapped it off at the hilt. "That'll stop anybody from interfering with our surprise package."

"Now what?" Dean asked, his two S&W .38 revolvers crossed at the wrists to steady his aim. The boy knew he was short on sleep and so was taking no chances on getting arm weary when he needed accuracy. "We looking for Leviathan?"

"There's no way of knowing where she is," Ryan said. "We're just going to head out of here."

Awkwardly, Mildred tried different grips on the parkerized Colt .38, the best of the bunch. To her sensitive hands, the gun was too barrel heavy, the action stiff, and the cracked tigerwood grip was very uncomfortable. The Colt was a single-action, not a double, but she had loaded in six rounds anyway. She didn't think there was much danger of a misfire. It wouldn't be long before the gun saw action.

"Which way?" she asked.

Shard gestured and took a step when a loud bang heralded the sharp cracking of a slug hitting the stone wall near them.

"Sec men!" Krysty cried, the longblaster in her grip booming in response. Down the corridor, a man toppled backward, a crimson stain on his chest.

More reports sounded, and the dull rattle of a .22 Thompson submachine gun, the small-caliber rounds impacting everywhere in a maelstrom of lead.

Ryan fired his rifle a fast five times. "The lock," he yelled, blasting steadily.

Thumbing in rounds, J.B. shook his head. "No way."

"When you have superior numbers and arms, attack," Doc said in that singsong way of his that meant he was quoting somebody. Yet his hands never stopped in their task of reloading. "When outnumbered, retreat, and attack later."

"When trapped, do the unexpected," Ryan added. Standing, he triggered the rifle and took off down the corridor at a full run. "Charge!"

Chapter Thirteen

Wild shots rang out, and the two groups were upon each other.

Blasting one man in the belly, the discharge of his pistol setting his clothes on fire, Ryan kicked another in the groin and received a brutal jab in the ribs. He reeled, feeling something snap inside.

"Incoming!" Krysty shouted in warning. She fired her blaster twice, then found J.B. in her sights and lashed out with the weapon to smash in the nose of an attacker. They were too close for blasters now, and everybody pulled out knives.

As two of the sec men closed in, Jak lashed out with knives and blood sprayed from the impact. Limply, the two dropped to the floor. Mildred shot a man in the knee and sternum. Dean sidestepped a saber jab then put his pistol into the man's ear and fired, the slug's exit taking a chunk of bone and gray matter with it. Doc elbowed a man in the throat, then ducked under a knife thrust. Bobbing and weaving, Jak knifed another.

Summoning his resolve, the Armorer grimly waded into the massed figures, punching and jabbing, kidneys, groins. This was no boxing contest with referee and bell, but a fight to the death using every weapon Mother Nature armed people with.

Two more sec men darted around Ryan and charged at Doc. Undaunted, the old man yanked a saber blade from a still warm body and swung it in a glittering arc to parry a vicious knife cut. Swiveling his own blade inward to protect his vulnerable wrist, Doc thrust his arm forward, the razor-sharp edge slicing one man across the cheek and opening the throat of another. Then two men tackled his arm and wrestled away the blade. Doc drew his blasters, killed one and wounded another.

Yelling as dramatically as possible, Mildred dashed across the cellar, hoping at least one of the sec men would follow her. Three did. But upon turning the corner and reaching a clear area, instead of collapsing in a faint or cringing in fear, Mildred drew her pistols and gunned them all down ruthlessly. Hastily, she reloaded.

Clumsily, Shard clubbed the sec men with his rifle, doing little damage. Then he froze as Doc raised a sword and lunged straight for his throat! The shiny blade went past Shard's head, missing by the thickness of a shave, and for one terrible instant, Shard saw a distorted version of himself reflected in the polished metal. Then the blade withdrew streaked with red, somebody gagged behind him and a sec man went crashing to the littered floor.

"Thanks," Shard panted, his heart pounding in his chest.

"Fight or get out of the way," Doc snapped.

Grimly renewed, the former prisoner waded into the fray, punching, biting, stabbing and clubbing like a wild beast.

With the sound of splintering wood, J.B. shattered

a rifle stock over a sec man's skull. The Armorer retreated to the wall as a knife wielder moved in for the kill. At the last instant, he danced out of the way, the blade shattering as it struck the stone wall. J.B. threw his arm forward, two stiff fingers going directly into the ocular cavity, crushing the man's eyeball like a ripe grape. He screamed.

The whole building shook as the hack room violently exploded, the door blowing off its hinges. Dust rained from the rafters and glass shattered in a hundred windows. Startled, the remaining sec men stumbled in the concussion, confused and dazed. Prepared for the expected blast, the companions finished them off with ruthless efficiency.

Doc dropped the saber and reclaimed his dropped pistols.

J.B. found the tommy gun and checked its cheese-wheel clip. "Thought you liked swords."

"My sword," Doc answered, dumping out spent shells and rummaging in his pockets for live rounds. "Not some rusty, bent saber."

"What's the difference?" J.B. asked, working the sidebolt on the Thompson.

"Blade man knows," Jak answered, pulling a knife from a cooling form. He and Doc exchanged glances and nodded.

"Where's the exit?" Ryan demanded, holding his aching side as he reloaded, the rifle held steady between his thighs.

Mildred saw the action and made a mental note to keep a watch on the man. If those ribs were broken, he could easily puncture a lung with too much exertion.

"What? Oh, yes. This way," Shard said, starting off.

J.B. stopped him with his gun barrel. "Is that the nearest exit?"

"Yes," he replied calmly.

Krysty nudged him with her rifle. "Then show us some other way out. They'll be expecting us to try that."

The former prisoner nodded. "Of course. Follow me."

It started softly at first, a distant yowl that steadily grew in power and volume until it was a banshee keen, a mechanical scream of strident power that built to a thundering howl and stayed there.

"The escape alarm," Shard said, trembling. "Every sec men will be rushing to protect the ward."

"And his kids," Ryan said, shoving him forward. "Good. Our plan is to leave, not start a revolution."

With J.B. on point, they took the other branch of the T-shaped intersection. A long corridor branched again, and then again in a confusing maze, which led them to a stairwell and a laundry. Clothes were boiling in big caldrons and drying on lines, but not a soul was in sight. He guessed that when the alarm sounded servants and slaves not in chains scampered for safety.

"What's out that door?" J.B. demanded, jerking a thumb at the laundry.

Shard blanched. "That goes to the dog kennels. We don't go there." He indicated the stairs. "We go down through the mill and out the chute used to dump the ville's waste into the river."

"Any guards?"

"A few."

"Armed?"

"No."

"You've considered escape before," Ryan stated.

Shard seemed embarrassed, as if caught in a lie. "Yes, it's true. At night sometimes, I dreamed of being free," he admitted sheepishly. "I'm a very bad slave, and wish to leave my masters."

Ryan slapped him on the back. "Good. That's halfway to being free. Not surrendering inside yourself."

Shard looked at Ryan with a strange expression, and clutched his rifle more tightly.

Mildred paused their progress. "It would make sense to have the garbage chute near the kennels. So why are we going this way?"

"Safer," Shard said. "Dogs would tear us apart."

"And slower," Ryan countered. "Aren't they released during an escape?"

"I...well, ah...yes."

Ryan motioned with his jaw, and J.B. took the point. "Then it's the one place we won't find any."

This was obviously new thinking to Shard, and he was hesitant to relinquish the standing order of "don't go near the dogs."

"We're getting out by going to the center," J.B. said. He hefted the tommy gun. "They won't be expecting this."

The kennels were deserted, the picket-fence enclosures for the dogs containing only the miasma of hundreds of animals. Suddenly, a hound dog with a bandaged paw limped into view from a doghouse. Ryan leveled his longblaster, but Jak stopped him.

"Not hurt us," the albino said knowingly. "Just old bitch."

Ryan relented and the beast watched them passing in silence, then went back to its bed and circled itself a few times before flopping down.

An office converted from a walk-in closet had been recently vacated, the remains of a meal on the desk top still steaming. Everybody grabbed a bite. On the wall near a centerfold, Dean found an empty gunrack, its locking bar swinging back and forth, keys in the padlock.

"These look familiar," J.B. muttered, examining the keys. "Yes, exactly like the ones I found on the coldhearts."

"So?" Krysty asked impatiently, halfway out the door.

The man smiled at her. "So it means one of the coldhearts once worked here in the kennels, and kept the keys." Taking them off the nail, he slid the most worn one off the ring and swallowed it. "You never know," he said. "Could be useful."

"Planning on getting caught again?" Mildred asked.

"We must hope for the best," Doc said, a blaster in each hand, "but prepare for the worst."

Rifle shots sounded somewhere not very distant, and a pack of dogs howled in hot pursuit, the noise trailing off quickly.

"Door," Ryan said, pointing at J.B., Doc and Krysty.

The rest of the companions stayed in the office,

their weapons ready to give protective cover fire for the three as they sprinted down the corridor to the door.

"Locked," Krysty said.

J.B. tried the keys on the ring, but none of them fit, so he used the lockpick. Turning toward the office, he tapped his chest twice with a closed fist, then gave a thumbs-up. The people at the door used their weapons to track the approach of the five.

"Dean, Jak, check the window," Ryan ordered, a hand on the latch.

The albino cupped his hands, and Dean stepped into them. He climbed the rough wall as Jak shoved him upward as high as possible. His head made it over the sill, and the boy ducked down to only peek between the iron bars. Dean then offered a clenched fist, flattened it and pointed at the ground. Jak brought him down.

"Big room ahead of us is clear," he reported. "Doors to the left, right and straight ahead."

"Dogs?" Jak asked.

"No sign of them."

"Good enough." Wincing with pain, Ryan eased open the door, and they moved through in single file.

"This place is huge," Dean stated. "What is it used for? Parades, or storage, or something?"

"Not used for anything," Shard said, stroking his rifle as if it were a rabbit's foot.

Mildred pointed to the walls. "Look there. Those faded numbers painted on the walls. That's the Dewey decimal system!"

"This was a library," Doc said. "Where are all the books now?"

Shard stared blankly. "Books?"

White-faced and sweaty, Ryan stumbled a bit, holding his side tightly. Mildred moved closer and gave him a shoulder for support. He said nothing, but accepted the assistance.

"Mildred, why would the kitchen be near the kennels?" Dean asked. "To feed the dogs?"

"Yes. But they also probably eat the dogs when they die."

"Of course." Shard smiled. "Roast dog is fine."

"Which way to the kitchen?" Krysty interrupted, scanning the distant walls for possible enemies.

"To the right. But the back gate is to the left."

"What's ahead?"

"That leads to the ward's private quarters."

"Don't want to go there," J.B. said, making a face.

Turning their backs on the door to the outside, they traveled deeper into the rapidly awakening prison. Reaching an intersection, they retreated while a group of armed guards passed by marching in formation. Turning the corner, Ryan encountered a sec man at a table assembling his blaster while drinking coffee. He left the body slumped over the table, head cradled in crossed arms as if the dead man were merely asleep.

"Won't fool a sergeant of the guards," J.B. commented.

"If they have one," Krysty noted.

"Doubt it," Ryan said, shaking his head to focus

his vision. "These folks rely too much on intimidation."

"Indeed," Doc agreed. "The guards are so positive that we are terrified of them, they assume that we would escape as quickly as possible via the shortest route."

"Sloppy," Jak agreed.

"I would have caught us long ago," Dean added.

Cutting through a storage room, then creeping down a flight of stairs past what smelled like a brewery, the companions froze as they spotted some slaves in gray rags listlessly mopping the floor.

Ryan asked Shard a silent question.

"They won't report us," he said. "That would involve meeting with the ward, a pleasure few survive."

"No reward for helping to capture intruders?"

"No."

"Stupe."

Staying on the far side of the hallway, the companions moved past the workers quickly. The men and women bowed their heads, refusing to even look at the armed people walking in their midst.

A locked door barred their progress for only a few moments, then they were inside a plush room of tapestries and carpeting. Sumptuous chairs, expertly patched in places, stood before a cold fireplace. A curtained alcove lay beneath a raised balcony and suits of old armor lined the walls in brickwork niches. It was a perfect place for an ambush, and Cawdor's instincts flared.

"Just down there," Shard said, starting to walk faster. "Only a bit more."

"Jak, shake the bushes," Ryan ordered, leaning against the wall.

The rest assumed combat positions as the teenager grabbed a chair and threw it. The crude wooden projectile hit the embroidered curtain, ripping it from the traverse rod and exposing three men in suits of armor, swords in their gauntlets.

"There they are!" cried one, starting forward.

At the cry, more men with crossbows popped up over the balcony on the second floor. Aiming at the armored sec man, J.B. cut loose with the Thompson, but the .22-caliber rounds bounced off the thick medieval armor. Mildred and Doc fired their .38 revolvers, the bullets denting chest plates and making the sec men stumble back a step.

A flurry of arrows hit the furniture around them as an older man with chevrons on his tunic called out for them to surrender. In response, J.B. hosed the balcony with a stream of .22 rounds, killing most of the archers. Then Ryan and Krysty cut loose with their Browning rifles. Neat holes appeared in the chest plates, and crimson sprayed onto the ripped curtain. The armored sec men fell to the floor, pumping blood.

"Plate metal armor?" Jak scoffed, kicking one to make sure he was dead. He was. "Stupe. Have blasters."

"Guards might not know that," Mildred said, dumping her two spent shells and sliding in fresh rounds.

"They do now," J.B. observed, struggling with the bolt to clear a jam. The bent shell popped free. "Doc, sweep the balcony, I'll cover."

Doc went up the stairs at a bound with blasters up and ready.

"Armor," Jak repeated in disgust.

"Against unarmed slaves, these would be fearsome and deadly opponents," Mildred said, watching Ryan. "The ville might be low on ammo for their blasters, and the baron might be trying to conserve rounds."

"But they got lots of black powder," Dean reminded them.

"Can't use it in modern blasters," J.B. said. "Fouls the mechanisms. And it won't work in an autofire."

"I didn't know that."

"Now you do."

"Clear," Doc announced, coming down. "You got them all."

"Good."

Krysty lifted a faceplate. The person inside was only a little older than Dean. "A child," she whispered.

"Tough," Ryan growled, "but take the job, and you get the pay."

"These are only trainees," Shard said, the unfired rifle still in his hands. "New sec men. Placed here as a precaution."

"Or else the guards know about the garbage chute." Ryan pressed a hand to his damp forehead. It was so hot in here, it was becoming difficult for him to think clearly, but he was getting an awful suspicion. "Shard, have you ever been to the laundry?"

"No. I work in the mines."

"Know anybody who has worked in the laundry?" Ryan beat the man with words. "Anybody at all? Ever?"

"No," he replied, backing away, "b-but we've all heard about the chute."

"From who?" Ryan demanded.

"Well, I—"

"It's a trap for runaway slaves!" Krysty declared, dropping into a combat crouch. "Dean, unlock the door! Whatever is past that curtain, we want no part of it."

Dean dashed for the door and flipped the latch. Instantly, a pack of dogs charged for the opening, their claws scrambling on the smooth stone floor. With a cry, Dean slammed shut the door, almost catching one of the beasts by the tail, and shoved home the bolt, but several had gotten through. The animals didn't bark or snarl, but silently ran straight for the companions. Everybody opened fire as J.B. triggered the Thompson, riding the chattering submachine gun in a figure-eight pattern, mowing the beasts down.

The last dog in, a brutish pit bull, turned from the carnage and sprang at Dean. He frantically dodged, and the beast only sank sharp teeth into his flapping vest. As the boy scrambled for distance, the animal leaped for his throat. Dean raised both of his pistols and fired. The dog slammed into him, and they both went down in a tangle of limbs. Rolling from underneath, Dean found himself streaked with blood. The pit bull lay where it had fallen.

"I got it," he said with a note of astonishment.

"Damn near," Jak said, pulling a leaf-shaped

knife from the dog's chest. The teenager wiped off the blade, and tucked it into his belt.

"Owe you one," Dean said solemnly.

Jak shrugged.

Suddenly, a pounding sounded on the door. "We know you're in there!" a muffled voice shouted. "Surrender or die!"

Kneeling, Krysty put a single round through the door at groin level. A man shrieked, and a few seconds later some fool put his eye to the hole. She fired again with the expected results.

Kicking aside the dead dog, Dean slid a chair under the latch, as Jak snapped off a knife inside the lock.

"That won't hold for long," Mildred said. "We better move."

"Double time," Ryan added, lurching forward, using his rifle as a cane. "Into the alcove!"

"We're going in?" Shard asked.

J.B. tightly wound the spring feed on the cheese-wheel clip of his tommy gun. "Unless you want to try and shinny up the chimney flue."

"But we know it's a trap!"

"And we might be the first to enter it knowing that," Ryan said, gritting his teeth, "which gives us an edge."

The alcove proved to be a short tunnel with a high curved ceiling and no windows. An ordinary door stood at the end of the passageway, a key in the lock.

"Forget that," J.B. growled, putting a single .22 round into the stout door.

At the impact the door opened a crack, and axes

swung out of slots in the walls, bright sparks flying as the blades glanced off each other, so tight was their passing. The axes churned the air for a while, then retracted into the walls.

Experimentally, J.B. fired at the floor with no results. He fired again at the door, and watched the blades carefully.

"Very nice," Ryan commented, resting against Mildred. "Never seen anything like it before."

"Sounded like it's powered by clockwork gears and springs," Mildred said. "Maybe taken off a church tower clock. Did you hear the clacking?"

"Of course."

"With some explosives we'd be through in a second," J.B. said, shouldering the Thompson. "As it is, we have to run for it."

"At least it isn't locked."

"We could don the suits of armor," Dean stated. "No, forget that. There's not enough to go around."

"Are you insane?" Shard demanded. "This is suicide!"

"There is a brief lag," Doc said, ignoring the interruption, "between contact and the blades."

"How long?"

"A second, maybe one and a half."

"So we have to get through instantly," Krysty said. "Any hesitation and we're dead."

The sound of chopping started coming from the room behind them.

"Together then," Ryan said, taking a deep breath. "We might need muscle, just in case there something blocking the exit."

"Such as a body?"

"Or more guards."

The companions bunched together tightly and held their weapons very close to avoid tripping. Licking dry lips, Shard kept glancing between the door in front of them and the one behind.

"Go," Ryan urged.

Charging over the short span, the companions hit the door in a crushing pile, digging in their heels and shoving for all they were worth. The wooden portal bent under the impact, holding for one long terrible instant, and then burst open just before the swinging blades arrived.

Tumbling to the floor, the friends rolled to their feet ready for battle, but they were in a deserted courtyard. The enclosure was bounded by a two-story-high wall of stone blocks topped with a spiral coil of razor wire, old and rusty, which only made the stuff more dangerous. To the right was a four-story building with grilled windows, behind which rose a castlelike tower. Eugene's dungeon. The siren was louder outside the prison, and the sky was a light gray, with yellowish clouds high in the sky.

"Rain in a few hours," Dean noted calmly. "That'll give us cover."

"Excellent," Doc said. "The acid will hide our tracks from the dogs."

"Hell of a choice," J.B. said. "Rain or dogs."

Returning to the door, Jak shoved a knife blade under the jamb to hold it firmly in place. "Has to slow for a heartbeat," the teenager explained in cold rationale.

"This is too easy," Krysty stated, her hair coiling and uncoiling. "Where are the sec men?"

"Inside searching for us?" Dean suggested.

She studied the high walls, a thin wind moaning through the bare stone turrets. "Mebbe."

"Keep moving," Ryan whispered. He shook and almost fell in spite of his makeshift crutch. "Got to find shelter from rain."

"Shard?" Doc demanded in a no-nonsense manner.

The man made a vague gesture. "Past the tower is the side gate. Guarded, not guarded, I don't know anymore."

Ryan took a tentative step and started to slump. Mildred caught the man and carefully placed her shoulder under his good arm and braced him upright. Shoving her pistol into a pocket, the stocky doctor slung his rifle over her shoulder and started to walk. Krysty and Dean moved beside them and stayed close by.

Hugging the wall for protection, the companions moved along as quickly as possible with J.B. in the point position, his stolen Thompson carefully switched from single shot to full-auto. The cold wind was getting stronger by the minute, dry leaves swirling about the isolated courtyard. There were water troughs and hitching posts for horses. Also an old gallows, the noose twisting in the wind.

Edging past the tower, J.B. called a halt, then urged them on faster. Coming into view was a huge door of riveted steel set into the stone wall.

"How are we getting through that?" Mildred demanded.

"Dunno," Jak said, frowning deeply.

"The…gallows," Ryan whispered faintly. "Use the rope…" His voice faded away completely, and the man went limp.

"To do what?" Mildred asked, shaking the wounded man, trying to rouse him. "Come on, Ryan. Use the rope to do what?"

"Hot pipe!" Dean pointed with his revolver. "Look there!"

Over by a tiered array of wooden crosses was a large familiar-looking canvas lump, big military-style tires clearly discernible under the stiff covering.

"Dark night, it's Leviathan!" J.B. cried. "We can blow our way out the door!"

Rushing over, the companions dashed underneath the canvas, and there was the massive tank, covered with hundreds of metallic cylinders.

"Run!" Krysty yelled, backing away. Instantly, there was a hissing sound from Leviathan and from the ground underneath them. The redhead weaved drunkenly and then dropped.

"No!" Mildred screamed in frustration. She suddenly realized that the entire courtyard had to be one huge trap! Holding her breath, the physician tried to race away on melting legs and fell onto the cobblestones, taking the unconscious Ryan with her.

Spitting curses, Doc collapsed, followed by Dean, Jak and Shard. In raw desperation, J.B. wildly fired the Thompson at the ropes holding the canvas awning in place, hoping to cut it loose and let in the wind to disperse the gas. But the shots ricocheted harmlessly off the granite and only a single rope was parted. The world began to spin around him, and the stubborn Armorer tried once more to trigger the weapon as he gently floated off into a bottomless hole of warm inky blackness.

Chapter Fourteen

The long windowless corridor was lined with wall torches and electric lights. A plush blue carpet covered the stone floor, and every five yards a grating closed off the passageway with sec men standing rigidly at attention behind iron kiosks. The lieutenant hurried along the corridor, the sec men rushing to open the grates for him, and then hurrying to close them behind. No password was asked for, or given. The dire expression on his face was more than enough security clearance.

The corridor opened to a small room with a squad of sec men in attendance. All gambling stopped as they silently watched his approach with growing trepidation. Two heavily armed guards flanked a high-vaulted portal suitable as a bank-vault door. The large sec men stood at parade rest, the butt of the M-16s resting next to the soles of their boots, the barrel held in a tight grip a full arm's distance from their spotless uniforms.

"Lieutenant Anders," the officer said crisply, "to see the deputy and lady ward."

"Password," the corporal guard muttered, his black face without expression. It was as if he had been carved from obsidian.

"Raincloud."

"Pass," said the white private. "And good luck."

The lieutenant paused, his hand an inch away from the door. "They're in a bad mood?"

"Been talking to their father," the corporal said, still staring straight ahead.

Sighing, Anders polished his boots on the back of his trousers, then exhaled into the palm of his hand to check his breath. Straightening his collar, and adjusting his dress uniform of Army fatigues with gold epaulets, he knocked firmly on the door and stepped through without waiting for a response.

WHATEVER FUNCTION the audience room had originally been used for was impossible to tell, after so many generations of decoration and alteration. There were countless tapestries and embroidered curtains, some hiding secret doorways, some covering blank wall space to confuse invaders. A fireplace large enough to roast a person stood on either side of the cavernous room, yet walking along the slim blue ribbon of carpeting Anders could feel no heat from the crackling flames. Overhead, the cathedral-style ceiling was dotted with crystal chandeliers, bathing the place in the unnatural illumination of electricity. A chained pack of pit bulls was growling in a corner, chewing on some femur bones and tiny skulls. In the opposite corner sat a strictly utilitarian nest of sandbags fronting a squat and ugly large caliber machine gun called a Maxwell. A three-man team stood behind the machine ready to unleash its awesome destructive powers.

Ten steps, pause, ten steps, pause. Anders exactly

followed the formula for approaching the presence
of the ward and his heirs. Their massive chairs
rested on a raised marble dais. In one chair sprawled
the lady ward, half dressed as usual, although
heaven and hell save the commoner who noticed her
lack of clothing. Young servants were brushing her
hair and massaging her feet as Amanda sipped wine
from a golden chalice and stared angrily at the lieutenant. Not a good sign.

Beside her was the deputy ward, in full formal
regalia, tassels on his boots, plumed hat, waistcoat,
vest, ruffles and cape. He appeared to be a dandy,
a fop, as they used to say, but in truth he was a
brutal commander, and the deadliest blade known.

Deputy Ward Richard Coultier was sitting forward on the edge of his chair, using an oily cloth
to polish a predark saber of astonishing sharpness.
An even worse sign. The anger of the son of the
ward struck like lightning, coming from nowhere
without warning, and the saber was his preferred
death tool. Once it left the scabbard, it was never
returned without first tasting blood.

Anders was somewhat relieved to note the curtain
hanging behind them was closed, cutting off any
possible view of the ward. At least he wouldn't have
to cope with that today.

Removing his helmet, Anders bowed to the heirs
of the ville, low for the son, lower for the Lady, and
he damn near kowtowed to the closed curtain.

"My lord and lady, I come to report bad news,"
he said in a single breath, the words almost gushing
out.

Richard glared, and Amanda dashed aside the chalice, red wine spraying over the floor.

"We know! What happened to them, Lieutenant?" Amanda shrieked. "Where are they! Where? Where?" Her hands formed claws upon the wooden arms of her chair, her expression radiating an insane madness beyond words.

"Milady, we went into the courtyard as soon as the sleep gas was gone," Anders said, his heart pounding in his chest. His right hand was tucked into his wide leather belt, and surreptitiously fingering a derringer, ready to blow out his brains before becoming a toy for Eugene.

"And?" Richard growled, drumming his manicured nails on the curved arm of the chair.

"And they were gone," Anders finished lamely. "There was no sign of them."

"Unacceptable," Amanda spit. "Who led the guards to collect them?"

"Corporal Phinious."

"Kill him," Richard commanded, daintily straightening his cape.

"No," Amanda corrected. "Strip him of all rank and send him to the mines."

"B-but, my lord!" Anders stammered. "The slaves will kill him with their bare hands!"

A new chalice was given to her. The blonde raised the golden cup and took a sip. "And your point is?" she asked sweetly.

"What I want to know is," interrupted Richard, "did they escape, or were they rescued?"

"Both actions are unthinkable!"

"Yet one must be true. Either the gas had no effect…"

"Impossible." She paused. "Or perhaps we have a mutie in the ville. Somebody immune to the vapors who removed their sleeping bodies."

"Before the guards arrived? Also impossible," Richard snorted, gripping the sword at his hip. Golden tassels dangled off the pommel and silver threads entwined the scabbard in ornate finery.

"They aren't inside the tank," Anders reported. "We can see through the front window, and there's nowhere for even a single person to hide."

"That you know of."

He admitted this was true.

"So Ryan and his people are free," Amanda said, handing away her chalice, uncaring of who took it. "Search for them, Lieutenant. Inside the ville and in Detail. Send scouts into the Wheel and an ambassador to the Sons of the Knife. Offer the cold-hearts anything they wish, but those people will be found."

Reclining backward, Richard said, "Place a reward of freedom and food to the slaves. Interrogate the gaudy sluts and servants, torture thieves, slaughter whole families! But find them, or else find us a way into their locked vehicle!"

"We try our best," Anders said, avoiding eye contact. "But the doors resist our best thieves, and the metal is proof to saws and acids. May I use explosives?"

"Not yet. What about the windshield?"

"We could probably smash through," the sec man said, "but then we would still have to get past the grating. It's made of a predark metal beyond our knowledge. Some sort of super steel."

"An alloy," Amanda said softly to herself, "or an althropic composite."

"My lady?" Anders asked, puzzled.

She waved the matter away.

"Continue in your efforts to gain entrance, Lieutenant," Richard ordered.

"And bring us success soon, or else you'll beg to be turned over to Eugene," Amanda finished in a soft purr. "Do you understand?"

"At once, Your Highness," he said, blanching. "Certainly. With all due speed."

Richard grandly gestured with the saber. "Then go."

"And report to us at sundown," Amanda said, smiling at the trembling man, "with good news."

Spinning on a heel, the sec man marched away on trembling legs, his camou fatigues splotchy with sweat stains.

When the lieutenant was far enough away, Richard turned to his sibling. "Do you think he told us the truth?" he asked, testing the edge of his weapon on a thumb. The steel drew a thin line of blood and, satisfied, he sheathed the blade with a flourish.

"I could smell the stink of fear on him," she answered. "Yes, he told the truth. And was yet brave enough to face us with failure."

"Does that mean he does not fear us enough?" Richard asked, a tinge of eagerness deepening his voice. "Perhaps we should reorient his attention."

"Later, my sweet," she promised, resting a dainty hand on his thick arm. "First, we must find the people who control the tank. With it at our command, nobody could stand before our troops.''

"We could rule the world,'' he burbled, "from coast to coast!''

She smiled at the ignorance. "From sea to shining sea.''

"Yes. Yes!'' He raised a clenched fist, then lowered it and glanced nervously about the room. "Do you really think Ryan is still here, even if free?''

"Naturally,'' the woman said in total conviction. "He admitted that he was a former ruler. He'll want the Citadel.''

The deputy ward turned red. "Never! Death is too good for them!'' He stood, flourishing his sword. "By Father's blood they shall all die for his impudence!''

"Rabbit stew,'' Amanda said, toying with her pearl necklace.

"What do you mean?'' he demanded hotly.

"The recipe for rabbit stew, dear brother,'' she said, crossing her knees, her gown rising to expose a great deal of creamy thigh. "First, catch the rabbit.''

"Perhaps we should flood all of Novaville with sleep gas and then have the sec men sort the bodies,'' he suggested. "Many would die, but how could he escape that!''

"How did he escape this time? Besides, if our guards are unconscious, then who shall do the work? Am I to do a slave's task?''

He kissed her hand. "No, of course not. But they must not escape!''

"That vehicle is the key to everything we want.''

"I only wish I knew how they locked its doors when they were asleep."

"Some clockwork mechanism, or a comp."

Richard snorted. "Bah, comps. Machines that think? Fairy tales for fools and peasants."

"If you say so, dear brother," Amanda demurred as a servant refilled her chalice from a silver tureen. She took a sip and frowned.

"Too sweet," Amanda said, pouring the brew onto the girls kneeling at her feet. They were drenched to the skin, but ignored the action and made no move to clean themselves. Gushing apologies, the servant hurried off to the kitchen for another bottle.

Turning slightly, Richard glanced at the closed curtains. "Perhaps we should awaken Father and ask his counsel."

"He'll be cross," Amanda spoke quickly. "He hates to be disturbed."

"Do we have another choice?"

She sat back. "No, we don't."

"Captain of the guards," Richard said loudly.

The little man scurried into view from a curtained alcove. The dogs responded to his passage, but didn't try to attack him. "Yes, my liege?" he asked, bowing. "How may I serve?"

"Clear the room. My sister and I are going to awaken Father."

The man clapped twice, and everybody departed quickly, even the sec men at the machine-gun nest. Alone in the great room, the heirs ascended the few steps of the dais to the next level and pulled the cord to part the heavy curtains.

IN RAGGED STAGES, he started to become awake, distorted images swirling around him like a fevered nightmare; the Ranger...the ivy...Leviathan...trap! As the last wisps of sleep departed, cold adrenaline surged and Ryan came fully awake, scrambling for his rifle. It was nowhere to be found.

Sitting upright, he found himself on a pile of rags forming a crude bed on a bare rock floor. The rest of his group was also nearby on rag beds. None of them appeared to be hurt, or constricted in any way. Glancing about, he realized they were in a cave of some kind, the light coming from oil lanterns set into holes in the irregular walls. It was quiet and cool, very restful. That was when he noticed his side didn't hurt much, and exploring fingers found he was expertly bandaged. It was a little difficult to catch his breath, but the pain was almost entirely gone. Also, he seemed to have been washed and dressed in clean clothes. His own clothes, the rips sewn and holes patched. Rubbing his chin in contemplation, Ryan was shocked to find himself shaved. Even his Army boots were polished. What the hell was going on here?

Some wooden tables formed a square under a hanging lantern, and stumbling over Ryan discovered their weapons lying there. Not the ones they had taken from the hack room, but their personal weapons: his Steyr SSG-70 and SIG-Sauer, Krysty's Ruger, Jak's big bore .357 Magnum, and Doc's oddball LeMat and swordstick. It was all of the supplies and equipment they had when that blond bitch gassed his people after they saved her from the bikers.

He lifted his pistol and checked the ammo clip. Incredible. The blasters and knives appeared to have been cleaned and oiled, and there were boxes and boxes of ammo, a lot more than they had taken from the hack room. There were even some HE grens and an old box of dynamite, the coil of fuse lying nearby, but not too close.

"What's going on here?" he asked aloud, shoving his blaster into its holster.

His voice acted as a clarion call, summoning the rest from their induced slumber.

Yawning mightily, J.B. staggered over. "What's going on here? We pass out in the courtyard and wake up in a cave?"

"Lightning hit us, and the courtyard collapsed?" Krysty suggested, her hair in knotted tangles, a sure sign she wasn't fully cognizant yet. "Or did J.B. hit something with his tommy gun?"

Then she stared at her hands. "Clean nails? Hey, I've been bathed," she said as a fact. "And the rips are mended."

"Blasters are over here," Ryan said, shouldering the Steyr.

With cries of astonishment, the weapons were reclaimed.

"Our own weapons?"

"Hot pipe, look at all the ammo!"

Pockets were stuffed.

"Better also check them for blocked barrels," Doc said, peering into his pistol. "Maybe this is an intelligence test of some kind."

"Mine's clear," Ryan announced, closing the SIG-Sauer.

"Clear," Krysty said.

Mildred closed her target pistol. "They're fine, you old coot. Don't go paranoid on us."

"Even paranoids have enemies," Doc stated loftily. "Besides, how do we know this ammunition is still viable?

Weighing a full box of .357 bullets in his palm, Jak examined a round, then slid a single bullet into his blaster and fired. The Magnum discharge sounded like thunder in the confines of the cave, and the slug blew a hole in the wooden table the size of a fist. The furniture toppled over with a crash, and a leg cracked off in pieces.

"Seems okay," the teenager announced, reloading his revolver.

"Fool," Doc snapped. "You could have blown off a hand."

"Know another way to test ammo?" Jak asked bluntly, snapping shut the cylinder of his Magnum.

Doc glared at the teenager, then relented with a grudging smile. "No, sir, I do not. My apologies."

After acquiring the grens and dynamite, the Armorer slid his shotgun over a shoulder and then paused, looking at the Thompson .22 submachine gun lying next to his Uzi 9 mm submachine gun. He patted the tommy gun fondly but reclaimed the Uzi, studiously checking it over for damage.

"J.B.?" Dean said, tucking away his Browning automatic, his vest once again bulging with ammo rounds.

"Yeah?"

"Can I have it?" he asked, pointing.

J.B. waved the boy on, and Dean took the

Thompson. Cradling the ungainly blaster, he experimented with different grips until finding a proper balance. "Heavy pump," he grunted. "I have to wind this key before firing, is that right?"

J.B. showed him how. "And work the bolt."

"Like this?"

"That's it. But be careful! It snaps into place like a rattrap."

"Gotcha."

"I also found it shot to the left, so take that into account."

"Okay." The boy lifted the weapon and peered along the sights. "This will take some getting used to."

"But it's the best thing for .22 rounds," J.B. told him.

There was a tap on Dean's shoulder, and he turned.

Jak was holding a box of 12-gauge shells and the pump-action Mossberg. "Mine now."

"Fine by me."

"Wonder who our benefactors are?" Krysty asked, sliding the Ruger into her belt. "And why aren't they here to greet us? Obviously they're on our side."

"Mebbe, mebbe not," J.B. said. "Could be fattening us up for the kill."

"Winter hogs?" Jak asked, tucking a knife into his boot.

"Exactly."

"And who says they are not here with us?" Doc countered, holstering the LeMat. With his frock coat on, pistol holstered and swordstick in hand, the old man felt safe again, the alien cold that sometimes caressed his soul and threatened his sanity kept at bay.

"We've been rescued, cleaned, washed, our wounds bandaged and given back our weapons." Ryan looked around them, studying the walls. "I think we've been hired as mercies."

"For what job?" Dean asked.

"To kill the ward," a strange voice said, "and his hellish children." With a rumbling noise like a hungry stomach, a section of the rock wall disengaged and swung aside. A tunnel beyond was filled with people in the patched clothing of slaves.

J.B. and Dean dropped low, their choppers at the ready, as the rest of the group assumed a combat stance. Fingers rested on triggers, ready to fire on Ryan's spoken command.

A group of five people entered the cave, their hands raised. "Don't fire, we mean you no harm," a lean tall man said.

"That remains to be established," Ryan replied coldly. They were dressed as slaves, but also wore blaster belts and knife sheaths. Empty at present. Making a decision, he lowered his rifle barrel. "However, you have definitely grabbed our attention for a while."

"If you are the ones who rescued us and brought us here," Krysty added, her eyes narrow slits of concentration.

"We are," said a tiny redheaded woman.

A hand still on his weapon, Ryan waved them toward the chairs. "Sit, and let's palaver."

"Thank you, Mr. Cawdor."

Ryan stared at her.

"Yes, we know your names," she said, taking a seat. "We have known about you since the lady ward brought you here in your own tank."

Jak hawked and spit on the stone floor.

The large man with the square jaw curled a lip in disdain. "I see you feel toward the heirs as we do."

"Bullet in the head," the teen said with feeling.

"We would prefer something slower, and much more painful."

"But her death is more important than revenge," the slim brunette hastily added. The other visitors agreed.

"And who exactly you are?" Mildred prompted, holstering her blaster and leaning against the wall, arms crossed.

The brunette touched herself. "I'm Lisa, the large man is Troy, the thin man is Clifford, the hawk is David and the redhead is Kathy."

Ryan and the others had no problem putting faces to names. And the hawk was right. David carried an expression like an attacking bird of prey. Ryan had a feeling he would be a difficult man to beat in a fight.

"No numbers?" Krysty asked.

"We're the resistance," David said proudly, thumping his chest. "We're free people, and people have names, not numbers like vehicles."

"Hallelujah," Doc rumbled in his stentorian voice.

"We have a proposition," Lisa said, resting her elbows on the table.

"I'm listening," Ryan told her.

Krysty stayed behind him, her .38 plainly in view,

while Troy stood to the rear of the brunette. He was balanced on the balls of his feet, his large callused hands hanging half closed at his sides, seemingly capable of anything. The others moved a little bit away from the leaders. Nobody spoke for a while, and the tension grew thick in the air.

"Where are we?" Mildred asked. "In a dead-head?"

The people looked at her in surprise.

"That is correct," Kathy replied. "This is a tunnel of the coal mine that was exhausted decades ago. The heirs ordered it sealed off, but we left an air shaft open."

"And now it's one of our bases," Clifford added.

Ryan heard a small pause there and guessed it was actually their only base of operations. Lie whenever possible. It was the first rule of negotiating.

"And the sec men can't find you?" Dean asked in disbelief.

"The excavations for the mines are miles deep into the mountain beneath us," Clifford said smugly. "With hundreds of side shafts and dead-heads."

"Resembles a tree root," Troy spoke knowingly.

"Sludger?" Jak asked.

"Timber boss."

"Good job, 'cept dust."

"You got that hot, chum."

One big and black, the other slim and pale, the two men nodded at each other in a friendly manner and Mildred could feel the tension ease in the cave. Because he was reticent to the point of absurdity, she often forgot how intelligent Jak was. He had done this deliberately to smooth the way for Ryan.

"Besides," Lisa said, "how could the heirs find something that doesn't exist?"

Ryan almost smiled. "Official denial. The slaves can have no hope, if they don't even know there is an underground."

"Even saying the word *escape* is punishable by death," Krysty added.

"Exactly."

"Give me the bottom line," Ryan growled, laying the Steyr on the table between them. Talk nice, but look menacing. It was the second rule of cutting a deal. Another valuable lesson from the Trader.

"You want to leave," Lisa said, ignoring the presence of the longblaster. "We want to be free. Help us, and we help you."

"We're armed again," J.B. said bluntly, tapping his Uzi. "What's to stop us from leaving this pit?"

Troy snorted in sour amusement. "Nobody can leave Novaville. Once past the walls, there's only one way out of the compound, and the heirs have been lining it with traps for lifetimes as protection against the Beast, should it decide to come here."

"That's why the coldhearts set an ambush for travelers on the road," Ryan said, comprehension flaring. "You're too well protected. I had wondered about that."

"Many times the Sons have tried raids," David said succinctly. "And they always fail."

"You'll never reach the flatlands alive without the machine," Lisa stated forcibly. "That is a fact.

Solid as the stone around us. And we have it. Not
the heirs, or the sec men, but us.''

"You do? Where?'' Doc asked innocently.
Sometimes, even the wise let slip important things
if you asked casually enough.

She stared at him. "I'm small, but not a child.''

"My apologies, madam.''

Ryan waved the trifle aside. "We kill the heirs
and the ward, and you give us back Leviathan, is
that it?'' he asked her.

"Just the heirs. They control the sleep gas.''

"Should be easy enough to avoid the canisters,''
Krysty said, her hair tensing in unease.

"They can release it anywhere, at will,'' Clifford
said bitterly. "From the walls, the floors…and nothing stops it. Predark gas masks, wet cloth, spices,
drugs, nothing.''

"It's the only real hold they have on us,'' David
stated, hunching his shoulders. "Men with blasters
we can fight with pavement stones, drown them in
our blood if necessary.''

"But any act of rebellion, even to disobey a direct
command from the heirs, and you awake in the
tower.'' Kathy hugged herself and shivered. "At
dawn, whatever remains is nailed to a cross in the
courtyard for all to see.''

"Then how did you get us away from them?''
J.B. asked.

Lisa reached in a pocket and withdrew a small
glass vial partially filled with a swirling milky fluid.
"The heirs drink this and walk through the gas unaffected. My father stole some, and we have been

saving it for the proper time. For the right people. You."

"We aren't mercies," Krysty said. "We fight only when we have to."

"As do we all."

"Or when the odds are right," J.B. countered. "And six against hundreds is a poor gamble."

"Dozens against hundreds," David corrected. "We can fight. Will fight. Have fought." He patted his empty holster. "We have blasters, put together from the pieces of broken weapons gathered over the years. We have ammo, knives, explosives! But we need people trained in combat to direct our army."

"An army of whipped slaves, not warriors."

"An army of men," Troy said grimly.

"Think of it as an investment," Kathy said. "Novaville can be your new home. You can stay here, or travel and use it as a haven to come back to in lean days. Blasters, fuel, ammo will be yours for the rest of our lives."

"That much at least we can guarantee," Lisa said. "The ward can't match that. In words, yes, but not in deeds."

Settling back into his chair, Ryan seriously considered the proposition. He knew everybody was watching him and kept his face strictly neutral, but to himself Ryan admitted that he didn't like the whole deal. Only a fool willingly undertook a desperate battle.

However, he had spent a lifetime in the Deathlands with the Trader bartering for supplies, cutting deals with looters, and making treaties with warring farmers. Ryan had once faced down armed cold-hearts with an empty blaster, and killed the man who tried the same on him. Many were the jackals who thrived, not by force of arms, but with lies and deceit. Ryan knew by the fact that he was still alive, that while he might not always be able to detect a lie, he was positive he would know when somebody was telling him the plain unvarnished truth. The companions couldn't leave without Leviathan, and they would never get it except by assisting to overthrow the rulers of the ville. That gave him only one option. Like it or not.

"Done." Ryan held out a hand, Lisa took it and they shook. Her grip was firm, but slightly damp with sweat. It wasn't hot in the cave. Nervous sweat? Suddenly, he had the vague feeling there was something important she wasn't telling him, something she was holding in reserve. He would have his people ready for treachery. More so than usual.

"Liberty, equality, fraternity," Doc said.

"Now we're going to need some information," Ryan stated, resting both hands on the table. "Maps of the ville showing every known attack point with the gas, and everywhere you have dug tunnels. We need to know how many sec men we're facing, what weapons they have and what kind you have."

The others murmured among themselves.

"This is a lot," Lisa demurred. "If this information falls into the hands of the heirs, we'll be destroyed.

"You ask a lot," Krysty reminded. "We aren't fools, or suicides to charge blindly into battle."

"And leave me the vial," Mildred said.

"No. You'll get it just before your attack," Lisa countered.

"I'm a physician, a healer," Mildred explained to their puzzled expressions. "I might be able to analyze the formula and duplicate it. Make enough for everybody."

Conflicting emotions played across the brunette's face.

"No," she decided. "The risk for betrayal is too great. You get the antidote when we say so, not before."

Mildred shrugged in acceptance.

"The ville sec men have blasters," Krysty said, holstering her weapon. "Without Leviathan, we're going to need an equalizer. Something unexpected. Can't conduct a revolution with sticks and rocks."

"Sure can," Jak drawled, pulling up a chair. "Lose."

"Our loquacious teenaged friend is correct," Doc said, leaning on his cane. "Without proper weaponry our efforts are for naught."

"We need a key," Ryan said thoughtfully. "J.B., what can you do with this dynamite?"

The Armorer inspected the top stick in the wooden box. The waxed tube was glistening with silver dewdrops. He replaced it with extreme care. "This is really old. It's sweaty nitro. Dangerous stuff. I can probably stabilize it into plastique. Should yield a couple of pounds of C-4."

"Not enough," Ryan stated, cracking his knuckles. "Any more in stock?"

"That's all we have," Lisa said. "And two men died stealing that much."

"Well, I can make lots of black powder," J.B. told them, scratching under his hat, "if you folks can get me some sulfur. The charcoal we can make from slow-roasting wood, and saltpeter we dig up out of latrines."

"I know the technique for turning black powder into gunpowder," Mildred said. "It isn't plastique, but it explodes better than black powder."

"Couple of hundredweight of that and we're in business," Ryan announced.

"Nails for shrapnel," Jak said.

"Explosives from night soil?" Lisa asked, staring at the companions as if she questioned their sanity.

"Close enough. Crystals form under deposits of waste. The older the better. The crystals are saltpeter, one of the chemicals needed to make black powder."

This news was received with excitement.

"Unfortunately, we have no latrines," Clifford said glumly. "The night soil of the ville is flushed into the river."

J.B. exhaled and tilted his hat backward. "Great. Well, what about silver? Coins, cups, anything will do."

"We can get some, yes," Lisa said. "But for what purpose? Any supplies needed we don't buy, we steal."

"Then steal me silver," J.B. ordered. "And white sugar. Lots of it. All you can."

"There is beet sugar," Kathy said hesitantly. "But it's reserved for the heirs, and it's much more closely guarded than ornamental metals."

"Get me enough, and I can make us explosives."

"From silver and sugar?" Troy demanded.

"And water and sunlight and old rags, yes." J.B. tapped the wooden box of dynamite with a fingertip. "I'll use these as primers and centers. Should do the job just fine."

David frowned. "Use them to do what?"

"Get us more plastique," Ryan told them. "Plus, grens, ammo and anything else useful we can find."

"Never waste time trying to reinvent the wheel," Doc explained. "Why make crude weapons, when we can steal good ones?"

"Steal." Lisa chewed on the word. "You plan on raiding the ville armory?" Her words ended on a high note.

"Sure. Last thing anybody would expect."

"You aren't cowards," Troy admitted in spite of his reservations. "Invade the Citadel. I don't believe that has ever been attempted."

"Good," Ryan said. "Then security will be lax."

"Excuse me," Dean interrupted, stepping forward, "but I wanted to ask, what happened to Shard?"

"Who?" Lisa asked, furrowing her brows.

Krysty glanced around the tunnel room. "Shard, the prisoner who was with us. Where is he?"

"Shard?"

"Tall skinny guy," J.B. said. "Bushy beard."

The slim brunette looked at her associates, then directly at the companions. "I'm sorry, but we don't understand. There wasn't anybody else in the courtyard when we found you."

"Are you sure?" Ryan prompted with a scowl. "Mebbe he got away, or the guards captured him."

She shook her head. "Nobody."

Chapter Fifteen

Washlines heavy with laundry wove a crazed netting over the filthy street. Marching in formation, a squad of sec men tramped through the squalid huts, pushing aside everybody in their way with a complete lack of concern. An old woman fell sprawling into the mud and half-naked children ran screaming for their mothers' skirts. Strong men stood silent as the armed guards went by, many of them hiding a clenched fist behind their backs.

"This is it," a corporal said, pointing at a hovel.

The house was made from bits and pieces of plywood and sheet metal, the tar paper roof sealed with mud. The whole thing was bleached gray from exposure to the acid rains from the west.

One savage kick from a private and the door broke apart into kindling, pieces of wood still clinging to the rusty hinges.

Inside, a girl was using a bare stick to stir a pot of something cooking over a small fire of coal fragments. As the sec men entered, she dropped the stick and folded her hands, bowing as low as possible.

"Good sirs," she spoke to the ground, not daring to look directly at them, "command me."

"Where are the strangers!" the corporal demanded, wrenching her face upward. "We know they're loose in Detail. Tell us where." Underneath the layers of cooking grease and dirt, he saw she was a beauty indeed, and wondered why this one had never before been brought to the barracks for a week of bed duty. Sloppy recruiting.

"Strangers, good master?" She blinked, wringing her hands.

"Outlanders, pretty one," he stated, tracing her face with a finger. Her cheek muscles twitched, but she didn't flinch. "Mutie invaders come to kill us all."

"I haven't seen them, master. I'm a good prisoner!" the teenager pleaded. "I obey the law."

The corporal released her and moved aside. Stepping closer, a burly sec man slapped her across the face with the back of his gloved hand. She hit the dirt floor, sobbing wildly.

"Liar," the corporal said, a hint of a smile crossing his face. "Where could you get coal pieces, unless they were stolen?"

The young woman worked her lips a few times, but nothing come out. Everybody stole coal pieces; it was the only way to stay alive. Didn't they understand?

"Perhaps you gave yourself to the miners for scraps," the corporal taunted. "Crime. And now you lie. Another crime."

He smiled openly at her now, his blue eyes shining. "Mebbe a day with Eugene will change your words."

She grabbed his leg. "No! Please! I have no knowledge of strangers! I obey the law!"

The corporal snapped his fingers, and a sec man moved behind her drew a knife and slid it across her throat. Blood welled and the teenager fell backward, clutching her neck, bubbling crimson.

"Assaulting a freeman," the corporal said, wiping a spot of her warm blood off his boots onto her skirt. "Crime."

Going outside, the sec men found the marketplace empty except for a few stragglers, mostly cripples and young children. But as the corporal glanced at the crude homes he saw motion behind closed curtains and in doorways.

"The girl is dead!" he announced loudly. "As will be all traitors who help the invaders! Assassins come to slay our beloved ward!"

"Praised be his name!" the squad chorused.

"Then may the lord of us all guide their blasters," muttered an old man, leaning on a crutch. From under his ragged garment only one leg reached the ground.

In a fluid move, the sec man pulled his blaster and fired. The villagers watched in horror as the cripple fell to the muddy street, his rags shifting to show the countless scars on his skeleton-thin body.

"You will tell us their location!" the corporal screamed, brandishing his revolver. "Lying is a crime! Crimes are punishable by death! "

Silence greeted this announcement.

"The Deathlands scum aren't your friends!" the corporal screamed. "We are your friends! Tell us where they are, I command it!"

Nobody spoke or moved.

"Failure to obey a freeman, crime!" he bellowed

and gunned down two more people at random. "Squad, tear this street apart! Find me the invaders, or find me somebody who will talk!"

Eagerly, the squad began shoving people aside, entering homes and smashing furniture. Unarmed, the people didn't attempt to defend themselves, but merely bowed their heads and prayed for deliverance from the living hell of Novaville.

"HERE THEY ARE," Lisa said, hurrying into the tunnel, her arms full of paper bundles. Troy entered with her but stayed near the disguised entrance, a hand resting casually on his holstered blaster.

Placing aside their plates of food, mostly bread and boiled vegetables, the companions gathered around a table as the brunette spread out a map of the mountain valley.

"This is a survey map," Ryan said, placing a wooden mug on a corner to hold the paper flat.

Doc rubbed the paper between fingertips. "Excellent condition. Where did you find it?"

"There is a cave of bad air," Lisa said, "sealed off with a wall of brick. But there's a door, edged with tar, and anything in that cave doesn't age or rot."

"Methane," Jak guessed. "From the mine."

Mildred nodded. "No free oxygen. Paper would last for centuries in there. However, food stored in the gas would taste awful. Eventually become poisonous."

Lisa didn't reply, but her face was bright with awe at their great knowledge.

"Is the cave a library," Dean asked, "open to anybody?"

She shook her head. "None may enter but freemen. For a slave to do so is punishable by death. All crimes are."

"Like feudal Japan," Doc muttered. "Serfs and samurai."

Ryan carefully smoothed out some wrinkles in the rolled paper. The prison appeared to be a large rectangular structure, with high walls and lots of turrets. There was only one gate offering entrance, just north of a four-story building.

"That's where we got gassed," J.B. stated. "Near the crosses."

"And the gallows," Dean added. "What's that building, the palace?"

"The Citadel," Lisa said, scowling. "I don't know the word palace, but it's where the ward and his spawn live."

Krysty used a cartridge to measure the size of the land around the prison. "Four, no six hundred acres. Damn, that's big."

"Must need that much land to support a hundred," Doc said, thoughtfully rubbing the lion head on his cane. "If the acid rain ever stopped, they could feed thousands off a farm of this size. Maybe more."

"And if the rain came constantly," Ryan countered, shifting his patch to a more comfortable position, "as it does in parts of the Deathlands, then they couldn't feed a rat."

"What's this?" Krysty asked, tracing a ring of

tightly clustered squares encircling the huge farms. "A wall of some kind?"

"That's a wall," Ryan said, tapping a finger on a thick black line past the band of squares. "I'd bet these are rows of small huts, homes for the farmers and miners."

"Pigsties," Lisa snapped. "A reward for those who have worked hard enough to live in the sunshine."

"And act as cannon fodder against invaders coming over the outer wall," Ryan growled. "All villes have perimeters, but this is the first that uses its own people as part of it."

"I like your ward less and less," Mildred commented, making a face as if she had bitten into a lemon.

"We don't like him at all," Troy stated from the door.

"And nobody ever goes outside that last wall?" J.B. asked, fanning himself with his fedora. "Except the heirs, and mebbe raiding parties?"

"Not so," Lisa countered. "Some of the oldsters are allowed to hunt with bows in the forest outside Detail. The mountains mostly protect us from the acid rains, and many animals such as deer and bear have returned as in the predark days, although some are not-right and can't be eaten."

Ryan took the not-right remark to mean muties. Lost in the rad-blasted desert, he had once been so starved he ate a rattlesnake that had lain dead in the sun for days. But he'd never been hungry enough to risk eating anything mutie. The very thought made his stomach roil. "These hunters, their families stay inside as hostages."

"Yes."

"Any hunter ever leave in spite of that?"

She rubbed her face. "Once, very long ago. There's a painting on the inner wall showing what the ward at the time did to the runaway's family. None has tried again."

Krysty poured the woman a drink of well water, and she gulped it.

"The outer wall, how high is it, how thick?" Ryan asked, probing for weaknesses in the ville defenses. Ancient wrongs didn't concern him. The dead were dead. "What materials, wood, stone, concrete?"

"Stone blocks, like the walls of the Citadel. Two feet thick and twice the height of a man." Lisa produced a goose feather, and, dipping it in a colony of oily ink, drew a rough sketch on a blank space. "There's a walkway along the top fronted by a coil of thin metal that cuts better than a knife."

"Razor wire," J.B. explained. "Probably looted from the city you call Wheel. No way the prison stores could possibly have enough to cover a wall miles in length."

"Nobody makes anything anymore," Mildred snorted. "Humanity has been reduced to jackals feeding off a corpse."

"O brave new world," Doc whispered.

"And this is the only road," Ryan noted forcibly returning to the subject. "Describe it, dirt, gravel?"

"Flat and hard. Black as coal."

"Yellow flecks down the middle," Troy added.

He was partially turned toward the door as if listening to a distant conversation.

"Sticky in the summer?"

"So say the hunters."

"Asphalt," Ryan stated. "Good. Excellent, in fact. And it ends at the prison?"

"Yes. At the front gate. That is made of wood beams an arm's-length thick, handed together with iron and covered with numerous sheets of steel."

"Flexible and strong," J.B. mused. "Tough to smash through. Very tough for explosives, unless we had a lot." Then he grinned. "But Leviathan could blow it to pieces with a single volley of the 75s."

"Hear something?" Jak asked, joining Troy.

"Thought I heard sec men, but they're gone now."

Jak pulled out a leaf-shaped blade. "Let's make sure."

Troy glanced at Lisa. She nodded, and the two men slipped through the rock door, closing it tight behind them.

Shifting pages, the remaining companions studied another map, a much older one, the paper yellow and brittle from age.

"This is the interior of the Citadel," Lisa said. "We have no idea why it is white lines on blue paper. Perhaps an effect of the bad air."

"Architectural blueprint," Mildred explained, grabbing two of her plaits and tying them together behind her head to keep the rest out of the way when she bent over. "It was a cheap way to make multiple copies. Or least it was before laser printers and computers.''

Ryan rotated the paper toward him. ''Hmm, a lot of these spaces are blank. Probably a safety precaution in case prisoners got a copy. So they couldn't find weak spots to try to escape.''

Lisa flinched at the forbidden word.

''We can guess what's in these rooms forever and never get it right,'' Krysty complained. ''Whatever they were in the predark, surely they're something different now.''

''Apples never fall far from the tree,'' Doc said cryptically.

''Doc's correct. You wouldn't make a kitchen a horse stable, but you might convert it into a laboratory.''

''I see,'' Krysty said softly. ''Very good.''

''What does this matter?'' Lisa demanded, annoyed. ''We know where the armory is.''

''I'm betting you don't,'' Ryan said, glancing at her. ''I'll wager no slave has never been near the real armory.''

''Then how will you find it?'' she shot back. ''Magic?''

''Where are the prisoners not allowed to go?''

''Many places,'' Lisa replied, waving her hand.

''Show us. One of them will be what we want.''

''And how shall you know?''

Ryan stared at the blueprint as if envisioning the walls and corridors. ''Oh, I'll know.''

''How?''

For the second time in as many days, Ryan almost smiled. ''Because I'm an even bigger bastard than the heirs are. All I have to do is consider where I'd put my storehouse of blasters.''

"Throne room?''

"That's not what they call it,'' he corrected. "But yes. Only much too obvious.''

"But definitely close by,'' J.B. said, raising and lowering his fedora. "Mebbe near where they sleep?''

Ryan stabbed a blank area on the map with a finger. "Not close by, J.B.,'' he corrected. "Inside.''

"That's the ward's bedchamber.''

"Exactly.''

"They sleep in the armory?'' Lisa's voice took on a squeak.

"A pair of paranoids, like the heirs?'' Mildred scoffed. "Certainly. It was probably their nursery as children.''

"Bedchamber,'' Dean mused. "Going to be a lot of guards, no, wrong. That would defeat the whole purpose. It will only have a few specially chosen guards.''

Ryan slapped the boy on the back in approval.

"So our best chance to gain entrance would be during the day,'' Dean said, preening under the attention.

"Midnight,'' Ryan stated, circling the area with a broken piece of chalk. The white ring enclosed two corridors and a room with no doors or windows shown. "Yes, that's got to be it.''

Lisa recoiled. "We attack when they're both there asleep?''

"Infiltrate,'' J.B. corrected sternly.

"But why?"

Ryan folded his hands and looked at her again with the full intensity of his cobalt-blue eye. "Because that's when you're going to start the riot."

Chapter Sixteen

The dark sky was full of ominous clouds, heavy, black and pendulous, threatening to unleash deadly rain at any moment. The ground was soft underfoot, not mud, but freshly plowed. It was like walking on a pillow, then on something solid. The sec men didn't seem to care as they patrolled the fields like dogs on the hunt, shoulders hunched, weapons sharp.

Off to the side, a team of rag-clad slaves pulling a plow continued their endless journey of turning the soil in preparation of a late planting. Every day that good weather permitted, the farms were worked. Every scrap of edible plant meant more would survive the coming winter with its acid snow.

"Try there!" Sergeant Kissel ordered, pointing toward a barn.

A squad of men approached a haystack and began ramming wooden pitchforks into it.

"No blood yet!" one man announced, adjusting his grip on the wooden shaft for a better hold.

"Get every inch!" Kissel snapped, both hands on his blaster belt, fingers nervously tripping the handles of his blasters. "Don't miss a section!"

A guard appeared from within the barn, cradling an armful of iron and rope. He hurried over to the waiting sergeant, jingling every step of the way. "I found some hooks, sir," the guard stated. "And more than enough rope to do the job."

The sergeant didn't turn from the haystack. "Excellent. Then start dragging the sewers."

"In this weather?" The guard gave him a puzzled smile. "Sir, do you really think anybody could survive—"

Wheeling, Kissel backhanded the man hard, sending him to the ground in a tangle of rope and limbs. The noise sounded like a blastershot in the quiet stillness of the field. The other sec men tried to hide their sneers, and the slaves plowed on, neither slowing nor caring.

"Never question my orders," Kissel hissed, his breath fogging from the evening chill. "Especially in front of the slaves! Now get going, and you will do the job personally."

"Yes, sir," the guard replied, rising hesitantly to his feet. He flinched as the burly sergeant made a sudden move toward him, but no additional strike was forthcoming. "Yes, sir. Thank you, sir. Without delay."

As the guard hurried off across the plowed field, the jingling was drowned out by the sound of a low purr announcing the approach of a motorcycle, Kissel turned to salute.

Braking to a halt in a plow fold, Lieutenant Anders killed the big engine of the BMW motorcycle and kicked down the stand, his boots resting on the parallel lines of turned earth. The soil was gray on top, dead and sterile as the moon, but rich, black and alive underneath.

"I can see the lack of success written on your face," Anders declared with a scowl. When he removed his leather gloves, fresh blood left moist streaks on his embroidered silk cuffs, but no cuts or abrasions marked his skin.

"We're looking everywhere, sir," Kissel replied hastily.

"Up chimneys? Under floorboards? Inside the manure piles?"

"That was the very next place I was going to have the men check, sir."

"Do so," Anders said, scanning the darkening farmland. Kissel gestured to the bloody shirt cuffs. "Any luck with the prisoner you were interrogating?"

Anders took no notice of the remark. "The lady ward has contacted the scavengers, and they pledge nobody has climbed over the walls. Which means Ryan and his people are still in the ville. Mebbe even disguised as sec men. Or slaves."

"Disgusting." Then Kissel glanced about quickly, and stepped as close as he dared to an officer. "Or mebbe the rebels have them?"

"There is no underground of armed slaves," Anders said brusquely. "However, the matter is being looked into."

"By our spies among the slaves, eh? I hear that the armory was blown apart by Ryan, and hundreds of blasters are missing."

"You heard wrong," the officer answered, turning his collar to the cold. "That explosion earlier was the testing of a new cannon. Nobody died, and nothing was destroyed. Understand?"

Kissel went ramrod straight and saluted. "Absolutely. You can count on me and my men, sir!"

"I sincerely hope so," Anders said, kicking the BMW into life. The muted rumble shook him to the bone for a brief instant, then waves of warmth radiating from the engine soon vanquished the chill.

Forcing himself not to shiver, Kissel looked hungrily at the motorcycle, but said nothing. Such was the privilege of rank.

"If anybody asks, I'll be reviewing the guards on the south wall. Time is short," Anders added. "Our masters grow more impatient by the minute with our failures. If we don't find Ryan soon, our beloved leaders will consult with the ward over this matter."

The sergeant blanched, his eyes going wide.

"I concur with your opinion," Anders said, revving the throttle a few times to clear the carburetor. A single puff of dark smoke drifted from the fluted tailpipes. "If the heirs think there's going to be another food riot, a mass escape attempt or a full-fledged attack on the Citadel, then we're all doomed."

"Amen," Kissel whispered, then he snapped off a crisp salute. "We'll find them, sir, or die trying!"

"That's the general idea," Anders said. He drove off, following the planting gully, a black-clad bubble of heat in the rapidly descending purple darkness.

THROUGH A PAIR of predark military binoculars, Amanda watched as the lieutenant moved off on his bike toward the south. "He's doing a perimeter sweep," she stated.

"Or checking that damn bridge," Richard stated, squinting into the distance. "I told you we should have torn it down years ago."

"An escape route is only good if you can use it, dear brother," Amanda replied, tucking the binocs into a cushioned pouch. "It's there for our protection. Nobody but you and I know about the boat hidden in the river cave."

He grunted in reply, admitting neither that he was wrong nor she was correct.

A chill evening wind moved across the front of the Citadel, the grayish stone turning black in the evening light. The heirs sat in chairs on the front porch overlooking the execution dock. They knew it was always wise to be plainly seen by the slaves in times of trouble. It quelled unrest.

Large braziers heaped with coals lined the courtyard around them, deaf slaves wrapped in discarded furs fanning the smoke upward, and directing the heat toward their masters. Richard often worried about discussing important matters in front of the slaves, until Amanda discovered that a simple thrust of an ice pick rendered anybody permanently deaf. And with the adroit application of a sharp knife, their personal servants were no longer able to speak about what transpired in private bedchambers. Amanda took great pride in the fact that Eugene could only kill, but she was able to "fix" prisoners and make them more valuable than before.

Patrolling the courtyard were armed sec men, their longblasters wrapped in sleek furs to keep the bolt grease from congealing and hindering the firing mechanism. Autumn in the mountain valley was approaching with its usual savagery, and soon the acid snows would descend, piling tall drifts of burning white crystals.

Prominently off to one side was a large canvas lump, the stiff sheeting firmly tied down against the wind by numerous iron spikes driven deep into the granite cobblestones.

"There won't be an autumn crop," Amanda said, checking the figures in a ragged book. "We'll be eating horse by March."

"Unless we get their tank. Then we'll feast on the limitless supply of canned food from the Wheel."

"Hope for the best, prepare for the worst."

Richard tossed a leg over the arm of his chair and curled a lip. "That's what Father always told us. But he was weak! We'll rule this land, all of this land! We'll walk like gods among the lower classes, sowing death as befits our whims!"

As befits our whims? "You've been reading books again," she said angrily. "I told you that would damage your eyes."

"You read them," he snapped.

In consternation, Amanda realized he was growing suspicious of her again. Damn his paranoia. Gently, she reached out to stroke his unshaven cheek. It was like caressing a porcupine, but he responded by moving against her hand.

"I'm a mere woman," she purred. "What matters my vision? My whole purpose in life is to please you, my brother."

He grunted in acknowledgment of the statement, took her hand, kissed it and shoved it aside.

"Anders is a good man," Amanda stated, changing the subject to a military matter. Her brother was placated for the moment, but in the growing excitement, she was losing her control over him. He was acting more and more independent, taking charge, making decisions. Absolutely intolerable. She would either have to finally give herself to him, which meant losing her greatest hold on the heir apparent, or arrange for their public marriage. An equally disgusting idea.

"The lieutenant? He suffices," Richard grunted, tugging a cloak tighter about himself. His sword was thrust cumbersomely under the arm of the chair, making it almost impossible for him to draw quickly. However, twin black blasters nested in a double shoulder holster. He had loaded the clips himself from their precious stock of predark ammo: Glasers and Talons, horrible bullets that entered a body and then shattered, spreading out an internal wave of bloody destruction.

"About Anders…" Amanda started again. "Perhaps this is the time for us to grant him a promotion."

"What? There hasn't been one since Father's accident!"

She agreed with a nod. "Anders is ambitious. We must promote him, or kill him."

"Kill him, then," Richard said, twisting the pommel of his sword.

"Competent men are few these days," she reminded him.

"We have no need of such," he replied haughtily. "Fear has always controlled Novaville. Fear of us, fear of Eugene, fear of the scavengers, of the Sons, of the Beast. Our slaves feast on fear as we do bread.''

The lady ward looked over the assemblage of men and women fanning the flames for her comfort. None dared look back at her or her brother, but there was an air of unease, a sense of tension, the normal feeling of their total surrender was no longer palpable. Amanda felt oddly vulnerable, and didn't like it one bit.

''What is the status of our gas?'' she asked quickly, her hand going for the electronic switch in the pocket of her clothes.

He sniffed. ''There is enough, no, there is more than enough.''

Amanda kept a neutral expression to the bad news. That was their private code. When in public, if either of them added a negative response in the middle of a sentence, it meant the entire sentence was a lie. So there was just barely enough gas in the vaults to protect them.

''Emergency storage?'' she asked pointedly.

''It's finished cooking, no, it was finished yesterday. There's all we should need and more.''

Blast! More bad news. Nervously, she rose from the chair and crossed her arms. Her long blond hair was piled high on top of her head. Her gown was the purest white, her slippers crushed velvet, the sawed-off shotgun tucked into her sash delicately covered with the finest silver filigree.

''They can't have gone,'' she declared aloud, referring to the missing captives, as if trying to convince herself. "So they must still be here. But where? And what are they planning?"

"Escape is most likely. Unless they're really Sons of the Knife, paving the way for the coldhearts to try another raid."

"Paving the way, how?" she asked. "We're on full alert. That only makes us harder to attack."

"Right now, yes," Richard countered, squinting slightly as a stray breeze brought smoke to his face. In the courtyard, a whip cracked, a slave screamed and the fanning increased vigorously. "But after ten, twelve hours we'll be tired," he went on. "Hell, mebbe they're sacrifices, trying to make our father use up all of the spare gas."

Damn, what an unpleasant idea that was. "No," she decided. "The tank is the target. It must be. I think we had better have the guards prepare all of our wall weapons."

"Whatever for?" Richard asked, honestly puzzled. "Their vehicle is already inside."

Both turned toward the canvas tent. It was beyond the circle of braziers, rich with shadows, and from underneath the sheeting came the noise of workmen banging steadily.

"Appears as if it's still there, doesn't it?" Richard said in satisfaction.

"Do you really think Ryan will fall for the same trick twice?" Amanda asked.

"Even if he's told the tank isn't under the canvas," Richard said with a smirk, "he'll still have to send people to double-check. Whether it's Ryan himself, his brat or bitch, we'll be ready."

"Unless they avoid the gas again. It only repelled

them last time," Amanda glowered. "And if they should find out where their machine really is and get it started, how will we stop them from reaching the northern pass without the wall blasters?"

"Bah. The defensives along the main road—"

"Are designed to keep the invaders out, not prisoners in." She rubbed her lip, gently adjusting her new tooth. "We should triple the guards in the tower or, better yet, have them remove the tires."

Richard blinked. "Remove? Why not just slash them? It's a lot easier and faster."

"Because we'll need the tires to operate it ourselves," she spit in ill-controlled fury. "And that large a size is hard to find intact. Those are military tires, not merely ones from a truck. Destroying the tires would be stupidity. Removing them will retard any attempt to escape."

"Yes," he said, smiling slowly. "I see. It should take them at least an hour, perhaps more, to put them back on. And in fifteen minutes we could flood the entire ville with gas."

Richard took her hand and kissed it. "So wise, and yet so beautiful. You will be a worthy queen."

"If we survive," Amanda replied sourly, reclaiming her hand. It was sloppy with spit, but she dared not wipe it clean.

"If? But surely everything is under control."

"Not quite. We have the tank in our possession, true, and are finally inside, but we still can't turn on any of the systems!"

Richard dismissed the matter with a cavalier wave. "Ryan, or one of his people, will tell us where the hidden switch is located. Or the correct command code to type in, or whatever the secret start-up procedure is. If not, then I'll assign our best techs to the problem.''

''Best remaining techs,'' she corrected hotly. ''The experts were killed trying to get through the booby-trapped hatch in the floor. We need Ryan alive, just in case. Or else all of this might prove to be pointless. We'll own the ultimate weapon, but won't be able to turn it on!''

''Annoying, but true,'' Richard said thoughtfully. ''However, I might have an answer to that. How long till sundown?''

She looked at the sky. ''An hour or so. Why?''

''Captain of the guards!'' Richard barked loudly.

From out of the shadows, the robed fat man scurried over. ''Yes, my lord?''

''Summon criers and have them spread the word. At the evening bell, we'll kill a random slave every hour until Ryan and his people are turned over to us alive. Alive, mind you. If they're dead, then every child in the whole ville will go to the twisters!''

''At once, your highness,'' the trembling man said. He bowed and scuttled inside the prison fortress.

''Brilliant, dear brother,'' Amanda breathed, sitting upright from eagerness. ''The slaves will have no choice but to give us the outsiders.''

''With Ryan comes the tank, and then we'll have the Wheel, and the world beyond.''

She laughed. ''Ryan might even turn himself in to save innocent lives!''

"The fool." He chuckled. "And then, he is turned over to Eugene?"

"Of course, my sweet," Amanda purred. "But not before we play with him for a while."

"Excellent," Richard said, giving a feral grin. "Excellent."

RYAN AND THE OTHERS were testing their supplies and strapping on weapons when J.B. and Mildred burst into the tunnel.

"Have you heard?" J.B. asked. "Mildred and I were checking on the molds for the explosives when a miner brought us the news."

"A slave killed every hour!" Mildred explained. "They must be insane!"

"Desperate and insane," Ryan agreed, pumping his shotgun to chamber a round. "That's why we're hurrying."

"We have forty-five minutes remaining," Krysty said. "How did the molds come out?"

J.B. and Mildred slid the bulky packs off their backs and laid the canvas satchels gently on the stone floor. "They're okay," the Armorer replied. "A few cracked, but, dark night, is sugar candy hard to work! Forms at 314 degrees and blows at 316. That's why I had it made in a side tunnel far away from us. Could have ignited during the pouring. Or the cooling, or when I opened the mold."

"Forty-five minutes to do what, exactly?" Mildred asked sternly. "Escape?"

Ryan used a strip of black cloth to tie his hair back off his face. "To attack the Citadel."

"Now? Hours ahead of the plan?"

"Yes."

"You're insane," Lisa said, as if it were a fact beyond questioning.

Leaning against the stone wall, Troy nodded his agreement.

"The sooner we hit," Doc countered, smearing lampblack over the silver head of his cane, "then the less prepared they are."

"And the lower the chance that a slave will crack under the strain of seeing friends and family die, and betray us to the ward." Finished with his preparations, Ryan walked over. "How many bombs cracked?" he asked.

J.B. removed his fedora and scratched his head. "Six. Can't use them for anything but fireworks. They won't explode, only spray out wads of sparks."

"A diversion?" Dean asked, loading another clip for his Browning Hi-Power and shoving it into his lumpy vest.

"Too chancy," Ryan decided. "Better leave them behind."

Lisa and Troy both spoke. "We'll take them."

Ryan waved them on.

"Six are broken, which leaves us with..." Doc prompted.

"Nineteen." J.B. rammed his hat back on. "It's not plastique, but when it goes, it'll sure ruin somebody's day."

"Shrapnel?" Jak asked, holstering his .357 Magnum pistol and drawing the oversized bowie knife.

"Couldn't find any nails, so I used broken glass. Rubbed the pieces with sewage, too."

Jak stopped honing the curved blade. "Sewage?" he repeated, taken aback.

"The sewage infects the wound," Mildred explained. "Kills the victim days later."

Ryan clapped his hands. "Heads up, people. We're moving fast and don't want to leave anything important behind. Everybody give me an equipment check."

"Got the bombs," J.B. said.

Jak patted a pocket. "Garrote."

Dean raised his butane lighter. "Ready, sir."

With Krysty's assistance, Mildred shrugged herself into her med kit. "Flashlight is fully charged."

"Lisa, are your people prepared to do their jobs?" Ryan asked. "We only get one shot at this, and we're behind schedule already."

"We'll be there when called," she stated. "Have no fear about that."

Ryan looked hard at the slim brunette. "If we fail, you fail," he reminded her.

Lisa didn't reply, but stepped closer and placed a tiny vial of milky fluid into his hand. Troy watched the passing with something akin to anguished grief.

Ryan pocketed the vial and moved toward the hidden doorway of the tunnel. "Let's go kill a baron."

WHEN THE COMPANIONS were gone, Troy reached into a pocket and withdrew a small packet of cloth. Accepting it, Lisa unfolded the piece of soft linen, exposing a small red piece of plastic with wires.

"We removed it from under the control board," Troy said nervously.

Holding it by the edges, she lifted the square for a closer view. The details of the workmanship were amazing. "And the armored vehicle won't start with this missing?"

"So far, yes."

"Good."

Troy blurted out, "We should destroy the thing! Whitecoats brought down the sky and killed our forefathers. All science is evil!"

"Perhaps," she admitted, carefully laying the red square back on the protective linen. "Yet this is how we control the wasteland fighters. They'll do as we ask, but only for as long as we have possession."

"And when this is over, then what?" he asked, fighting the urge to smack the thing from her grip and grind it under his sandal. "We just give this to Ryan and let them leave?"

With a neutral expression, Lisa gingerly wrapped the delicate piece of predark technology in the cloth and said nothing.

Chapter Seventeen

"I got him!" cried a dirty slave, bursting into view from the mouth of the coal mine. "Me! I got him!"

In a brick kiosk, the sec man on duty spun at the shout, a hand on his blaster. He scowled at the scrawny man running toward his post. Hopefully it wasn't another flood. The water that seeped through the stone walls of the mine was the ville's only reliable source of drinkable water. Filtering by a couple hundred yards of stone removed most of the pollution from the acid rains of the outside world.

"Got what, slave?" he demanded, then gave a start. "Not Ryan?"

"Yes!" the man replied proudly, coming to a halt. "We were mucking against the winter damp and there he was! So I shoved over a timber and the tunnel caved in. He's trapped in a deadhead with no way out. Come and see for yourself."

The sec man grabbed his long blaster and shoved the slave ahead of him. "Show me, and you better be right."

"The ward promised a reward of freedom for capturing the outsider," the slave said over a shoulder.

"And you'll get it," the guard growled, prodding him with the muzzle of the blaster. "If it really is

Ryan, and he's still alive. If not, your own children will be the first killed.''

"He's alive. You bet! This way, sir. This way!"

At the entrance of the mine, the slave grabbed an oil lantern from a half-filled rack of them and lit the wick with a glowing piece of oakum. Directing the cone of light ahead of them, he scrambled into the main tunnel, with the guard following close behind. They went down several levels, following a zigzagging maze of ever-narrowing tunnels, until reaching a branching intersection of tunnels. Here a dozen lanterns hung from wooden rafters supported by buttressed timbers anchored into the living stone. Milling about was a crowd of slaves clustered in front of a recent collapse, the tools of their lowly trade still in callused hands.

"Here! Right here!" the slave announced, moving through the crowd. He patted the sloping pile of pale rocks, tan stone and ebony-colored coal-bearing ore. "He's behind this!"

The sec man scowled. The debris reached from floor to roof and looked as solid as the mountain it came from. There wasn't even a breathing hole drilled in the walls, or a single crack to let air through, and that was bad.

"Start clearing it away," he ordered. "We've got to get some air in there before he dies!"

"Yes, sir!" The slave placed the lantern into a niche, positioned to shine on the avalanche. "Will you be getting more guards?"

"What in hell for?"

"He has a blaster, sir. A big one. But it didn't go off like regular one. It stuttered like an old man."

"Machine gun," the guard muttered, clutching his bolt-action rifle. He wanted the reward from the heirs of no duty for a year to the guard who found Ryan alive, but he had no intention of dying for a year of relaxing.

With a stabbing motion, he pointed at the cluster of slaves. "You, you and you, start digging. You and you, get more timber and shore up the roof! We don't want another collapse. You, go get the duty sergeant and summon more guards. I'll stay here."

The slaves moved with unusual haste, but the sec man never noticed, already dreaming about a full year of sleeping late and bedding any female slave he wanted.

Ryan! Alive! It was a miracle.

FIVE HUNDRED YARDS away, a crowd of slaves was shouting and jumping about in wild excitement.

"Over here! Here!" a woman cried, a nearby group of slaves rolling hogshead barrels and dragging wooden boxes over to block the sagging door of a splintery barn. "We got him trapped inside!"

Sitting on a plow, sipping a cup of field coffee to stave off the nighttime cold, Sergeant Kissel gagged and spit out the brownish fluid. "Ryan?" the sergeant demanded. "You have Ryan?"

The slaves stood in front of him, dancing from foot to foot. "Found him in the silo! I want the reward!"

"I found him," a young man countered rudely. "I want the reward."

"Me!"

"I!"

Standing, the sergeant cuffed them both to the ground. "I'll decide who found him after we got the bastard in chains! Understand?"

They whimpered acknowledgment as a shot rang out from the barn.

"Shitfire, he's armed and that's a .45," Kissel cursed. A large-caliber slug like that would go straight through his flak jacket at close range. "Sentry! You there!"

In the distance, a guard pointed a questioning finger toward himself.

"Yes, you, you damn fool! Bring troops and alert the Citadel. We got Ryan boxed!"

The sec man's face contorted with greed, and he took off at a frantic run.

Kissel checked the load in his blaster and worked the slide to chamber a round, then eased back the hammer into the firing position. "Frag Anders and the bike he rode in on," Kissel growled. "I'll make captain of the guards by midnight. And then it's payback time."

DEEP WITHIN the Stygian shadows of a filthy alleyway in the marketplace of Detail, David wrapped the eyepatch around Clifford's head, while Kathy artfully arranged his wig of long black curly hair. It was the flank skin of a sheep, but from a distance, nobody should be able to tell. Charcoal lines made Clifford's face appear older and heavily scarred. Dressed in repaired clothes from the guards' laundry, the skinny man held a rifle of ancient manufacture that was so badly rusted most of the internal parts no longer existed. It was beyond unrepairable, but still looked deadly potent. But the S&W .38 revolver in his belt was fully functional, even if it only held three live rounds.

"Done," Kathy said, knotting the black string used to hold the wig in place.

"Ready?" David asked.

Breathing deeply to charge his lungs with oxygen, Clifford nodded yes, then paused. "If…" He started again. "If anything happens, tell Troy I love him."

In the darkness, David gripped his shoulder. "Of course, my friend, but you'll be fine as long as you keep moving and stay on the route we mapped for you."

All over the city alarm bells sounded, causing enough noise to wake the dead.

"Hurry," Kathy urged. "One of the Ryans has already been found. You must go now!"

"Death to the heirs," Clifford said, then took off into the street. Instantly a hue and cry formed in his wake.

"It's him! It's him!" cried dozens of people. "Invader! Outlander!"

Guards charged out of doorways with blasters in hand, but hesitated to fire. To kill Ryan meant their own deaths from the hated and despised Eugene. Shoving slaves out of their way, the sec men desperately tried to follow the darting man, his telltale eyepatch identifying the outlander to them in a single glance. A wild chase began.

HIGH ATOP the parapets of the Citadel, a lone guard standing near the alarm bell shivered from the cold in spite of the thick bearskin coat he was wearing.

Retrieving a hand-rolled cigarette from a pocket, he placed it in his mouth and lit the tip from a match, cupping both hands around the tiny flame as protection from the wind. On the ground they might only be getting a mild breeze, but way up there with nothing to act as a buffer, he was washed in a steady stream from the mountains.

The cigarette finally caught, and the guard inhaled the smoke with true satisfaction. He smiled in contentment, then frowned and started to wave his arms and legs about. He tried to grab for his blaster, but it was buried deep under multiple layers of fur and leather, impossible to reach with any speed. The precious cig dropped from his gasping mouth as he continued to dance above the floor. After a few minutes, his struggles lessened and finally stopped as he went limp, but didn't fall.

Grunting from the effort, Ryan finished tying off the wire garrote around the man's neck, the strands buried deep in the mottled skin. The corpse stayed where it was, firmly attached to the flagpole.

Ryan whistled twice. Moving out from behind the chimney flue, the rest of the companions got to work. With a soft clatter, J.B. removed the cover from an air vent and stepped aside. Stripping off his vest and weapons, Dean gave them to Krysty and wiggled into the opening. The boy just barely managed to crawl inside the cramped aluminum duct. When he was safely inside, J.B. secured the cover back on and the rest departed for the ground.

In the ville below them, alarm bells were ringing, the soft crackle of small-arms fire sounding steadily, and an irregular splotch of light seemed to be a barn engulfed in flames.

IN THE AUDIENCE ROOM of the Citadel, both the massive fireplaces loudly crackled with huge fires, slaves wearing only loincloths constantly adding small logs to maintain the conflagration. Tables laden with different types of food were arrayed before the dais, and the heirs supped off golden plates held by silent slaves. Taking one bite from a succulent beef rib, Richard tossed the morsel aside and laughed as the dogs fought over it. Amanda was chewing her way through a pile of chicken legs, her lovely face scrunched into a thoughtful scowl.

"Have we done everything we can?" she asked, swallowing a tiny mouthful.

Richard belched, and wiped his mouth on a silk sleeve. "Yes, of course we have. Now shut up. The slaves will bring us Ryan within the hour."

"And if they don't?"

"Then we start killing them." He took another rib. One bite and it went to the dogs. Their stomachs grumbling with hunger, the slaves in the room struggled to keep themselves from diving to the floor and fighting the pit bulls for the food scraps. They would be allowed to eat after the heirs were done, even if it was only bread and bloody juices mopped from the dirty plates.

At the other end of the room, the iron-banded door slammed open and in rushed Captain of the Guard Ian McGregory. The bald man came scurrying toward them at a full run, his robes of state billowing around his legs. He jerked to a halt before the dais and bowed almost as an afterthought.

"My lord and lady!" he panted, flushed with the exertion of running. "I bring bad news! There have been reports of Ryan being captured."

Sucking loudly, Richard freed a piece of meat from between his teeth. "That's good news, you ass. Are you so feeble a short run has scrambled your brain?"

Toying with a strand of her blond hair, Amanda took a sip from her silver goblet. "Or did you mean to say, he is dead?"

"The reports say alive," McGregory gushed, bowing apologetically. "However, I have received reports of him in the east, north and southern sections of Novaville, all at the exact same time."

"What? Impossible!" Amanda stated. "Has this information been confirmed?"

"I double-checked before reporting. It's true. A one-eyed man with black hair and blasters has been seen."

"It's a feint," Richard declared, wiping a hand clean on his shirt, "to lure us away from the south wall."

Petulantly, Amanda dashed her chalice to the floor. "Or more likely, the fuel storage dump."

"He's going to ignite our stock of gasoline to cover their escape!"

"Or as a prelude to their attack."

"Where is Anders?" Richard demanded, standing and buckling on his blaster belt.

McGregory smiled uncertainly. "Unknown, my lord."

"Then this your responsibility, Captain. Find Anders or Kissel. Have them split our forces. Send half here to protect us, split the other half again, and send in one group to defend the fuel storage, and hold back the rest as reserves in case it explodes."

Amanda nodded at the wisdom of the arrangement. Her brother was a fool in most matters, but survival wasn't one of them.

"However, don't remove the guards on the tank," she said. "And elevate the order on Ryan and his people to kill."

"My lady?" the man said, confused. "But I thought—"

"Do it," Richard commanded. "They should go to Eugene, but this isn't the time. Shoot on sight. Bring us their bodies."

"Yes, my lord!" The bald man bowed and started to leave.

"One moment, Captain," Richard said softly.

Frozen in place, the man turned slowly. "Y-yes, my lord."

In slow deliberation, the son of the ward drew one of his blasters and fired. McGregory flinched, but felt no searing stab of pain. But a slave slicing a loaf of bread at the dining table dropped the carving knife, staggered backward and fell over, gushing blood.

"We said a random death every hour," Richard stated, holstering the blaster. "And it will continue until the outlanders are lying dead on this floor before us. I'm a man of honor."

"I just want them dead," Amanda stated. "You

have until dawn. After which there will be a new captain of the guard.''

Forcing a smile, McGregory acquiesced and depart with even greater haste then his arrival.

THE ROOM WAS DARK and smelled slightly of mold and mildew, like a damp cellar, sealed off and forgotten. Off in a corner, a bolt holding down a metallic screen twisted to the left, the right and then steadily turned counterclockwise. A hand reached through the grilled opening of the air vent to catch the bolts before they disengaged and fell to the floor. With a muted screech of rusty metal, the grating was forced off, angled sideways and pulled into the air duct. There was some scuffling, then, swinging out his legs, Dean wiggled free of the confining duct and dropped to the ground, his stocking feet hitting the concrete with soft pats. He stood in the blackness, trying to listen with his whole body. There was no sound, except for the thunderous beating of the heart in his chest.

Shielding the lens of the flashlight with his palm, Dean moved amid the boxes and shelves of the storage room, easily locating what he was assigned to find. Moving to the door, he prepared his tools and knocked on the wood just below the hinged inspection hatch, a small affair no larger than a few inches.

A surprised grunt came from the outside, followed by the scraping of a chair leg on stone. Then the hatch swung aside and a squinting face appeared in the opening framed by light. There was an almost musical twang and the sec man stumbled backward, a crossbow quarrel embedded to the fletching between his eyes.

A few seconds later the door swung open and Dean came out, pocketing one of J.B.'s lockpicks. A crossbow was dangling around his neck, along with a full quiver of quarrels. Sliding on his boots, Dean removed the dying guard's ring of keys and headed down the corridor.

The lock on the side door was already oozing oil, and the key worked silently. He pulled it aside, admitting a gust of cold air and the rest of the companions. Ryan patted the boy on the shoulder, Krysty returned his vest and blasters and J.B. took back his picks.

"This way," Mildred, directed consulting a map. "Two levels up, one corridor over. Third door."

"Guards?" Jak asked, knife and blaster at the ready.

"None," she replied. "We're coming in backward, remember?"

"Two on two coverage," Ryan said, the silenced 9 mm SIG-Sauer out and level. The bolt action Steyr SSG-70 was riding in its usual position across his back. "Silent penetration, one yard spread. Doc on point, Jak back of him. I'll take the rear. Dean, J.B., Krysty and Mildred, take the crossbows."

"Arrows," Mildred said, tucking a crossbow between her thighs and, holding the string with both hands, cocked the weapon. The launching lever locked into position with a loud clack.

Dean handed them out. "Two quivers each."

The physician tucked a quarrel snugly into the notch. "Ready."

"Check," Krysty said, expertly holding the weapon slanted upward, a hand laid alongside the lever, but not actually touching. Metal blasters got stubborn with age as springs weakened. Wooden crossbows got feisty.

Doc holstered the LeMat and unsheathed his sword. The normally shiny blade was a dull gray from a mixture of ash and bone glue. Perfect for nightcreep work.

"So let us do the deed which must be done," he said quietly, "dark and bloody, this cold night."

Staying near the walls to retard visibility, the companions swept through the deserted halls of the Citadel, advancing down corridors, up stairs and through spacious rooms lavishly decorated. They meet with no resistance.

In a chilly corridor lit only by hanging oil lamps at both ends, Ryan raised a hand and closed it into a fist. Everybody stopped. Then he lifted a finger and twirled it in a circle. The others gathered close.

"This feels wrong," he said. "They must have everybody out searching for us."

"Idiots," Jak agreed, snowy hair masking his features.

"Then they took the bait about the gasoline tanks," Dean said.

"Appears so."

"Or this is another trap," Ryan countered, feeling the tiny hairs on the back of his neck rise. "I don't trust the heirs any more than I do the slaves. Haven't meet this many crazy lying bastards since those folks in Maine."

Suddenly, Krysty sliced the air with a flat hand

and conversation ceased. The ceiling above them was vibrating slightly, making the hanging lanterns twitch at the end of their chains. The noise steadily increased until the ceiling rumbled with the sound of marching, then it briskly faded away in the direction they were heading.

"That was a freaking army," J.B. said, tucking his glasses more firmly onto his nose as a prelude to combat. "The heirs must have called in the reserves."

"Leave?" Dean asked.

"If we could get past the wall without Leviathan," Ryan said, "we would already be gone. We're in for the full count, boy."

Krysty spread the map flat on the floor and Jak brought a lamp closer.

"Any way to circle past the bedchambers and reach the armory from the other side?" Ryan asked, studying the old map.

"We can cut through the garage," Krysty replied, pointing the way.

"Won't they be expecting that?" Dean asked worriedly.

"It's too small for Leviathan," Ryan said. "Only bikes and such there. Nothing a prisoner could use to escape."

"Hell, there's not even anything there we want now," J.B. added. "Just a place to go through."

A sec man in old worn sneakers stepped around the corner, the rubber soles noiseless on the stone floor. He was holding a steaming mug in both hands and gasped when he spied the group huddled around the map on the floor. Doc lunged, stabbing him through the throat with his sword, the blade slicing through to the other side. The mug dropped from nerveless fingers, and Mildred caught it in midair. Hacking for air, the guard stood there, motionless with the pain. Jak moved behind him and thrust a leaf-shaped blade upward into the base of the head where the spine met the skull. Then he twisted the knife and the guard went limp as if a switch had been thrown. As they lowered the body to the floor, Dean was amazed at the lack of blood from the attack and filed the move away for future use.

Flat against the wall, Ryan hissed for their attention and held up two fingers, then pointed around the corner. J.B. and Doc moved out of the way and let the others bunch together. Ryan directed Krysty and Jak to go left, Mildred and Dean to the right. They nodded agreement. Taking a breath and holding it, Ryan held up one finger, then two, then three. In unison, they stepped around the corner.

The two sec men, lounging in front of a door, turned at the sudden movement and a knife handle sprouted from the forehead of one, while the other staggered about, his chest full of quarrels. The companions converged upon the guards and disposed of them quietly.

Going to the door, J.B. listened, heard voices and went to the another. Unlocking the door showed it was a utility closet full of mops and buckets. The bodies were dragged inside and he locked the door to hinder their discovery.

"Double time," Ryan whispered, taking the point position.

Mildred stopped him. "Somebody is getting tortured in there," she said, tilting her head, "and I recognize the voice."

Ryan scowled. "Eugene?"

"Sounds like Shard."

Another agonized moan wafted to them from inside, then there was the cracking sound of a whip.

"I'LL NEVER TELL where Ryan is," Shard gasped, choking for air between each word. The chains clamped about his wrists pressed deep into the flesh, cutting off circulation. His hands had gone numb hours earlier. They were the only part of him that didn't hurt. He tried again to rest his feet on the ground and failed. A nearby brazier glowed with heat, iron rods thrust deep into the pile of red coals, and the slave wondered how much longer his captor would wait before using them.

"For the hundredth time, I don't care about him!" Anders stormed. "How do you turn on the great machine? You must know! Tell me!"

"Only...Ryan..."

The whip laid fire across his bare back, and Shard bit back a cry. "That the best you got?" he mumbled weakly. "My sister...hits harder...."

The lieutenant tossed aside the whip and grabbed an iron rod. The end glowed white-hot and sizzled against bare flesh. The pain was beyond words, engulfing Shard's whole body. He screamed.

"You're a fool!" Anders growled, putting the iron back into the coals. "Tell me and you live! I don't work for the heirs, I want this ville for myself! But I need the tank to kill them."

Then his tone softened, and he raised a cup of

wine to Shard's cracked lips. "Show me how to operate the great machine, and you can be my mechanic." He smiled. "You'll have women, food, anything you want!"

Shard spit into the cup. "Anything except freedom."

Throwing the cup aside, Anders grabbed the whip. "I want to know where they got the tank," he demanded, walking around the chained man, striking him repeatedly. "And are there more of them? How do you operate the device that tells of the approach of other machines? And what other booby traps does the vehicle have aside from the bomb on the belly hatch?" Anders dropped the whip. "My patience grows short, as does the time. Tell me or die."

"Do it," Shard whispered, having trouble keeping his head erect. His strength was fading, and soon the pain would claim him. "Kill me. I'll never betray a friend."

"Friend?" Anders sneered, slapping him. "Nonsense. You never met him before the tower room."

"They treated me like a man," Shard whispered, blood dribbling from a broken nose, "not a slave. That is worth more than anything you offer."

"Oh, you'll soon beg to talk." The sec man pulled a medical instrument into view. The blade gleamed in the light of the brazier. "This is one of Eugene's favorites. I've seen him use it on many subjects. Now it's my turn."

"I escaped once," Shard said out of the blue, playing his last card. Raw desperation flooded his body with the strength to speak clearly.

Lowering the instrument, Anders stared. "What?"

"Got out. Over the wall. Made it to the forest and got captured by the scavengers. They tortured me, too. Had to bed a female mutie, a stickie, or else they would have roasted me for their dinner." Shard squinted as if trying to focus his blurred vision. "Always thought you looked familiar. Are you my son?"

With an insane snarl, Anders threw away the medical probe and drew a dagger from his belt when the door behind him opened unexpectedly.

"I told you not to disturb me!" Anders screamed.

"Too bad," Ryan said clearly.

His face distorting into a rictus of shock, the lieutenant turned, fumbling for his blaster, and a flurry of quarrels slammed into his chest. The impaled sec man grappled with empty air and slumped onto the brazier, his clothes instantly igniting. Burbling screams, the man tumbled to the floor, the gushing blood from his wounds extinguishing the burning uniform.

Dean bolted shut the door, as J.B. removed the chains. Krysty and Mildred eased Shard to the floor. Doc started to look for anything to serve as bandages.

In no great hurry, Ryan walked over and shot the twitching officer once in the head with a silenced 9 mm round.

"Not real..." Shard breathed. "You're not here...."

Mildred gave him a sip from her canteen. "We're

real enough,'' she said softly, ''and you're coming with us.''

''Freedom,'' Jak stated, massaging the chafed wrists. The skin was purple and cold, not a good indication, but it started responding to the ministrations.

''Dying...''

''Oh, you're beaten badly,'' Mildred said, peeling back the bloody clothing to examine the wounds. Doc handed her a relatively clean towel, already torn into strips, and she began to bind the worst of the cuts. ''But you aren't going to die. That fellow must have been afraid to go too far and kill you before he got the information.''

''Information you didn't have,'' Ryan said. ''Why'd you do it?''

The battered lips formed a smile. ''Buy you a chance....''

''Bought yourself more than that,'' Ryan announced. ''After we ace the heirs, you got a seat in Leviathan for as long as you want.''

A ragged cough shook the man, flecks of blood staining his lips. ''Too weak...never make it...''

''I'll carry you,'' Doc said, dropping his backpack of supplies. He tucked his swordstick into the bundle, making sure it was secure.

Done with the bandaging, Mildred waved him on. Easing his arms under the man, Doc lifted Shard seemingly without effort. ''Come, sir, this way to the egress.''

''No!'' Shard whispered, reaching out a trembling hand. ''Don't go to the courtyard! Canvas tent... trap. It's not there....''

"We know," Ryan said, placing the dead sec man's revolver into Shard's grip. "Leviathan is in the armory."

He held the weapon tightly, trembling as if it weighed more than the whole world. "No, the tower."

"What do you mean?"

"It's in…the tower."

"Which tower? Not Eugene's tower?" Krysty asked, hoping she heard that wrong.

A weak nod.

"Are you sure?" Mildred asked, touching his forehead to see if the man was delirious with fever. "No mistake?"

Another nod. "Heard them talking. Said it was last place you would look."

"They got that right!"

"Gaia, it's on the other side of the ville!" Krysty cursed, her hair curling wildly. "Where the riots are."

Ryan picked up Doc's pack of supplies. "Then we better get moving. Time is against us now."

"What about our deal to kill the heirs?" Dean asked. "We're so close to their room!"

Starting for the door, his father said, "Deal's off. The bastard rebels lied to us about having control of Leviathan. They can go kill the heirs themselves. It's not our problem anymore. We're going to get our vehicle and leave this rad-blasted pit."

"Not good," J.B. said, shifting his backpack of homemade explosives. "This isn't good."

"Nothing's ever…good," Shard remarked. "Only different levels of shitty."

Chapter Eighteen

His longblaster slung over a shoulder, barrel down to protect the insides from the dew, a lone sentry stood trembling slightly in the cold. His brick kiosk was alongside the main road leading to Novaville, and the thick walls helped cut the wind some, but not much. He knew there used to be glass in the windows, but a wad of C-4 removed it all, plus the sec man inside, and only the sentry had been replaced. It was too difficult to make glass these days, was what the quartermaster said. But the sentry believed the lack of glass served the dual purpose of keeping him cold, and thus more alert, and saved supplies. Why put in expensive glass that would only be blown out again in the next attack? The cheap bastards. He heard somewhere that glass deflected bullets, so it would actually be helping to protect the man who protected the ville. This far away, the high perimeter walls of the ville were only visible during the day, and then only as a thin line of black cutting across barren fields and the smooth black macadam of the main road. A misnomer if ever there was one, because this was it for roads. It was all they needed, and more than they wanted.

A stove made out of cinder blocks and filled with glowing coals radiated waves of heat that the gust-ing wind nullified. Stamping his boots, he unsuccessfully fought back a yawn. An old brittle piece of plastic with holes cut for head and arms served him as a poncho against the night mists. It didn't work very well, and he longed for the day when he would reach the vaunted rank of corporal and get one of those fine bearskin coats. Now that would protect a man just fine.

The belt buckled outside his poncho was looped with leather strands to hold cartridges for the rifle, and his hip bulged from a single gren. On a shelf was a plastic toolbox, the lid sealed shut with candle wax. That was for emergencies only, and it hadn't been used for months, the last time being for those fragging bikers bastards. They had almost made it halfway up the main road before dying. Damn dumb asses. Between the unclimbable mountains, the cliffs and the cannibal scavengers, Novaville was impregnable. But then, his job wasn't to fight off invaders, but merely live long enough to sound the alarm. Grim work, but better than patrolling the mine, or gutting slaves on the execution dock.

A low rumble, like far-off thunder, sounded, and he went to the window for a look. But the sky seemed clear, stars bright, with no sign of the low yellowish clouds that marked another acid rainstorm. Then something caught his attention on the horizon. Far down the road, past the first set of traps, near the bargaining gate was a dark shape moving his way. Cursing his lack of binocs, the sentry squinted to see. The object seemed too tall for a pack of bikers, but could be a truck. Didn't see many of them these days, and good luck for the

driver. The heirs would confiscate the vehicle and
give the sec man a reward of any women on board,
and a percentage of any booze or tobacco. This
could be his lucky night!

In a silent explosion of wood, the vehicle plowed
through the gate and bounced onto the road proper.
Immediately, a dozen concealed crossbows released
a flurry of barbed arrows streaking across the asphalt at knee level, more than enough to blow even
the toughest predark military tires. The black shape
didn't even pause under the assault.

Watching in horror, the sentry stared as the shape
rolled onto the bridge stretching across a ravine.
This trap had never failed. There were two bridges,
actually, a slim one just barely large enough for a
motorcycle to roll across, then a nice big spacious
one built of canvas and hollow pipes. Even the
weight of a single man would make the bridge collapse, sending the invaders tumbling into a pit full
of iron spikes. It had taken the slaves hours to lay
enough planks over the ravine so the lady ward
could roll that huge outland machine across the trap.

Just then, the dark shaped dropped from sight.

The sentry laughed in victory, then stared as the
angular craft rose again, rolling back onto the road
and proceeding toward the outer wall of the ville in
undiminished speed.

Snatching the coal oil lantern hanging from a nail
in the wall, the sentry blew out the flame and
ducked low. From the floor, he reached up and
snatched the plastic toolbox on the shelf, hugging it
to his chest in an irrational moment of panic.

Then grim necessity seized him. Fingernails

scratching the wax from the joints, the sentry pried loose the lid on the plastic box and ripped it off. Nestled inside was a Veri pistol and three flares. Stuffing the first fat cartridge into the hollow tube, he shielded his face with an arm, pointed the box into the sky and fired. The pistol thumped loudly, and the flare was blown high into the starry sky. One flare meant strangers, possibly danger.

It detonated into a brilliant white glare, slowly parachuting downward, riding the wind like a kite. While it was airborne, he had the second flare loaded and launched. Two meant an armed attack, send troops pronto.

The dark shape rumbled past the kiosk, shaking the walls and making the thatched roof collapse in sections, sending stalks of tar-coated hay everywhere. He stayed in the corner, praying for his life, and the thing moved onward.

The moment it was past, he shoved a hand out the window and sent off the third flare. It was a signal he had never used before, and had spent his whole adult life hoping not to. It as the signal for disaster, invasion and much much worse.

Then a blinding flash of light slashed across the kiosk, slicing apart the masonry. A terrible pain seared in his stomach, and he tried for a scream when the grenade in his pocket detonated, blowing his steaming guts across the rubble in a grisly crimson spray.

AS THE TROOP of armed sec men marched around a corner, J.B. darted from behind a pile of rotting garbage and across the dark street, taking a defensive position.

He whistled low twice, and the rest of the companions followed him with Krysty on rear guard.

"These guys aren't too sharp," Mildred commented. "I've seen better guards in hotel lobbies!"

A dull clanging noise rose from atop the Citadel. Then, softly, a siren started to howl, growing in pitch and volume until its strident scream split the night apart. Lights started coming on in every window of every home, doors burst open and half-dressed men stumbled into the streets, weapons in hands.

The companions retreated farther into the safety of darkness.

"They finally know we're here," Krysty said, her pistol steady in a combat grip.

"Took them long enough to notice," J.B. retorted, one of the homemade sugar bombs held ready, its long fuse dangling like the swing hoist of a petard.

Cradled in Doc's arms, Shard shook his head.

"Not for us?" Jak asked.

The patient winced as Mildred reached over to tighten a bloody bandage. "Invaders," Shard wheezed. "Ville's under attack."

With both of his longblasters extended like the horns of a bull, Ryan smiled. "Better coverage for us."

"Chaos is the friend of thieves," Krysty agreed, her hair moving to its own secret rhythm.

"No," Mildred countered, the expression on her face lost in the shadows. "Remember, the Beast is dead, the Sons destroyed. Who else is there who would dare attack this fort?''

"Don't know," Shard replied.

"Mayhap some new enemy," Doc espoused, slightly shifting the position of the man he carried. "Raiders, mercies. The list of palliards who hate and/or lust after this locale must be nigh infinite.''

"Bastard hope so," Ryan muttered, doubtfully eyeing the mounting chaos in the streets. A trio of sec men struggled to roll a black powder cannon into position before the very door they had left only moments ago. Ryan checked the status of his weapons.

"Forget silent, we're going hard," he announced. "Kill on sight. I'm on point. J.B., cover our rear with the bombs. Mildred and Dean, cover Doc and Shard. Something big is happening, something more important than us escaping or a slave rebellion, and I want no part of it.''

THE RANGER ROLLED unstoppable along the road that led to the primitive city. Land mines constantly exploded under its rebuilt treads, causing more smoke and noise than damage. Twice a barrage of glass bottles filled with coal oil smashed onto its hull, covering the patched-together tank with flames. This was unfortunate as it greatly increased the vehicle's visibility, but it did little else. The drones had done their job properly, and while not up to its original standards, the General Electric Ranger Mark IV was functional.

The Ranger had patrolled the ruins of the city and the desert sands of Ohio, wandering aimlessly, unable to locate any hint of the unknown invaders who had destroyed it. Then a radio signal began to weakly broadcast from the area ahead. The Ranger's main computer recognized this was a nonmilitary fortress full of civilians. However, if they were assisting the enemy, they were to be considered traitors and dealt with accordingly.

Bypassing another disguised pit, on the forward vid scanners the Ranger detected a crude wall of tree trunks embedded into the dirt atop a low hill: the outer perimeter of the civilian fortress. Activity bustled along the oak palisade, high probability security personnel preparing weapons. Radar indicated a low percentage of steel, scant iron, absolutely no depleted uranium and no high-energy sources that might power lasers or microwave beamers. Lowtech weapons only, certainly no danger to the adamantine hull of the Mark IV.

Then a slash of brown erupted from amid the bushes to one side of the road, and the Ranger rocked under a brutal impact, but penetration of the hull wasn't achieved.

Another copse of bushes trembled, and this time the cameras saw a telephone pole barreling toward the tank. The end was sharpened to a point, and the rear feathered like an arrow. Military records instantly identified such as an arbalest, a medieval antisiege weapon. Cumbersome and slow, requiring a ten-man crew to operate and load it, it was only useful against stationary or unusually large targets.

All this was done in an electronic microsecond, while the laser turret traversed quickly, but not fast enough, and the pole slammed into the Ranger. The tank shuddered as splinters exploded from the collision. Again, penetration wasn't achieved, couldn't be achieved with this primitive device, but diagnostics showed the rear radar and a vid camera were annihilated. Unacceptable.

The transformers boosting to full power, the laser cannon traversed in a full circle, pumping out gigawatts of condensed light. The surrounding countryside was set on fire before the computer was satisfied this potential danger was neutralized and proceeded onward.

SNUG INSIDE an underground bunker cut into the side of the hill, a sec man pressed his face tight against the plastic periscope and tracked the approach of the Beast. The distance was considerable, maybe four hundred yards. Too far at present, but with its current speed, in less than a minute the Beast was going to be utterly destroyed. Wards, heirs and guards for generations had prepared the defensives of Novaville, waiting for the day when the Beast would finally turn its terrible attention to them. Well, this was it and they were ready.

"Get set," the corporal said, mentally calculating trajectory and speed.

"Not in range yet," the private stated nervously.

"We fire where it *will* be," the corporal snapped, "not where it is. Distance plus velocity, remember?"

The private nodded.

"You got the safety removed?"

The young guard displayed the iron bar. "She's ready to go."

"Good." He turned back to the periscope. "Grab the rope and wait for my signal."

"Yes, sir."

"Pull early, and I'll have your balls for breakfast."

In the tiny mirror of the scope, the Beast was still on the access road just passing the first marker. The road to the ville was lined on both sides with stones, certain ones dabbed with different colors of paint and carefully paced off to exact distances so they could serve as target markers. Red for entering the kill zone, yellow for prepare and green for go.

Maintaining a regular speed, the cannon of the angular machine was rotating steadily, ready to laser-blast anything dangerous. The corporal smirked at the thought. A fat lot of good a laser would do against his weapon! The other defenders might as well go home; this was a done deal.

"Just a little bit more..." he said.

The private gripped the rope tighter and braced his boots on the broken bricks set in the dirt flooring.

"Ready...." The corporal took in a breath and whispered, "Now, Private."

As hard as possible, the sec man yanked on the rope. It resisted for a split second, then yards of it dropped inside the bunker.

On the hillside, the rope snaked away, dragging along a stout stick from a large hasp that was connected to a gate in front of a disguised tunnel. The unlocked gate swung open, and a boulder rolled into view, closely followed by dozens more. The avalanche cascaded down the hill, gathering speed and momentum. There were no trees or bushes in the way, every obstacle painstakingly removed decades ago. It had taken hundreds of slaves months of grueling labor to gather the collection of boulders into the pen, the very ground lubricated with their blood as tired bodies got crushed underneath. Tested on several occasions against the Sons of the Knife, the boulders tracked straight and true and they converged on the tank, shaking the ground in their thunderous approach.

THE FIRST ROCKS smashed into the Ranger, almost tipping the machine onto its side, denting the composite armor and destroying a sensor array. But instead of retreating as expected, the tank boldly charged, dodging around the largest rocks, and the second volley missed it completely. As the last of the boulders rolled across the road and into the forest, the Ranger backtracked their most likely course to the small tunnel in the side of the hill. Infrared sensors found two humans nearby, and it bathed the area with the laser until the grass burst into flame, the soil blackened, the exposed rocks softened and flowed like steaming mud. Muffled screams came from the melting bunker, but soon stopped.

"THEY FAILED!" shouted a sec man standing on the catwalk inside the wooden palisade of the outer wall.

On the ground, Sergeant Kissel grunted at the news, but nothing more. Rule number one for any commander was never to show surprise. The men always had to think you knew an event was going to happen and that everything was under control.

Torches lined the area before the gate, the ground littered with ammo boxes and supplies. The sprawling market of Detail was completely empty of prisoners and totally wide open, granting an invader easy access to reach the inner stone wall and the castle of the ward.

"Seal the gate!" Kissel ordered in a booming voice.

With twenty men pushing and swearing, the tremendous portal was firmly shoved into place. Then a stout wooden beam more than a yard thick was slid across the gate and into iron loops on either side. Next, iron bars were rammed into niches set in the cobblestone street and levered up against the stout beam.

"That should hold it," a private said proudly, pounding it with a fist.

An older bald man sneered at the youth. "Balls, it'll ram right through."

"Two feet of oak covered with steel chains?" he cried. "That gate took years to complete!"

"We're all dead," the bald man said with a sigh, "and you know it."

Walking closer, Kissel fired from the hip, and the bald man dropped to the ground, gushing blood.

"Stinking traitor," he spit, holstering his piece. "You there, take his blaster and ammo. You two, shove the body aside. We'll feed him to the scavengers later on. After we kill the Beast!"

A ragged cry rose from the troops, but it seemed to lack some conviction.

Kissel cupped hands around his mouth. "Wall sentry," he bellowed, "give me a call!"

"It's past the red marker!" the man shouted down, binocs to his face. "Took minor damage from the rocks!"

"Battle stations!" Kissel cried, drawing his blaster.

Racing to the battlements, the guards amassed along the catwalk, crouching to hide their numbers.

"Where are the RPGs and recoilless rifles?" a corporal asked, loading his longblaster. "The bazookas, the LAWs?"

"Back on the main wall."

"But we need them here to stop the thing!"

"Go complain to the heirs. All we got is these!" He glared at the black powder rocket he was stuffing into a rusty launcher. Two feet long and made from lead pipe, the homemade rockets were crude and had a tendency to veer wildly in flight, often returning to kill the very men who launched them. Missile post was a punishment detail, not a promotion.

Plus, the launcher was merely a beehive array of car tailpipes welded together. A score of thick green fuses fed from the end of the corroded steel and were tied together into a single thick tail. A gunner with a magnesium road flare was ready to light the fuses and then run like hell in case the launcher exploded, as so many of them did.

"It's approaching the yellow marker!" the sentry called out. "Range, two hundred yards!"

Climbing onto a horse, Kissel rode to the nearest catapult. A team of men was tying off the ropes as he galloped closer to the huge contraption.

"What is the status, Corporal?" Kissel demanded.

"Ready to go, sir!" the man answered, snapping a salute. "Number one is loaded, two is being loaded."

"Range is set for…?"

"One hundred twenty, and one hundred yards."

He stared at the fresh-faced guard. "Don't miss, lad, these are our best hope now."

"We'll get the bastard, sir."

"Passing yellow," the sentry announced, holding the binocs with both hands. "Almost at the green! Range, one fifty!"

Somebody handed Kissel a rifle, and he counted slowly to three. "Open fire!" he commanded.

Every man on the wall cut loose with their blasters, rifle and pistols, throwing a hail of lead at the tank. And in spite of the darkness and distance, dozens of rounds ricocheted off the armored hull.

"Wasting ammo," a private muttered, levering in a fresh round.

"Luring it in closer," a corporal replied, spraying 9 mm Parabellum rounds from his chattering autoblaster.

"Ready at the cats!" Kissel shouted, reining in his horse. "Prepare to release!"

Swords slashed at ropes and the catapult arm jerked upward, slamming into the stop bar and sending the cargo in the basket hurtling high over the wall. Lost in the starry sky, the collection of wooden kegs with hissing fuses rained upon the tank with pinpoint accuracy, and it was coated with booming explosions, the dense smoke masking the effect of the barrage.

"Reload the catapults! Launch the rockets!" Kissel shouted, and the fuses were lit.

Spraying sparks and smoke, the rockets streaked away into the night on tails of flame. A few angled toward the woods, one went straight into the ground and detonated in the dirt, another spiraled off to nowhere, but the rest zoomed in straight and pounded the Ranger with satisfying accuracy. A second salvo was released, then a third, as the cheering men on the wall emptied their blasters into the inferno.

Then out of the smoke rolled the Beast. Every external antenna was removed, radar gone, its video cameras reduced to sparking trash and dangling wires, but the hull wasn't visibly breached. It headed directly for the gate, the laser cannon angling upward and strobing at the palisade.

Blind, or with their heads on fire, screaming men tumbled off the catwalk and plummeted to the cold ground.

IN THE CITADEL, Amanda and Richard raised their heads from studying the map on a table as McGregory entered the audience room.

"Well?" Amanda snapped. "What's happening out there?"

"Report, Captain!" Richard barked.

"The situation is poor, my lord," McGregory said. "The outer defenses have failed. The sec men hit the tank numerous times with rockets and bombs to no real effect. Even the boulders did little damage. The guards are preparing to retreat to the slave cottages in Detail and continue fighting from there.''

"Is it through the gate yet?" Amanda asked.

"Not yet, no. But soon."

"Acceptable," Richard said, returning his attention to the strategy table. Colored markers of different types and tiny flags covered the map of Novaville. A black box sat prominently near the gate in the wooden palisade.

"Deputy Ward, you are wrong," McGregory heard himself saying. "I'm duty-bound to tell you that I believe the fight is hopeless unless the guards get those bazookas! Even just one could make all the difference."

"No," Amanda said, moving a marker from the palisade to the inner stone wall. "Those are for our personal protection."

Richard shifted another. "We'll destroy the machine in the market square. There's no need to waste precious supplies."

"I only hope it's enough." McGregory sighed, accepting a cup of wine from a kneeling slave girl.

"Explain yourself!" Amanda demanded hotly. "Our father, the ward, personally designed the ville defenses!"

"But he hasn't seen this thing, my lady," McGregory said wearily, "and I have."

Chapter Nineteen

In ruthless efficiency, Kissel dispatched the last of the screaming men with a pistol and silence returned to the battlefield. The huge wooden gate was pierced in several places by burning holes and the Beast on the other side crashing repeatedly into the resilient barrier. Each attempt bent the crossbar more and more, widening the cracks in the weakening timber. Only the iron locking bars held it in place, and when those went, so would the gate.

"Everybody who can see, back on the wall!" Kissel shouted, dumping his spent cartridges and reloading frantically. "I want every rocket we've got launched right now! Do you hear me? Now!"

Less than a dozen sec men stumbled up the ladders to the catwalk. Many more stayed where they were, wandering aimlessly or sitting in the dirt, clawing at their dead eyes. Then there was a deafening crash and the burning gate exploded off its hinges.

The horse beneath Kissel went wild with fear at the sight of the machine, rearing wildly. The sergeant struggled to maintain his seat in the saddle, but tumbled off, almost getting tramped under the slashing hooves.

Cursing bitterly, Kissel stumbled away and drew

his revolver, then from out of the smoke the Beast was upon him, towering over the sec man like a metal building. Its laser traversed to the left, pulsed once, and a catapult burst into flames, while it continued to roll toward Kissel, crushing the bodies of guards under armored treads.

Screaming in terror, Kissel threw away his blaster. "I surrender! I surrender!" he whimpered, raising both hands. "Don't kill me!"

The Beast loomed before the shaking man, its cannon swinging to point at him directly. Openly weeping, Kissel braced himself for death, and the machine rumbled off, leaving him unharmed amid the wreckage and carnage of the defeated troops.

"Alive. I'm alive," he whispered in shock. Then shouted. "It doesn't kill if you surrender!"

But there was nobody alive to hear the news. The catwalk was lined with smoking bodies, and most of the blind had long ago crawled away out of earshot.

A sudden crushing shame for his act of cowardice hit the sec man, icy fear knifing into his stomach almost making him retch. But nobody had seen, nobody had heard. Grabbing weapons off the ground, Kissel reclaimed his horse and galloped out the smashed gate of the fiery palisade, heading for the distant mountains.

SMASHING ASIDE a split-rail fence, the Ranger rolled into the marketplace of the civilian town. Single-story cabins of scrap wood and tar paper lined both sides of the common. Produce was strewed about and carts overturned. The area had been vacated in a hurry, yet every cabin door was closed, a most singular incongruity. The Ranger slowed, wary of a trap.

Across the market, a corporal stepped into view from behind a water barrel, drew a Veri pistol from his belt and put a single round into the air. He died a microsecond later, the charred corpse reduced to little more than ashes with boots. But the Ranger slowed, knowing something was about to happen.

Then the front of the cottages violently disintegrated as fifty muzzle-loading cannons fired in unison. The barrage of iron slammed into the tank, rocking it back and forth, as waves of gray smoke flooded over the market. Inside, relays cracked and the repair drones bustled to fix burgeoning short circuits. Bright orange tongues of flame stabbed into the murky smoke as a second volley hammered the tank, and it tipped over, exposing its belly. Unsure of what to do, the Ranger fired the laser randomly, but unable to traverse, it could only hit the earth and sky, not the enemy to the sides. Hydraulic systems began to leak thin red fluid on control boards, and the drones rushed to fix potentially dangerous leaks.

The sec men in the ruined cottages redoubled their efforts to load the cannons, swabbing inside the hot barrels with damp rags to kill any lingering sparks before pouring in fresh bags of black powder.

The main computer of the Ranger considered a million options and chose a direct tactic. All auxiliary power surged to the gyroscopes, increasing the revolutions to the maximum and then beyond. The rocking of the craft stopped altogether, and in majestic slow motion, the Ranger righted itself, the treads slamming onto the ground. Now the cannon swung to attack.

Dropping their wet nimrods, the armed sec men tried to flee from the cottages and failed.

ON THE EASTERN SIDE of the ville, a platoon of sec men hurried along a dank alleyway, struggling to carry a bulky, canvas-wrapped object approximately the size of a small car.

Calling for a halt, the sergeant advanced to the stone wall and began to run his hands over the rough surface as if fondling a lover. There was a click.

"This is it!" he announced, as a section of the wall disengaged and swung aside to reveal a large tunnel. "Everybody in!"

The platoon scurried inside as quickly as possible, the last man pausing at the entrance with blaster in hand, making sure no slaves saw their departure through the wall.

"What is this?" asked the corporal as the secret door closed with an echoing boom.

"Private escape route for the ward," the sergeant said, raising the lantern higher to spread out the light. "Built generations ago in case of a slave rebellion."

The corporal glanced around them. "This is big enough for the Beast to move through!"

"That's why we're going to trap it outside the wall," the sergeant replied. "Just in case it can find the passage."

Emerging out the other side, the guards found a horse stable, a blacksmith shop, a gaudy house and dozens of the usual slave cottages. But no people; the area was deserted.

"We'll set up in the brothel," the sergeant directed, starting across the muddy street, his boots squishing in the filthy muck.

A layer of gravel lay scattered around the gaudy house, rendering the ground more solid and less prone to make drunken customers slip and soil their uniforms. A single kick from a private rendered the front door passable, and the platoon swarmed inside. The main room was filled with patched couches and a bar made from stained planks laid across several hogshead barrels. Clearly, the establishment had been vacated recently, as a spilled beer still dripped onto the sawdust-covered floor.

"Move these couches," the sergeant ordered. "We'll set up here."

An area was cleared in front of the broken door, and the canvas-covered object was set down with grunts of relief. In practiced movements, the platoon busied itself unwrapping the thing. The massive autofire weapon consisted of a cylindrical firing chamber, the eight 20 mm barrels joined in a circle, a top-loading ammunition box and a squat motor, supported by a heavy tripod. It was the pride of the ville, a Vulcan minigun salvaged from the back of a predark military wag the lady ward had found outside the ville. In the light of the oil lamps, the predark superweapon gleamed like polished death.

"Bring some wine barrels from the cellar," the sergeant ordered. "They'll help hide us."

Then he turned. "You there, take cover behind

the bar. Be ready to give protective fire in case of a mishap.''

The man with the RPG launcher slung over his shoulder saluted and moved with due haste. Two more guards carrying the huge rounds for the weapon followed closely.

Kneeling, the sergeant assisted the corporal with attaching the wide ammunition belt. The dull gray cartridges for the Vulcan were thicker than a cigar, and weighed considerably more than lead or steel.

''What are these made of, sir?'' a guard asked, jockeying the belt feed into position.

''Don't know. But the heirs say it will punch through the armor of the Beast like it was flesh,'' he said, watching the work in progress. ''Here now! Tighten that bolt, or the first round through will be our last!''

The top hatch was closed and locked in place, the firing bolt thrown and the safety unlatched. Dangling wires were carefully attached to a collection of car batteries, and a light glowed green on a small panel.

''Armed and loaded, sir,'' the corporal reported crisply. ''What is the plan of attack, sir?''

''We wait here until it goes into the tunnel,'' the sergeant said, lighting a cigar.

''Begging your pardon, sir,'' the corporal said hesitantly, ''but is that wise? Wait until it is past us? Why not fire broadside? It's an easier target.''

''You're a fool. Tank armor is thinnest in the back. That's our best chance to blow it to hell, when it's moving away from us.''

''So, now we wait?'' the corporal asked.

"Yes."

"Hate waiting," the man grumbled.

The sergeant blew a smoke ring at the open doorway. "Trust me, you'd hate dying a lot more."

IN THE WESTERN courtyard, a sergeant slashed with his sword, cutting loose a team of mules from a gunnery carriage. Working like slaves, guards struggled to position the antique muzzle loader on the cobblestone courtyard before the huge iron gate. Mostly salvaged from museums and parade grounds, the predark weapons had each been painstakingly rebuilt to function fully and had slain many bikers and muties over the years. There were already forty assorted cannon placed in a broad semicircle in the courtyard, teams of frantic gunners preparing for the battle.

More and more wags constantly arrived, carrying shot and powder. When unloaded, the wags were rolled into position and toppled onto their sides in front of the cannons to hide them from direct sight, hopefully fooling the Beast for a few precious seconds until the fuses could be lit. Along the rooftops of buildings, in every window and doorway, swarms of guards with long blasters were ready to give cover fire and confuse the tank with multiple targets.

"In position and loaded, sir," a corporal announced, sweat pouring off the man in spite of the chill night air.

"Good. Wait for my command," the lieutenant replied, slamming a clip into his rebuilt AK-47. "And shoot any man you even think is lighting a fuse early."

"Sir?"

"We only get one chance at this," the sec man stated grimly. "One chance. We stop the Beast here or die trying."

JOSTLING THROUGH the plowed farmlands surrounding the odd stone fortress, the Ranger was apprehensive that nobody had attacked while it was crossing the open fields. Logic dictated only two possibilities: the defenders of the enemy had fled, or much more likely, they were gathering their forces for an ambush.

There was no sign of a gate or door in the tall granite wall, but that was to be expected. Any openings would be on the other side of the stout barrier, where an invader would have to pass more traps and weapons before reaching the portal. And this wall would be much more trouble than the wooden fence. The layers of granite blocks forming the six-yard-tall barrier were so dense that its sensors couldn't properly register the thickness. The Ranger guessed at a thickness of six feet, but it could be a lot more. And while its polycyclic pulse cannon could blast its way through anything given enough time, it would be at a cost of mobility and power unwise to expend at the present moment. Although its attackers were using primitive weapons, the tank had already sustained minor damage, and it would be unwise to risk further disablement that could jeopardize the mission. General order 147J/82: Unless the proper authorization codes were issued, anyone or anything attacking or escaping from the redoubt was to be terminated with extreme prejudice at all cost. There was no other option for the robotic Ranger. It would pursue the invaders forever.

The radio signal from the wheeled tank it was pursuing was still coming from ground level, roughly in the middle of the approaching compound. Since there was no obvious superior choice of direction, the Ranger arbitrarily headed to the left and began circling, searching for the entrance, pausing only for a moment to pulse its laser at the top of the tallest tower to remove any possible sentries or video cameras from observing its progress.

A SCREAMING MAN on fire plummeted past the window of the Citadel, distracting the heirs from their work for only an instant. Glancing into the courtyard, Amanda noted the guards scurrying about, dragging a single massive cannon in front of the Citadel.

Everywhere else, slaves were running amok, dashing back and forth, carrying bundles of worthless possessions or their wretched children, totally out of control. For a split instant, the lady ward thought she saw Ryan in the crowd, but then he was gone. She stepped away and closed the shutters. She had to have been mistaken.

"And you said the cannons had no effect?" Amanda demanded, returning to the conversation.

Standing by the map-covered table, McGregory spread his arms. "None that we could see, my lady. There might have been internal damage, but there's no way for us to know."

"How far away is it?" Richard asked.

"About ten minutes."

"Dearest brother," Amanda began sweetly, "I suggest we use the rest of the bazookas and LAWs, including those from the outlanders' vehicle."

He questioned her. "Take the missiles from the launch pods also?"

"No. Those can't be fired by hand. Just the light antitank weapons, and those fiery things."

"The HAFLAs," he said explained curtly.

She smiled, knowing how much he enjoyed correcting other people. "Those are the things. The HAFLAs."

"Granted," Richard said. "Captain, have sec men get them from the armory. Not slaves, mind you, guards. The ones you most trust. And you are in charge of the matter."

McGregory smiled in relief. "At once, my lord! Certainly!" He hurried from the room, the attending slaves parting before him as if he carried disease.

"And perhaps we should prepare the outlander tank for our departure," Amanda added, moving closer to her sibling.

Bending over the table, Richard partially turned. "Leave our ancestral home?"

"Prepare to leave, darling," she corrected, lightly resting a warm hand on his bare arm. "Purely as a precaution."

"Never!" he spit, shaking her off. "I'd rather die than betray our beloved father."

Amanda took a stance. "And what if the slaves use this opportunity to start a rebellion?"

He went back to studying the table. "The guards will slaughter them."

"While fighting the Beast at the same time?"

Richard moved more cannon to the front gates. "Then we'll use the gas."

"Of course. But later on—"

"Not later, now. Right now."

She blanched. "What?"

"I will immediately release the sleep gas outside the stone wall," he stated. "The slaves outside will fall asleep, but that doesn't matter. They won't be assisting in the defense of the ville anyway."

"Their bodies will line the roads," she said, thinking aloud. "Perhaps slow the advance of the Beast. Legend says it won't kill if you surrender. This could work.... No, it won't. Have you forgotten the guards with the Vulcan? If they fall asleep, they can't operate the gun!"

"I gave them the antidote," Richard said, shifting the position of an oversized brass cartridge outside the eastern section of the stone wall.

"Before this trouble began?"

"Yes. Anticipation is the cornerstone of victory."

Amanda watched her brother for a long time before speaking. "Most wise," she purred, pressing her soft body against him. "Father would be proud."

Richard moved another piece inside the Citadel and smiled briefly. "How nice of you to say so, sweet sister."

STAYING IN THE SHADOWS of a tack shop, Ryan and the companions watched the growing bedlam on the streets of Novaville, waiting for an opportunity to move unnoticed. But it wasn't forthcoming. Slaves dashed about in every conceivable stage of dress.

People were screaming. A glass window was smashed. Far off, a cannon boomed and a bell started to clang. A coal oil lantern was smashed, setting a cottage on fire. At the smell of the smoke, horses stampeded from a corral. A group of rushing sec men turned a corner, and a gang of prisoners in chains jumped them, using the iron links to strangle the guards to death. Fistfights were everywhere, blasters spoke constantly and a weeping woman with a bullwhip was lashing at anybody near her.

Crouched under a window, Ryan frowned at the madness. "This is getting worse," he observed. "Not slowing down."

"Good," Jak drawled, peeking out the door crack. "Hides us from heirs."

"Unless a random slug blows off your head," Krysty pointed out. "But Ryan's right. This has become a full-blown rebellion, not just a simple uprising."

"Lisa and her people must be doing their job," Mildred said, pouring some water from a canteen into her hand and then rubbing it on Shard's face. "Whoever the invaders are, they must be giving the sec men a hard fight."

"D-death to the heirs..." Shard whispered, sitting limply in a wooden chair.

"The ward won't allow this to go on much longer," Ryan said, pulling the vial from his pocket. He thumbed off the stopper and took a sip of the milky fluid. It tasted sweet at first, then burned its way down his throat like undercooked moonshine whiskey. Trying not to gag, he passed it around and everybody forced themselves to take a sip.

"Ghastly," Doc rumbled. The last in line, he tossed away the empty vial. "If that does not kill us, nothing will."

"Agreed," Ryan scowled, scouring his mouth with his tongue. He wanted to hawk and spit so bad it was an ache within him, but he knew better than to waste a single drop of the sleep gas antidote. "So let's move. And leave the crossbows here. We don't need silence anymore."

Krysty, Dean and Mildred divested themselves of the cumbersome weapons along with the quivers of arrows. Then, pushing open the door with the barrel of his Steyr, Ryan took the point. The rest followed him into the street, Doc with Shard in his arms, J.B. and Mildred giving them protective cover. At the sight of the weapons, dashing slaves arched around them, some reversing course and running away in the other direction.

Then a ragged man charged into view carrying a melted rifle in a blistered hand. "The Beast is here!" he shouted, waving the steaming blaster stub. "It's at the wall! Run for your lives! The Beast is here!"

Ryan stared hostilely at the blind guard as he stumbled off into the chaotic throng.

"He said 'the Beast,'" Dean said hesitantly. "Could it be?"

Her hair tightly curled, Krysty nodded dumbly.

"Impossible," Mildred stated. "After we dropped a building on it? It must be another tank."

"Let's not stick around and find out," Ryan said, grimacing. "Double time, people. Shard, which way?"

The wounded man pointed. In a two-on-two cover formation, the companions moved through the me-lee, avoiding conflict with the slaves whenever pos-sible, and chilling any sec men who came their way. Soon the stink of a dog kennel filled their nostrils, and Shard directed them to the right, past a behead-ing block, and then to the left.

"Square one," J.B. growled, his hands tightening on the grip of his Uzi.

The canvas tent was exactly where they remem-bered, but even if they had been interested in check-ing it, slaves had torn the material and they could see nothing was under the canvas but gas canisters and still forms lying on the ground.

The five-story tower dominated the courtyard, the gallows to one side, the bloodstained crosses to the other. A large garage door was partially hidden by ivy, its windows covered with plate steel. Two sec men stood guard, both armed with pistols and shot-guns. They constantly swept the crowds with the scatterguns, and shot anybody who dared to get close.

"Take them," Ryan said, leveling the Steyr.

The companions did the same with their blasters, and on Ryan's command cut loose at the same time. The guards were slammed back against the door, spouting blood in a dozen different spots. The older guard managed to fire his shotgun once, and then collapsed onto the street. A slave snatched it from his grip and raced away, whooping and howling, brandishing it like a trophy of war.

Hitting the wall alongside the door, Dean stood

guard while J.B. took the keys from a guard's belt and unlocked the door.

The room was cavernous, covering the whole ground floor of the tower. The floor was stained with the grease and oil from a hundred vehicles, the walls lined with shelves and stacks of boxes, the entire place brightly illuminated by electric lights. But none of that mattered when they saw what was prominently sitting in the middle of the floor.

"By the Three Kennedys!" Doc roared, clutching Shard so tight the man whimpered in pain.

It was Leviathan, intact and undamaged, glistening as if washed and waxed, surrounded by slaves busy removing the very last tire.

Chapter Twenty

In a hundred different locations outside the stone wall, a soft hissing began to sound from the ground. Fleeing slaves toppled over in piles, fell down stairs and plummeted to their deaths from the scaffolding in the mine. Sec men rolled off horses, and officers tumbled from moving motorcycles, many of them mangling limbs and wheels with grisly results. In less than a minute, a profound silence encircled the ville, punctuated only by the crackle of small fires, labored breathing and the soft whoosh of distant rockets launching from the top of the Citadel toward the predark war machine battering at the massive iron gate.

IN THE GARAGE, J.B. raised his shotgun and fired a round into the air. "Put those tires back on!" he shouted. The kneeling slaves froze at the booming discharge, then hurried to do as they were ordered.

"Look out!" Krysty cried.

J.B. turned as a snapping whip wrapped its leathery length around his gun barrel and the blaster was painfully yanked from his grip. He heard his hand crack, and saw his index finger was bent backward into an unnatural angle. He clumsily raised the Uzi.

Laughing, Eugene snaked the whip around his

obese form and lashed out again, entwining the leather around J.B.'s throat. Turning purple, the Armorer clawed at his neck, gasping for breath.

Ryan swung the SSG-70 in a short arc, pointing the big-bore barrel toward the sneering eunuch.

"Shoot me," Eugene chortled, his bloated belly jiggling obscenely, "and your man dies! Now drop your weapons and surrender!"

A pistol cracked, and the whip was torn from the eunuch's grip in a spray of bones and blood. He stumbled backward, screaming in pain and clutching his shattered hand when the Steyr boomed. Eugene flew backward, his face no longer whole.

In a flurry of motion, Mildred was at J.B.'s side, along with Jak, one of his many knives cutting the man loose. Doc stared down at the man cradled in his arms, and the smoking pistol peeking out from his bloody bandages.

"Dead?" Shard asked softly.

"As a doornail," Ryan replied, jacking in a fresh round. "Good shooting."

He smiled weakly. "No problem."

Then a wail came from behind the stack of boxes along the wall.

"Master?" a man asked, walking over to the faceless corpse. The blood on the concrete was spreading into a pool.

"He shot the master," a woman accused, pointing at the companions.

"Kill them!" another shrieked. "Kill them all!" And the people charged, shooting weapons, a pack of snarling dogs at their heels.

"Take cover!" Ryan shouted, dropping into a

crouch. The rest of the companions dived into combat positions, their blasters firing steadily.

THE WESTERN GATE WAS glowing a dull red, sending off waves of heat, and a terrible glare shone from the other side brighter than the sun.

Shielding their faces, the sec men on the battlements fired their blasters blindly between the stone turrets, not willing to risk losing their sight by looking directly at the Beast. Staves were shoved into pry holes, and men strained to tip over vats of boiling coal oil. The fluid sloshed over the rim of the vats and hundreds of gallons rushed down fluted gullies to pour over the war machine below. The heat of the laser cannon ignited the oil and the Beast was engulfed in a fireball. More oil was poured down, while the guards steadily fired their blasters and tossed what few grens and plastique they had.

STANDING ON THE ROOF of the Citadel, a lieutenant grimaced at the sight. It was impossible to see through the flames, but the fact that the gate continued to grow hotter was a strong indication their weapons were having little effect on the predark monster. It was yellow-hot now, glowing like a furnace. Soon it would reach white-hot, then soften and melt.

"Corporal of the guards!" he yelled.

Lowering his binocs, a man hurried over to the officer. "Yes, sir?"

"To hell with waiting. Hit the bastard thing with everything we have!"

"But sir, the deputy ward ordered us—"

"Fuck that jackass, and his bitch sister!" the officer stormed, placing a hand on his holstered blaster. "Hit it now! With everything! And that is a direct order."

The corporal saluted and raced to obey, but filed away the comments for future consideration.

FROM THE PARAPETS, a bugle sounded a clarion call, and men rushed to obey. It sounded once more, holding the last note for a good while, and as it died, the whole wall jumped as explosive charges removed the hinges of the gate and the sizzling iron portal thunderously dropped to the ground.

The Beast charged out of the inferno, its laser pulsing at anything that moved. A flimsy barricade of overturned wags barred its path, and the tank lumbered forward to crash through when the radar began to beep wildly in warning. But it was too late.

"Fire!" the sergeant screamed, brandishing a torch like a rifle.

The short fuses of the hidden cannon were lit. They weren't the dainty field guns hidden among the slave cottages, but garrison guns, the bulwark of the ville's armada. These monsters needed four horses to move them, took a charge of ten full pounds of black powder and fired cold-iron balls so enormous it took two strong men to lift them into the muzzle. When they spoke, the world trembled.

At point-blank range, the titanic cannons roared. Ragged pieces broke off the angular hull of the Beast with a screech of tortured metal, and the laser winked out.

Victorious cries came from the amassed troops,

and again the cannons vomited flame and iron. Masked by the thick swirling smoke, the fiery daggers of the discharges reached out to starkly silhouette the Beast. The bugle sounded a brief tone, and more troops joined the fight, firing their blasters from the battlements. Wet nimrods were rammed down hot maws to extinguish sparks, barrels were packed to the bursting point and the cannons roared, their carriages leaping from the cobblestones by the force of the discharge. Rockets streaked in from every direction adding to the hellstorm, blasters never stopped, the dull thud of grens mixed with the sharp whomp of plastique and huge arrows from the gigantic arbalests disappeared into the roiling smoke.

Then the fiery lance of a LAW streaked in from atop the Citadel, closely followed by the four whispering black birds of the HAFLA, the deadly missiles leaving contrails in the foggy air. The volley became a barrage, a fusillade, a bombardment.

The destruction seemed to go on forever, the lake of smoke swamping over the guards high on the stone wall. No longer able to see where to point their weapons, the sec men held their breath and waited, weapons at the ready. Nothing seemed to be moving in the dense cloud of discharge fumes. The gray smoke was slowly thinning, but it would take minutes before they would know the results of their trap.

STEPPING OVER the bleeding bodies of men and dogs, Ryan walked to Leviathan and rapped on the side of the tank with the butt of his rifle. ''It's over," he announced loudly. "Come out and finish putting the tires back on."

Doc bent and spoke to the people huddled under the vehicle. "You will not be harmed," he rumbled, using a polite, but firm tone. "We are on your side. Just fix the tank, then you can run away if you wish."

Several of the cowering slaves remained where they were, unsure of what to do. However, the rest crawled out from under the vehicle and slowly started to assemble the wheels, constantly glancing over their shoulders at the armed people standing around them. Reloading her pistol, Krysty surveyed the garage with a practiced eye, searching for any more possible trouble spots, when she stopped and carefully walked over to a dead man. The ground was coated with brass cartridges from the Uzi, and walking was a tricky matter.

"Will you look at this," she stated, and took the revolver from his warm hand. "I'll be damned."

"Found something?" Mildred asked, pocketing her spent shells and loading in fresh rounds.

The redhead nodded. "This is the exact same type of blaster I lost in the city. Smith & Wesson Model 640, .38-caliber revolver, nickel-plated, adjustable sights, J style frame, combat trigger." She searched the man for bullets, finding the unexpected bounty of an untouched box. Then she solemnly laid the Ruger on his gaping chest in exchange.

"Thank you," Krysty said, hefting the revolver. "The balance is perfect, not nose heavy like that blasted Ruger."

"Dirty," Jak said, wrinkling his nose as if the weapon smelled.

Krysty smiled. "So it'll take me a while to clean properly. Worth it. Fits in my palm like it belongs there."

"At last your arm is complete," Doc muttered sardonically, wiping some blood off his swordstick. "My compliments, Sweeney, on the good fortune."

Asking a silent question, Krysty looked at Mildred, who shrugged in response. "I think it's from an old play," she said.

"I'm going to check inside," J.B. said, walking among the dead. "Make sure everything is working."

"Watch for traps," Ryan warned, never taking his vision off the slaves. "You there, tighten the nut more."

The slave nodded and did as requested.

"Fellow slaves, hear me!" Shard said, sitting against a packing crate, bullet holes forming a pattern around him in the battered wooden slats. "When you are done, you can all follow us out of here to freedom. These aren't the new masters, but your liberators!"

"The guards also have blasters," a brave soul pointed out.

Shard laughed in scorn. "And who would dare to try and stop Leviathan, killer of the Beast!"

The workers whispered that among themselves like a litany and the work proceeded faster.

"How many tires do we need to move?" Dean asked, joining his father.

Ryan scowled. "At least six. But we better have

eight, though, just to be safe. The rest we can throw in back and put on when we get the chance.''

Father and son watched the work proceed, and the lug nuts of the eighth tire were being tightened when J.B. popped into view from the rear doors of Leviathan and whistled sharply. The companions hurried over curiously.

As the interior of the tank came into view they gasped in shock. The inside of the war machine was completely different. Velvet drapes lined the armored walls, hiding the lockers and supply racks. The floor was cushioned with a soft carpet, the chairs more resembled red velvet thrones and red tassels dangled from damn near everything.

''Check the console.'' J.B. laughed. ''They got gold leaf and silver embellishing the bastard controls!''

''Gaudy house,'' Jak said, a wry smile on his face.

''I wouldn't know, son,'' Doc intoned. ''I have never been to anyplace as nice as this. Other than the Grand Hotel in Vermont.''

''Hey!'' J.B. called. ''Look here! The ammo bins for the 75 mm recoilless rifles are packed to the brim.''

''Full here,'' Jak added, checking the ammo boxes of the port .50-caliber machine gun.

Dean rushed to the rear. ''So are the 40 mm rapidfires!''

''They rebuilt and reloaded everything,'' Ryan said in wry amusement. ''Must have been planning on using it as their private war wag.''

Mildred laughed. "We should thank them for the gifts before we leave."

"If we have missiles again," Krysty said, trying to activate the launch controls, "then we can put a couple of these babies into the Citadel." She fumbled with the switches, but couldn't get a response. "Somebody start the engines, I want to get a reading on these."

Ryan moved for the driver's seat, checking for traps first, but the chair and dashboard were clean.

"We have a problem back here," Doc announced, looking inside a cabinet. "All of the MRE food packs are gone."

"What did the heirs replace them with?" Mildred asked, sounding concerned. "Roast quail? Caviar?"

He closed the door. "Nothing. The locker is empty."

"That's trouble," Dean said, his stomach giving a soft rumble. He never seemed to be able to get enough to eat these days.

"Rather have bullets than food any day," J.B. said, toying with a golden tassel attached to a trigger assembly. "Hope they didn't mess with the feeder mechanisms."

"Damn fools," Doc agreed dourly. "You double-check the guns, I'll go check on Shard and the Pep Boys."

Cursing softly, Ryan tried again to start the engines, but nothing happened. "Something's wrong," he stated. "We got no power to the diesels."

"I'll check," J.B. stated, and, removing a hatch, he wiggled under the console. Tense minutes passed as he muttered to himself and twisted uncooperative wires.

"Well?" Ryan demanded as the Armorer crawled back into view.

"Try it now," J.B. suggested, dusting off his hands.

Experimentally, Ryan pulled the choke and pushed the start button. Instantly the big engines roared into life, the console coming alive with indicators and quivering dials.

"We have missiles," Krysty announced, tapping an indicator. "So what was the problem?"

"The fuse to the ignition was gone," J.B. replied, taking a seat at the starboard .50-caliber machine gun. "No problem. These things always have spares in a plastic box nearby. Don't want to get trapped in the middle of a battle because of a lousy piece of plastic."

"We got eight," Doc said, tossing a tire into the vehicle. "Help me get these on board."

Dean and Jak jumped to assist in the task, while J.B. and Krysty kept watch at the blasterports.

With the aid of Mildred, Shard carefully climbed inside the craft, moving as if his bones were made of glass. He could only stare about the tank in awe. The physician tenderly directed him to a wall seat and helped the man operate the safety belt.

"It's like a dream," he whispered. "Truly, you are the parole board."

"Not quite," Ryan said, starting the diesels. Under the floor boards, the twin power plants rumbled in barely restrained fury, softly vibrating the entire vehicle.

Tires bounded into the tank through the back doors, the men grunting from the exertion.

"Ready," Doc announced, slamming shut the rear doors and shoving home the lock.

"Eight?" Cawdor asked.

"Check. Two at each corner, one behind the other."

"Good." Ryan shifted gears. "J.B., man the left machine gun, Jak take the right. Dean and Doc, rear rapidfires. Krysty, load the recoilless rifles with AP shells. Mildred, watch over Shard. We don't want those wounds opening up again."

Everybody moved with a purpose. Spinning the steering wheel, Ryan directed Leviathan around in a halting circle until it faced the garage doors. Thick chains were wrapped around iron stanchions, locking the aluminum doors firmly in place. Ryan put the pedal to the metal and the tank crashed through the thin plating into smoky night.

"Is it safe to be on the streets like this?" Shard asked, sounding worried. "What about the guards? The ward and his heirs? Surely they'll want revenge for killing Eugene and reclaiming the—" he paused and nearly smiled "—our tank."

"As long as the sec men are busy fighting the invaders," Ryan said, checking the radar screen which was clear, "they won't have any chance to bother with us."

J.B. added, "The guys trying to get in are always a bigger concern than the folks trying to get out."

Shard nodded at the wisdom.

"Can't storm the front gate," Krysty said, checking the rearview mirror. "That's probably where the main fight is. We can blow a hole through the wall at any point with the missiles, but I sure hate to use them up.''

"Go down that street," Shard said, pointing to the right. "I know of a private escape tunnel for the ward.''

"Anybody else know?" Ryan asked sharply.

"The door is hidden." Then he frowned. "But I don't know how to unlock it.''

"Just show me where," Ryan said grimly, working the clutch and gears. "I'll get us in.''

As Leviathan rolled away into the night, the waiting slaves broke ranks and looted the bodies of clothing and weapons. Dashing into the streets, the armed slaves separated to spread the word of the coming freedom.

WITHIN THE BANK of smoke masking the western gate, a faint shape could be seen in the thinning haze. The updraft caused by the glowing gate was forming a breeze that was quickly dissipating the discharge fumes of the half-score cannons.

Some of the troops tried to dart into the smoke for a better look, but quickly backed out, hacking and gasping for breath.

"It lives!" a man screamed, running out with both hands outstretched, clawing the air, his eyes dead-white orbs of cooked flesh. There was a flash of light and the man vaporized.

A blazing rod of destruction, the laser swept the yard at chest height, sec men, gunners and cannon all disappearing in its vitriolic energy beam.

The guards not slain in the first sweep threw away

their weapons and fled. Its armor buckled and battered, leaking hydraulic fluid and oil, the Beast rolled after them, crushing the remains of the mighty cannons under its armored treads, vaporizing the swift and blinding any who dared to glance its way.

Then the machine paused, spying a tall building of stone and brick standing prominently within the fortress. The Beast traversed its turret and concentrated its polycyclic laser on the base to remove a potential danger.

A TREMOR SHOOK the Citadel, the windows cracking, suits of armor falling from their wall niches to break apart on the floor in noisy crashes. Whimpering slaves huddled under the map table.

"It's melting the foundation," Richard cried, righting himself as the floor titled to a greater angle.

"We have lost a battle, not the war," Amanda said, grabbing her holster and blaster, heading for the door. "Summon the guards! We'll continue the fight from the tower!"

Richard turned, spitting in rage. "And leave Father alone with the rabble?"

"You fool," she screamed furiously. "Father is dead!"

"What?" he whispered, backing away from her madness.

"Dead! You idiot! Dead. Has been for years. I killed him myself when he refused to make me his queen! Even after I gave him a son!"

"Lies, all lies," he started, then saw the mocking triumph in her face, the face that looked so much like his own.

"You bitch!" the deputy ward roared, wildly firing his pistol.

Lady Ward Amanda Coultier of Novaville fell to the floor, hugging her stomach, holding in a spill of intestines. "Fool," she croaked, blood running from her mouth. "We could have…ruled the world… together…."

One final shot resounded in the audience room stopping any further traitorous words from the madwoman.

Going to his chair, the deputy ward ripped off the seat cover, exposing a red lever. Wrapping both hands about the switch, he pulled it upward until there was a metallic crack and the lever broke away clean.

"There's no stopping it now," he said, slumping to his knees. "We're dead, they're dead. Everybody is dead."

DEEP UNDER THE Citadel, the antiriot gas of the predark wardens erupted from its storage container as the primary seal was permanently ruptured. Following the path of least resistance, the gas poured through a maze of pipes hundreds of years old, and thousands of yards long, hissing into every street, every building. The vapor wafted along the ground, constantly rising higher, cresting doorsills, then windows. A thousand cubic yards of chemicals swirled into the smoky atmosphere of the ville unnoticed until it was far too late.

Slaves toppled to the floor and out windows, sec men dropped as the gas floated past the flaming ruin of the barricade, down the raised concrete embankment and out into the fields. Galloping horses shattered legs as they were engulfed, snarling dogs became drowsy then somnolent, the wounded and the dying mercifully ceased their screaming, wrapped in the anesthetic arms of the soporific.

Lisa and Troy collapsed trying to gain entrance into the armory. Clifford became insensible chained to the wall of a jail cell. David and Kathy succumbed firing their stolen weapons at escaping sec men. Deputy Ward Richard went limp at the foot of his gilded chair, the Citadel crashing down around him, as the very rock it was built upon dissolved.

Men, women, children, young or old, whether they quietly accepted their fate or cried in fear, fired their weapons or hid under furniture, it made no difference. Some held their breath, while others formed crude masks from wet clothing, but these only offered the briefest of respites. Eventually, the gas seeped into their pores and they were unconscious. Only minutes after the gas release, dead silence filled the ville, from the leaning tower to the still burning timbers of the palisade.

Then from out of the swirling smoke and gas came the Ranger, its black angular form moving like a nightmare through the fiery desolation. Sleeping people lined the streets, but the machine moved ever onward, uncaring of the bloody carnage the armored treads left in its wake. It was very near to the source of the enemy radio signal, and getting closer.

Chapter Twenty-One

Violently, the disguised door to the secret passage in the stone wall exploded across the intersection, showering the sec men in the brothel with hot shrapnel. Caught by surprise, they wasted precious seconds recovering and by then Leviathan was in the street and moving away. Holding torches aloft to spread the light, guards ran into the night. Some cursed, some knelt and fired their blasters.

"Attack!" screamed the sergeant standing in the doorway, blood trickling from an ugly gash in his cheek.

The Vulcan minigun awoke with a roar, unleashing a solid stream of rounds that stitched a line of black holes along the granite wall and across the rear end of Leviathan.

THERE WAS a double bang, and two holes appeared in the side of the tank.

"Damn!" Dean cried in shock. Then he jerked about and sure enough there were two exit holes in the flapping wall tapestry and the hull behind.

Doc angled the vented barrel of his weapon and tripped the rear 40 mm rapidfires. He hosed the suspect building with high-explosive death. Both sides of the street erupted in a series of fiery detonations, and the deadly buzz of the Vulcan stopped, replaced with screams of pain.

"Keep going," Doc shouted, working the bolt to clear a jam. A brass shell popped out of the breech and hit the carpet. "They will not bother us again."

"Good," Ryan said, scrutinizing the buildings they passed for any furtive movements. The area seemed to be deserted. Then he noticed the bodies sprawled in doorways and out windows. "They gassed the whole place!"

"Heirs," Jak growled menacingly, as if he were about to hawk and spit.

Experimentally, Mildred took in a deep breath from the breeze coming through her blasterport. "Not affecting us," she said. "That antidote must work."

"What did they hit us with?" Dean asked, sticking a finger out the hole in the composite armor.

"Might have been depleted uranium rounds," J.B. said, nesting his glasses onto his nose with a finger. "Don't know exactly what the stuff is, but it's hellishly good armor, and the only thing that can get through it is DU slugs."

"We got that?" Jak asked, rapping the hull.

"Hell, no. Wish we did."

"Could that be what the Ranger was covered with?" Ryan asked, bumping over rubbish in the road. He was trying to avoid as much of the debris as he could, but the stuff was everywhere. They had only eight tires and losing one now could be deadly.

"Sure," the Armorer said. "Why not?"

Zeroing the trim on the front 75 mm rifles, Krysty frowned. "Then it might still be functional."

"That sec man did say 'the Beast,'" Mildred added nervously, "and that's their term for the robot tank."

"Hold on," Ryan said in a whip-crack tone, and he slammed his foot on the gas pedal. Leviathan dramatically increased in speed and noise. "Shard, fastest way out of here!"

Groaning with the effort, the man lurched from his seat and staggered across the tank to grab the back of the driver's seat.

"Take that corner," Shard replied, pointing. "No, that one, sir, and follow the small road. It ends at the palisade. There used to be a gate once, long ago. But it's been walled over."

"Another secret door?" Ryan asked, switching on the powerful headlights. This far into the slave quarters, there were few lanterns hanging from posts on corners. It was getting more and more difficult for him to avoid the unconscious people strewed in the streets.

"Not secret," Shard answered. "Useless."

Downshifting, Ryan took the corner on four wheels, rubber screeching. "Explain," he snapped.

"The road on the other side leads to nowhere." Shard paused in thought. "Or so we have been told."

J.B. snorted. "Wouldn't trust that blond bitch if she said the knives were sharp."

MOVING. THE RADIO signal was moving to the southeast.

Locking a tread, the Ranger careened in a new direction and took off around a stone tower with a broken garage door. The thin metal stripping was bent outward, and the main computer reasoned this was where the enemy tank had been hidden. Pivoting, the front video cameras showed the garage was full of munitions and mechanical equipment, a perfect location for its own repairs for the damage incurred by the attacks. Hydraulics were at fifty percent normal, oil pressure was near critical, but still at functional levels. Only one video camera remained, and the motion detectors no longer existed. But the laser was fully operational and that was what mattered.

THE BARRACKS BUSTLED with activity. Every sec man who took the antidote had gathered here, the farthest point in the palisade away from the approaching Beast. All had blasters, and most had been smart enough to grab food or ammo. The good times were over here. The heirs were dead, and they were leaving.

Then the door burst open and a guard backed into the room, staring into the street as if hell itself had appeared. A cold night wind blew into the barracks, whipping clothes and extinguishing candles. Only the crackling fire in the hearth was undisturbed.

"Sweet Jesus!" the guard cried, colliding with a table. Bottles and mugs went flying, adding to the litter on the dirty floorboards. "It... It's..."

"What? It's what, you triple-stupe fool?" a corporal demanded, stuffing cans of food into a sack by the light of a lantern. He wore a bandolier of ammo slung across his chest, and two holstered automatics. "More guards? Some slaves?"

"The Beast!" the guard screamed, cowering in a corner and covering his face with both hands. "Don't look at it! You'll go blind!"

"THERE!" SHARD GESTURED, pointing straight ahead at a two-story house with bars on the windows and motorcycles parked in front. The building was crawling with sec men, dropping boxes of supplies, yelling orders and scrambling for weapons.

"There?" Krysty asked in disbelief, leaning forward in her chair. The headlights of Leviathan bathed the entire area with brilliant white light, dimming the coal oil lanterns to merely reddish points.

"Yes."

"The guards' barracks?"

"Good way to block a hole," Ryan said, steering around the still form of horse. "Looks like the place is only made out of pine boards. Don't waste a missile."

"No problem," the redhead agreed as she pulled the lever and the vehicle bucked as the twin 75 mm rifles fired in unison.

The whole building blew into pieces, exposing the wooden barrier beyond. Moist green moss-coated areas, and a piece of the second floor yet clung to the palisade, loose boards dropping like autumn leaves. But a ten-yard section reaching to the ground was lighter in color than the rest, and Krysty oriented the recoilless rifles there. They volleyed again, and the patch in the palisades simply disintegrated under the assault.

Crunching over rubble, the tank bucked through the jagged hole. Breaking timbers loudly scraped across their hull. The sideview mirror snapped off. Splinters sprayed in through the blasterports, somebody howled in agony underneath the floor, then they were through and moving fast.

A two-lane asphalt road stretched out before them, the cracked surface disappearing into the trees. Krysty lowered the rifles and fired a third time. Spewing gouts of rock and dirt, the trees were uprooted, but stayed standing, their limbs intertwined through decades of growth.

Pumping the clutch, Ryan hit the gas and Leviathan rammed into the forest, branches and bird nests smashing on the protective ironwork grid over the front windshield. The tank plowed out of the trees and instantly dropped down a steep incline, going straight into a river, the force slamming everybody into the seats. Water sprayed skyward from their arrival, sending a tidal wave across the river that sloshed onto the asphalt road on the far bank.

The advance of Leviathan noticeably slowed, and Ryan downshifted to account for the loss of traction from the mud.

"Seal the ports!" he ordered, hitting the wiper blades and clearing the windshield. "Don't know how deep this goes. We got a snorkel, but I don't know if this thing is really waterproof."

"Now is no time to find out," Mildred warned, watching the surface of the stream climb higher and higher toward the windows.

Something on the console beeped suddenly, and Krysty stared at the circular screen, puzzled for a moment. "Sonar?" she said aloud.

Rising from the dark waters, a horrible segmented

creature appeared, the many mouths of its three mis-shapen heads snarling and hissing.

Ryan hit the brakes, as Krysty triggered the left 75 mm rifle. The HE round caught the mutie in the chest, blowing open its chest in a grisly rain. Reeling from the strike, writhing in pain, the aquatic mutie thrashed about as it slithered beneath the turbulent waters.

"River snake," Shard said, watching a gobbet of flesh slither off the window leaving a slimy trail. "Didn't think they existed anymore. Haven't heard of them for years."

"Hope there's not too many more," Ryan said, grinding gears and putting the tank into motion. "Wasted two shells on something we can't even eat."

The water level continued to rise to a dangerous level, then blessedly receded and the vehicle lurched as the front wheels encountered asphalt again lumbering onto the road.

"Made it." Mildred sighed.

The radar beeped.

Muttering a fast prayer, Krysty checked the glowing green screen. There was a big blip directly behind them, heading their way, slow but steady.

"The Ranger is back," she called out. "Range... mile and a half, mebbe less."

"Any chance we can lock a missile onto the radar signal, and fire them at the thing?" Dean asked hopefully, holding a stanchion with grim determination.

"Mebbe this war wag can," his father replied, flicking the wipers again, "but we've never had enough time to study the controls well enough. Running is our best bet.''

The companions held on tight as the output of the engines rose to a mechanical roar, and the speedometer needle hit the red line. Trees and brush flashed past in the darkness, the bouncing headlights making the road surface barely discernible. Occasionally they collided with something, weeds and grass having grown out of the ancient cracks in a natural carpet of greenery. But Leviathan plowed through everything in its blind haste to escape, bulldozing aside hedges to unexpectedly reach salvation.

''It's a bridge!'' J.B. cried. ''Dark night, now we're cooking!''

''Mebbe,'' Ryan said, grinding gears and hitting the brakes to slow their speed.

Fully illuminated in the headlights, the box girder assembly was covered with vines, moss and general corrosion. Its age was indeterminate, as was its structural integrity.

''Think it can it take our weight?'' Mildred asked, trying not to hold her breath.

''Two thousand yards,'' Krysty announced, intently watching the beeping radar screen.

Ryan shifted into low. ''Let's find out.''

At a slow creep, Leviathan gently rolled onto the bridge. The struts groaned as the front tires put their full weight on the roadway, and Ryan slowed. When nothing adverse occurred, he started again, moving even more cautiously. A ghostly wind blew over the tank, moaning softly, and as they reached the middle span the steel girders began to sway slightly under their tonnage. Cresting low on the horizon, a silvery moon flooded the valley with unearthly light. Through the windows and blasterports, the companions could see a tiny thread of sparkling blue stretching along the distant valley floor.

"This is a gorge, not a valley," Mildred said, touching her heart. The physician disliked heights, but had no intention of showing her fear.

"How deep do you think it is?" Dean asked, craning to get a better look.

"Thousand feet, or so."

"Spam in can." Jak frowned.

"I beg your pardon?" Doc said curiously.

"It's an old armored cavalry phrase, tank soldiers actually, that precisely covers this situation," Mildred explained, obviously pleased to know something the time traveler didn't. She mashed two palms together in a smack. "Spam in a can."

"How graphic," he said, returning his attention to the world outside.

"At least there's no way the Ranger can follow us," J.B. stated, removing his fedora and wiping the brim with a handkerchief. "It's too big and too heavy."

"Fifteen hundred," Krysty said, hunched over the screen as if trying to glean additional information by sheer force of will.

His hands white-knuckled on the steering wheel, Ryan said nothing, concentrating on not driving them off the side. A lot of the supporting members of the bridge had rusted completely away, and the guardrail was a thing of the past. One wrong move on his part, and they wouldn't have to worry about the Ranger, or anything else, anymore.

As their front wheels reached the other side, everybody sighed in relief.

"Goodbye, bridge," Doc said, tripping the rear submachine guns.

A stuttering stream of shells peppered the bridge, blowing away chunks of steel and greenery.

"Hold it!" Ryan yelled, brakes squealing. "Stop all firing!"

The guns ceased, and Doc turned, wearing a puzzled expression. "What is wrong? Remove the bridge and the Ranger can never follow us."

"Unfortunately we need that bridge intact."

"What for?"

"To leave. This is a dead end."

Abandoning their posts, the companions gathered to look out the front window. Directly ahead was a cul de sac, the road leading into a mountain pass with steeply sloping sides. This once might have been a highway for travelers, but that was aeons ago. Rain and snow had weakened the slopes and the mountainsides had slumped onto the road, dirt and rocks filling in the pass completely.

"That's why they never feared an attack from this direction," Shard said. "Who could make it over such an obstacle?"

"Not us, that's for bastard sure," Ryan stated, checking the side of possible avenues. However, the mountain range rose straight from the gorge. There was no cliff or ledge for them to drive along.

"Don't think we could even make it over that on

foot," J.B. commented. "Too smooth. We'd need climbing gear."

Everybody jumped as Krysty triggered the 75 mm rifle. The shell went deep into the earthen mound blocking the road, and the landslide shook from within, nothing more.

"We're not going to blast our way through, either," she groused, levering out the dead shell. It hit the carpet and sizzled on the material.

"Range," Ryan snapped, undoing his seat harness.

She looked. "Less than a thousand yards."

"We can go back," Doc suggested, the lion's head on his cane peeking between fingers. "Bedamned tank probably only wants Leviathan. It might not even recognize us as suitable targets. We could hide in the bushes and leave on foot after it goes."

"And then how do we get across the gorge to reach the next redoubt?" Mildred demanded hotly. "Fly?"

"Climb."

"A thousand feet? Straight down? We might as well jump."

The beeping on the radar was coming fast, almost a steady tone.

"Spam in can," Jak muttered, snapping the bolt on the big .50-caliber machine gun.

"Can't run, can't hide," J.B. muttered. "Gotta fight."

Striding to the rear of the vehicle, he replaced Dean and prepared the 40 mm rapidfire. "I'll try for the laser again. Doc, back me up."

The old man nodded.

"Thought you said it was pure luck that worked last time?" Dean admonished.

"Got a better plan?" the Armorer snapped.

"Yeah," Ryan stated. Busy in the dim light of the dashboard console, he activated the missile launch controls. "We'll hit it with everything we got. Mildred, see if you can angle a fifty to fire straight backward."

"Okay." The physician grunted, struggling with the rubber antivibration blocks of the breech to align the vented barrel. "It doesn't want to, but yes."

"Jak!" Ryan snapped. "Get the port blaster."

Turning off the interior lights to allow them to see into the darkness outside better, Krysty then killed the keening of the radar.

"It's here," she announced, resting a hand on the forward 75 mm rifles. Pointed toward the earth embankment, they were utterly useless for this fight. "Ryan, give me your SSG-70. I can snipe from the outside."

Grabbing the bolt-action Steyr off the floor, he tossed it to her. "Take Dean with you."

"Why?" the boy demanded suspiciously.

His father faltered at a reply, but everybody knew why. So that somebody might survive the battle.

There was a movement at the side door as it closed.

"Hey, where's Shard!" Mildred asked, glancing around.

"There he is!" Doc said, pointing out the louvered slots of the rear door.

Visible in the headlights reflected off the sides of

the pass, the wounded man was sprinting for the bridge, a bulky satchel strapped to his back.

J.B. checked the floor of the tank, then looked outside again. "He's got my bag of explosives!"

"What's he doing?" Dean demanded. "Running away?"

"No," Jak said, and he touched two fingers to his temple as a salute. "Crazy son of bitch."

"He's trying to save all of our lives," Krysty answered softly. "And I doubted the courage of a slave."

"Free man," Ryan said.

Mildred started for the side door. "We have to stop him!"

J.B. took her arm. "It's too late."

STOPPING IN THE middle of the bridge, Shard crouched amid the churned greenery as the Beast rumbled out of the bushes from the other side of the gorge. Its laser cannon immediately pulsed once, and the missile pod on top of Leviathan was vaporized.

"Twenty," Shard said, dashing out of concealment. He only hoped what Mildred had told him was true, or else this was for nothing.

The Ranger paused before the bridge, as if considering the matter, then rolled onto the structure. The bridge actually bowed under the robotic tank, small girders snapping.

"Fifteen," Shard panted, leaping on the back of the big tank and scrambling across its angular hull. Perfect for deflecting incoming rounds, the irregular hull offered good handholds.

"Ten!" he screamed as electricity crackled over the hull to dislodge the intruder. Limbs shaking, wounds reopening, Shard climbed across the turret, straddling the cannon with his bare legs.

A flurry of metal crabs scurried out of an opening, their razor-sharp pinchers snapping wildly. The Beast was almost off the bridge, Leviathan sitting there in plain sight. The tiny drones covered his body, ripping at his flesh, as Shard reached a count of one and stuffed the bag of explosives directly into the side exhaust vent of the laser cannon as it pulsed again.

For the briefest instant, Shard saw his hand vanish, then blackness took his vision and the whole world erupted.

THE MASSIVE EXPLOSION engulfed the Ranger completely, swamping the bridge in thunderous flames, the supports twisting like warm taffy. Its laser gone, multiple internal systems destroyed, the Ranger tried to backtrack for safety but Leviathan cut loose with its own firepower, aiming at the bridge, not the adamantine hull of the predark tank. Struts snapped, columns buckled. In a deafening cacophony of tortured metal, the bridge broke apart and dropped out of sight, taking the Ranger with it. Rushing to the edge of the broken roadway, the companions watched as the robotic guardian disappeared into the distance.

Ryan snapped binocs to his face and dialed for clarity. The Ranger and the pieces of bridge were still tumbling through the misty air of the gorge when he found them. Then they hit the river simultaneously. The bridge stabbing into the bed like the skeleton of a knife, the Ranger punching through the shallow stream and hitting the granite riverbed like a triphammer. Its hull burst into pieces, the mechanical guts spilling out. Something inside the wreckage detonated, finishing the task, and as the smoke cleared, the river waters were flowing over the impact point and there was nothing to be seen.

"It's dead," Krysty stated, her hair moving constantly from her conflicting feelings. "Kind of hard to believe, isn't it?"

"Yeah," Jak said quietly.

"He saved us," Dean added, his chest tight with emotion, but his face was a stern battle mask.

Krysty walked closer to the boy. She could feel his anger at the loss, his frustration and rage. "It's the cycle of life," she told him gently, "and he died a free man. That was more important to him than anything else."

Dean kicked some pebbles over the edge of the cliff. "I suppose," he muttered, not sounding very convinced.

Keeping a hand on top of his hat to stop it from blowing away, J.B. scrutinized the other side of the gorge. "You know," he said slowly, "we should have grabbed those depleted uranium rounds back at the ville. Those are probably the only thing in existence that could have easily stopped the blasted machine."

"A man stopped the machine," Ryan said, turning his back to the destruction. "Not armament or science. Just a man."

In silence, they walked to Leviathan. The remains of the missile pod on top of the craft were still glowing from the heat of the laser beam. The companions stopped at the open side door, but Ryan continued on to the blast crater in the mound.

He took a handful and rubbed it between his fingers. "Soft dirt. Mebbe we can blow steps into it with the recoilless rifles."

"Not get high enough angle," Jak said, rubbing his cheek.

"Sure can," Dix countered. "We'll use the tire jacks to boost her up a couple of feet."

"It should work," Doc added. "We can brace the undercarriage with the tires not on the wheels."

"Good idea."

"I better start making backpacks." Mildred sighed, climbing into Leviathan. "Looks like we're walking out of here."

Shivering slightly, Krysty crossed her arms. "Sure, only a couple hundred miles till the next redoubt."

"Better than being dead," Ryan stated, feeling oddly tired. "Come on, let's get to work."

Epilogue

Through the fuming, smoky ruins of Novaville came the scavengers. Erect bipeds, they stood hunched over, their skin deathly pale, animalistic fangs filling their wide mouths. They wore only loincloths of untreated hide, and carried clubs of tree branches with the bark removed.

The destruction of the ville was near absolute. The wooden palisade that marked the boundary of their territory was burning out of control, and the formidable stone wall smashed in countless places. The harder-than-stone black gate was melted.

Blasters lay everywhere, but they avoided those, knowing that when they barked they killed. But there were sleeping horses for them to gather, and there was food aplenty. The dead and the sleeping sec men were piled on litters and dragged back to the dwelling place to be cooked for dinner, or smoked in the great lodge and saved for winter. The unconscious slaves they respectfully detoured around. The Beast had slain hundreds, but not harmed the slaves. Clearly, they were his chosen people and to eat one would be to invoke terrible consequences.

In the crumbling base of a brick tower, the muties found a mighty altar of silver and jewels with a

wizened old man sitting in the chair. His skin was
wrinkled and tanned as leather, his eyes blank glass
orbs, his mouth sewn shut. Some of the stitching
along his neck had popped, allowing the cotton stuffing inside to burst out in wads. On his head was a
crown of gold and jewels. The scavengers bowed
deeply to the totem and left immediately, fearing to
disturb the god of the ville. None wished to chance
negating their great good luck this day.

The hated norms with their barking things of
smoke were dead, the walls blocking their land were
down and they had a banquet of meat, enough to
feed everyone for months to come. All hail the
Beast! Generous was the one-eyed god of the desert,
and the muties happily sang its praise as they began
the first ritual cuts into the screaming food.

It would be a good winter this year.

TAKE 'EM FREE
2 action-packed novels plus a mystery bonus
NO RISK
NO OBLIGATION TO BUY

Blood inheritance...

DON PENDLETON's

MACK BOLAN®

STORM FRONT

A homegrown terrorist group lying dormant for more than a decade rises to continue its war against the American government. Revenge against the Feds who stalked and shut down the Cohorts years ago is the first on its agenda of terror. The group's actions are matched bullet for bullet by the Executioner, who is committed to eradicating the Cohorts and its legacy of bloodshed.

Available in July 2000 at your favorite retail outlet.

Brutal civil war...

STONY MAN ™ 47

COMMAND FORCE

Stony Man is called into action as a rogue party of Albanian freedom fighters attempts to collect a blood debt on America's streets. The Free Albania Party has crossed the line from rebels to terrorists, and their thirst for retribution against the hard-line Western powers has reached crisis proportions.

Available in June 2000 at your favorite retail outlet.

GOLD EAGLE®

GSM47

Desperate times call for desperate measures. Don't miss out on the action in these titles!